Tayna's Dawn

Written by Marie Daley

Book 1 of The Adventures of Ryes and Garth

Copyright © Marie Daley 2015
Cover photo by: B Ramey
Author Photo by: Ellen Coulombe
ISBN: 978-1733184878

This is a work of fiction. All the events and characters portrayed in this book are fictional and any resemblance to any real people or incidents is purely coincidental. And if you do find Tayna, please invite me along to visit it with you.

Dedication

I dedicate this book to my dearest and closest friend, Ellen Coulombe. You were the one who pushed me hardest to finish this story. Thank you so much!

Also, to my very patient and loving kids: Alex Scott, Amber Farnsworth and Grace Lovely!

This page intentionally left blank

Table of Contents

This page intentionally left blank

Tears

Tair of House Clenons looked at his reflection in his desk screen, changing it to reflective mode. He clearly was of the noble class with his definite feline cast to his features; the commoners' features were far more plain and easy to distinguish as the Royals decreed centuries ago. He stood a little over two full measures tall and was lean and well-muscled as he kept himself in good physical condition. It was more than just personal pride that he kept in shape; he wanted to be ready in case the tides turned and physical action would be required to protect his home, life and family. He felt he should be constantly prepared and so had an isolated home which was well armed and defended, too. But his weak Dreamer Talent gave him no clues to work with to further hone his preparations. He felt he couldn't abandon Kahmarr with the rest of his family here. He'd have to stay and fight. He looked back to his reflection.

His ears were neat and rounded at the top, covered with his body fur and dyed with dark stripes and white stripes to accent his own natural medium-brown hair color. He thought they looked dashing, even if he wasn't seeking a new mate. And his dark gold eyes practically sparkled. His nose was properly flattened but not too wide, nor too low a dip at the end. And his upper lip split was even and neat when he grimaced at himself as he smiled. He looked at his claws, which he always kept sheathed, as was proper. He extended them to ensure that they were all properly sharpened with no splitting to indicate new growth. His hair was long, neat and swept back. He kept it secured at the base of his neck with a bejeweled filigreed clasp to keep it out of his face and out of the way. Overall he approved of himself and yet knew he still yearned for something more. He had no idea what that more might contain. He dialed back his screen to get back to work. He'd reviewed the schedules for shipments of his share of the family mercantile business and found no flaws. He started delving into the captains' reports to see if any new troubles were brewing. His brows knit as he saw what was being voiced and yet left unsaid in the reports before him; it was troubling and disturbing.

"Da?" a very familiar voice sounded from the door into his office, as she peeked her head around it, her curling flame-red hair spilled down towards the floor in a careless cascade. Tair was surprised but smiled, his heart lightened by this unexpected visit. He blanked his screen and stood up to quickly cross the large room to pull his oldest daughter into the room and into his arms.

"I have missed you so much, Tyra!" he exclaimed. She clung to him for a long moment, as if clinging for dear life itself. This alarmed him, but unless she opened up to him from within, he was not going to barge in to further abuse her using his Talent. The rest of his former wife's family had their way too freely with her for years already; he wouldn't add to her burdens. It was so much for a young one to bear. She would have to open up to him from within first.

"Come and let us sit and chat for a bit," he offered instead. She surrendered to his urging and let him lead her over to his comfy chairs and settee near the floor-to-ceiling windows. The garden outside was in full bloom, presenting an astounding vista which drew her eyes for a few heartbeats; the sweet smells of the blooms drifting in through the open windows. This was the garden where he had watched over her as she explored the outside world for the first time. She had grasped at the bright flowers and seemingly unable to decide what she wanted to do with them, once she'd crushed them in her tiny hands. Echoes of her loving laughter still filled his mind. He saw memories appeared to cross her sight too, and then she blinked, sighed and turned back to him as she took her seat. He gave her a nod and a small smile, sitting down next to her on the settee.

"I saw Elofin. Did you know it won't be long now before his Talent will open up?" she asked, mischief in her eyes as she diverted his questions. He frowned, wondering at her moods today. She was outright mercurial.

"He has been tested several times now and the Catalysts have all said he is Talentless. That is why he was given to me to raise." he replied, closely watching her. The gleam of mischief fled her eyes as she leaned towards him, placing her delicate hand upon his wrist.

"You MUST send him away from Kahmarr, Da! His mind and spirit are in great danger. And he must never return!" There were flashes of anger in the depth of her emerald eyes, which surprised him. "My own Catalyst Talent has told me the truth; just a few moments ago," she insisted. "I do not care what any other Catalyst might claim. Can you guess why?" she queried. He frowned for a few moments then a horrible thought came to light and a shock ran through him as it clarified.

"He has Empath!" he breathed out in surprise. She smiled sadly in response as she nodded agreement. "Kahmarr will kill him!"

"Whenever I must come home, I keep my own Empath Talent locked down tight. Kahmarr is cruel, grasping and a destroyer. That is why I felt his budding Talent so strongly. It echoed my own – soul to soul. I can awaken it in him, but not here, not on Kahmarr." He sighed in relief, knowing she had never been cruel to anyone. It was why he had always been driven to protect his first daughter every chance he got.

"So, you did not come all this way to talk about Elofin, since you didn't know he was an Empath until today. What troubles your heart my beautiful Tyra? How can your ol' Da brandish his sword in your service?" he teased. That brought out a warmer smile, lighting her eyes once more, but still sadness shadowed her face. His heart went out to her, wanting to know what troubled her so greatly.

"Word has gotten out that I am a Talent of One and now the great houses are vying to lay claim to me in any way they each can, before the Crown is officially informed and can decide the rest of my life. Somehow, Grandmother has decided that it is time I marry," she told him, then paused as her voice caught, unable to pass a lump in her throat. He took her hand in his, noting her claws were halfway out – a sure sign of her great distress.

A Talent of One was extremely rare and was an occurrence in the bloodlines once every twenty thousand years. It wasn't that she had one really strong Talent. She actually had been born with all fourteen Talents. In Tyra's case, none of her Talents were very strong, but still the potential for her to pass this unique genetic make-up on to her children made her invaluable and someone to be treasured. If the Families had their way, she would spend the rest of her life caged and out of everyone's reach, except whomever the Crown felt worthy to see her, or speak with her.

"You are barely sixteen years old!" he declared, his anger rising. "You should be deciding what to wear at the next party, not your wedding!" She suddenly threw herself into his arms and the floodgate of tears she'd been holding back opened. She cried out her heart to him. He held her wondering what he could truly do to protect her from the other side of her family? It wasn't like he was powerless. His own family's status even set closer to the crown than his former wife's, but he didn't want his family elders meddling further in her life, either! He pulled back to look into her emerald eyes, once again.

"He is OLD Da; ANCIENT!" she sobbed. "Why would Grandmother ever pick such an arrogant, self-involved, creepy, old...." He saw she struggled for more fitting descriptive words, without drawing from common, offensive slang.

"I get the idea. Who is this fell ancient ancestor Lin has chosen for your first mate?"

"Walmuss of House Oftirrin," she replied, wiping at her tears in distress. He gave her his pocket kerchief and she flashed a brief twitch which might have once been a smile in gratitude. It was like lead hit his stomach upon realizing whom she spoke of as her chosen mate. He could not believe his ears!

"He is as old as your Great-Grandmother! What is going through Lin's mind? You are only a child! It has to be part of some agreement between the two houses!" He knew Walmuss would use and abuse her horribly! He suddenly stood up; feeling a need for immediate action and not knowing what he needed to do first. "Who would know you came here?" he suddenly asked, turning to look at her.

"Mother is a strong Dreamer," she stated with a lop-sided smile, "remember? But she was the one who suggested I had not walked in your gardens in years." She seemed to gain strength by seeing him ready to take action. He wouldn't disappoint her now!

"He cannot be my first Da, please!" He stopped and frowned, knowing Mada was a willing conspirator seemed to ignite his own courage, as the rest of a daring plan instantly crystalized.

"Since we already have a family emergency and need to evacuate Elofin from Kahmarr, I would like to invite you to accompany me upon The Margiiti? Then you can help open up his Talent and coach him best in its use," he suggested.

"It would be my honor to lend a hand to save Elofin," she formerly replied, smiling so that her eyes lit up from within, once again. "He is my half-brother, after all. Family First!" He smiled as he returned to his desk to get things set into motion. It was his own family moto.

"Da, where do we go now?" she asked, after they had finally freed the ship from Victory Starport. She set her helmet into a storage compartment, followed by her gloves. She'd change into a ship suit soon and stow the rest of her space suit disguise later. Elofin went back to his own cabin to change. He'd been charged by the thought of heading out on a voyage instead of having to go to class and had been a willing conspirator. "Grandmother Lin will find us eventually," she pointed out. He grimaced with a nod of understanding.

"Normally I would agree, but if we're going to put you beyond her and Walmuss' reach, we'll need help." He sighed and was suddenly reluctant to reveal his plans, which in hindsight seemed inadequate. She nodded her agreement, puzzled.

"And?" she pressed, spreading her hands in invitation as Mada liked to do at times.

"We're heading out to a lightly colonized world named Tayna," he finally told her. Her brows knit, as it seemed she didn't understand his reasons, nor reluctance to speak about it. "First, to see if Elofin could be accepted into a Forester program. It will give him a new life on a new world with potential for him to build a solid future. Then we will see if you can be hidden away for a few years in cold sleep by an order of women established by Doran of House Forental. They have a hidden encampment where she serves out her sentence for a serious crime. Lin would never find you there and Walmuss would never be allowed to make his claim on you." She nodded, smiling, and closed her eyes. She was still for several long heartbeats, but finally she opened them and smiled for him. He sighed in relief.

"Not the most ideal environment, but yes, I will be safe from them there," she finally agreed. Inwardly a chill held her heart captive at the scenes she had just glimpsed of her future thanks to her Visionary Talent. "Elofin will have a good long life and will be serving the Crown Prince," she told him with a happy smile. She stepped closer and threw her arms around him, snuggling close. "I will miss you, Da."

"It will be a short goodbye. We'll be together again soon and I should have my family ready to help protect you from Lin and her plans by then," he assured her. She nodded her head at this in agreement.

"By the time I leave Doran's company, Grandmother Lin will no longer have the power to direct my life," she stated confidently, thinking it was the best way to assure her father as tears started up, again.

"Do not cry, Tyra. It will all work out," he said, trying to comfort her. He gave her a handkerchief to use. She grasped it and nodded against his chest, then pulled back.

"They are happy tears, Da! I am going to find my one and only there and he will have a good heart which is filled with lots of love for me and our family." He sighed in relief and gave her a hug.

"He had better be a man I would approve of for my daughter," he told her. She laughed and nodded her head, still crying.

"He will be," she assured him.

He never knew they were also tears she cried because she now knew she would never see her father, nor mother again in this life. Sometimes Talents could be a curse as well as a blessing.

A Sedate Life

"Truly Ryes, you must know Rowan will be fine. He'll be looked after by both Tanns and her daughter, Tennan. He will be Fine!" Rinna of House Itten pressed emphatically. "In fact Tennan can move into our room and stay here with Rowan, so she'll be able to take care of both of yours grandfather. Trust her. She's been taking care of her siblings for years; she can handle him."

Ryes was sure it would give Tennan a break from her mother and the chaos she knew sometimes reined in that house for a bit, but was still uncomfortable with the thought of leaving his side. And she truly did not know her cousin enough to trust her with his care. She was younger. Would she make the right decisions if something happened? She felt torn within; wanting to reach some decision where she knew her own true needs would be best met, too. She closed her eyes for a moment as a shudder coursed through her frame, as if an icy draft coming from the gates of the Demons' Realm itself! Myriad visions filled her head and for a few moments she was lost in them. Then suddenly it was as if she knew where she needed to be for her life to be true. It was nothing she could wrap her fingers around, but still the feeling was strong and sure.

"I don't know what it is, but I can't go with you this year, Grandmother Rinna," she finally stated, opening her emerald green eyes, squarely meeting Rinna's brown ones. It looked like Rinna was again wishing she had the Mind Voice Talent, as she strove to look deeper into her soul. Even if they weren't related by blood, she felt such a deep kinship with her that she might as well have been her grandmother in truth. Rinna knew her mind and heart almost as well as Rowan.

"You're getting close and it's scaring all of us. I've seen him watch you, as if his madness has you confused with your mother. It's no longer safe for you here, child!" The naked fear in her eyes somehow comforted Ryes in an odd fashion. Her courage crystalized and she knew she was the one to set her own life's course. And she would not run off to hide. She knew within that she needed to face this challenge squarely.

"I have the forest and he'll never be my match in my own element. I'll be fine, Grandmother. He'll never catch me there! Please trust me in knowing this one thing very well." They suddenly wrapped each other in their arms, trying to find an anchor where their hearts felt safe and secure once again.

"You don't think he'd try to hold Rowan as a hostage against you?" she whispered tensely, then kissed her ear.

"That would destroy Tanns' trust in him, and so his own home. I don't see him doing that," she whispered in return, tears now running down her cheeks. "And if he harmed Rowan, I'd find a way to make him pay dearly for it. He's terrorized the Village long enough. He's tried to frighten me and it has not worked since I was a child." Rinna pulled back to look into Ryes' eyes once again.

"This is not your burden. Leave this one to the Elders, at least," she started, but Ryes made a scoffing sound at hearing it and shook her head in denial.

"The Elders have let him rampage for what? Two decades? No, it'll have to be the men of my own generation who'll have to make him stop. He's getting old and someone will finally put an end to his murdering ways. I only pray to Ricmon that it will be sooner rather than later," she teased at the end, smiling again. It was their traditional game to name their favorite deities for the situations they were discussing. Usually they each picked a different one to counter the other.

"Better make it Aletagga, the god of wild good fortune, instead," she finally laughed out, tears in her eyes too. "If you change your mind, just take a few things, mount Honey and ask her to carry you out to us. Follow the road east or south and you will find us my Sweetling." Ryes stepped back, letting go with a lot of reluctance.

"I'll just have to get used to the sedate pace of life we have here when you're gone, once again," she returned, spreading her hands helplessly. "Not many villagers come all the way out here to bother us. We'll be fine."

"What about your follower friend?" she asked, her eyes glinting with hidden secrets whenever she mentioned him.

"He won't bother me. He just likes to keep tabs on what I'm doing at times," she shook her head, reminded again of Garth's more frequent presence in the last few months. "I don't feel any harm from him," she assured Rinna. She laughed at this, nodding in agreement.

"I meant, if you come out to meet us, either leave him to help with Rowan, or bring him along. We can always use a strong back and a quick mind. It seems to me that he has wanted to look out for you for years, but you don't know how to let him," she returned.

Ryes shook her head again, grinning mischievously as she bit her lower lip. "It's all right child, time will play out its dance for you both. Now one last kiss goodbye as it seems Darman's ready to roll out." They hugged and kissed and cried over each other one more time before breaking free so the Caravaners could begin their annual journey.

Ryes ran beside the slowly moving van for a while, waving goodbye once again, before they took the road heading east. Twenty-two vans passed her as she stood beside the road, each occupant granting her their farewells and blessings as they passed. She turned back for home, feeling lonely for a moment, yet feeling there was something in the air. This year's departure seemed very different. How was she going to fit back into the slow life which was Matlowe Village's norm once again? She craved so much more.

The orange-red light of Tayna's setting sun glinted brightly off the metal tip of the spear Ryes held in her hand. Her gaze traveled from the sun's rays in the west toward the ancient ruins to the north. They appeared as a thin, dark line, almost beyond the far horizon at this high advantage. A brightly tipped needle of a spire above it reflected its light back to her. It was where her father, brothers and sister were said to have died so violently under Korman's brutal claws. Her grandfather could still recount the tale of her mother's escape in a chilling narrative, with herself a tiny, helpless infant. Her mother died in a pool of her own blood here in the Village as her grandfather fought to save her life. Now Old Korman watched her with hooded eyes whenever he was near. She was sure he was making plans for her, as he tried before with her mother.

"NEVER!" Ryes vowed, with a low growl in her voice. She stood up to descend the tall peak, north of Matlowe Village. She slung her laden hunting bag over her shoulder, turning for home. When she reached the bottom she was surprised as Garth stepped forward. He offered her his hand, claws retracted, palm up. Ryes looked up to his face as she hesitated, feeling uncertain, then crossed his palm with her own - a sign of accepted friendship. Her heart was beating rapidly as she blushed.

This was the first time anyone had met her here at this time of day and Garth was not alone. The villagers, who were out with her today on their special hunt, were all here too! She'd thought they'd gone on to their own homes. There were questions in their eyes and for the first time she was embarrassed by her daydreaming. Was it vengeance she wanted, or an escape from this Village? Shyly she lowered her eyes.

"I usually bid my father and siblings a goodnight at this time of day," she explained, suddenly feeling very precarious and wanting to be clear with him and the others. Garth gave her a nod in understanding. She recalled him watching her go through this ritual from time-to-time through the years and saw he understood it now. He must have been curious before.

"Thank you for all your time and teaching today," Garth replied, then looked to the others around them, a silent goad. "Your wisdom will not be forgotten." He smiled genuinely, looking down into her emerald eyes. She blushed more deeply. She smiled in return, the light of her inner happiness showing in her eyes. She saw patience and more in his golden ones. She couldn't believe she was the hope for survival of the entire Village in this time of famine. She had never been given the chance of friendship with the villagers her age, until now. She hoped it would hold true after this current crisis. Garth stepped back and the remaining members of the hunting party came forward to offer their hands in friendship too. Her pounding heart kept her rooted to the spot in amazement.

"Thanks for the help," a tall young man she thought was named Torr said, as he stared down at her. She wanted to laugh at the silly expression he wore. Seeing the merry look in her eyes, his smile grew wider and he gave her a wink then stepped aside.

"I'll tell my mother that she doesn't know you at all," Maren stated with a smile, too. She knew her younger cousin, yet had never spent any actual time in his company before today. He had turned out to be a surprisingly fun person, who seemed to care for her after all. She sighed and gave him a return smile and nod, along with a murmured thanks. Aunt Tanns ignored her unless she needed help with gathering herbs or medicinal plants. She usually faced a cold reception in her home, so stayed away. The rest of her cousins took a queue from their mother and shunned her also. She barely knew any of them. It was partly why she was loathe to leave Rowan in Tennan's care.

The other hunters gathered around her were also mostly strangers, even if each and every face was familiar. She was unsure of some names, but each offered her their hands and made small comments and thanks. It'd been a good day's hunt with everyone bearing very full bags. A surge of loneliness she was unable to suppress rose up in her heart. All the years of living apart crashed down upon her, almost drowning her.

The hate had long been culled by the love of Tara of House Itten, who taught her when she was young that the pent up hate she then fostered harmed only her and no one else. She helped her come to terms with it and let it all go. Still, she never took the further steps Tara always encouraged – to make friends with the villagers – if she had then... Perhaps the belonging she had come to know today could have been hers all along? It caught at her and she was reluctant to part company, but it was getting late and her grandfather would be worried. So, she said her goodbyes and turned towards the Village, quickly trotting ahead of the larger group. A rising tide of conflicting emotions swelled within her heart as tears threatened to blind her eyes.

"She wasn't the farga we grew up believing her to be," Sabin commented to Garth as they walked a much slower pace. He smiled in response; his eyes glued to her lithe form until she dropped down into the Village proper.

"I'm sore everywhere! Does she always have to be on the run? I thought she'd never give us a moment's rest," Maren complained, as he caught up to his friends and rolled his shoulders to emphasize the aches.

"But the hunt was GOOD!" Ardis practically shouted, as she picked up her steps so she could pace the men. She walked next to Sabin. Her face betrayed her inner turmoil as she glanced over to see Garth's infatuation with Ryes.

"Yes, it was good," Garth agreed, glancing over to the others walking with him. "Karr's going to love this day's surprise. I'm glad we finally took your mother's advice, Maren. We should have asked for Ryes' help long ago." He gave Maren a smile and got a chuckle in response.

"My mom's been after us to do so for the last few weeks. I can finally go home and not face her anger," he admitted. "Actually it was grandfather who insisted she push us to ask Ryes. I heard them talking about it yesterday. I really knew so little about her before today. She's shy, but kinda fun."

"Yeah, let's talk about that! You were hoarding her attention all day long," Torr complained. "We were lucky to get a few moments with her at any given time."

"You were all scaring her!" Maren quipped back, laughing as he told them what she'd admitted to him earlier. "She stuck near me because she knew I was a safe, if a mostly unknown, person for her to be around," he boasted. The men gaped at him in surprise; a look of disbelief in their eyes.

"What do you expect?" Ardis demanded in disgust. "You men were practically falling all over her every chance you got. She's lived alone with Rowan since she was born and as I recall, didn't quite a few of you pull mean tricks on her when we were all little? That's why she's avoided us for years! She figured it was the best way to get out of a beating. And you expect her to trust you now?" she challenged them, humor and fire in her brown eyes.

"You were giving her plenty of mean looks yourself," Shadd scolded after having caught up and hearing the conversation. "There were so many things she was trying to explain... It's going to take me years to learn it all!" she declared, then sighed, "I only hope she'll hunt with us after the way everyone was behaving both today and from the past. I used to tease her too, but only because the older kids were doing it. Back then I didn't really understand it all."

"I'll go talk with her," Maren volunteered. He understood. He knew it wasn't that Ryes hadn't noted their overtures today, but that she hadn't known what to do about them; so she had stayed as close to him as she could, at all times. Other than the young cubs, she avoided the villagers for years. "I seem to recall doing nothing myself, when some of you cornered her one rainy afternoon in the old deserted part of the Village. She was beat up and it was weeks in healing back up. Grandfather kept her at home for months. And it was all over a toy flyer that one of the caravaners gave her. I've got a lot to answer for, myself," he admitted. He saw those near him hung their heads as they appeared to recall their own dark deeds of the past. Garth sighed and Maren recalled he'd been the one holding her down that day.

"I'll go with you, as I have much to apologize for, too. I can only hope she'll forgive us and continue teaching us her hunting ways," he stated. "I can't believe how well she knows the forest and all the plants and animals. It's almost as if she were a Forester from out of the old stories."

"I have that cape of marl fur," Sabin offered, appearing to get an idea. Torr raised an eyebrow and scoffed in surprise. "She's saved lives here today," he asserted, glaring at Torr as he thumped his bulging hunting bag. "It's well worth my sister's life any day."

"That's true. Maybe a gift for all the trouble we've been to her for so long? Do you think she'll accept it, or throw it back in your face?" Ardis challenged. Shadd nodded in agreement.

"Would a gift like that be too obvious?" she voiced, crowding closer to the others.

"She's not that type of person. She probably wouldn't know what to do with a gift from one of us. If she hadn't already forgiven us all long ago, she would've never taken us out today," Maren asserted. "She has no idea what to do with so many people focusing on her. Give her time. I'm sure she'll learn to trust us and may become a true friend." Garth smiled at this, giving him a nod.

"I have something I'd like to give her, too," he added in afterthought. Maren immediately thought of the second beltknife Garth had spent two years perfecting. It was exactly like the one he carried, only smaller and daintier. He had once told him that he intended it as a gift for his first mate. And he knew that Garth wanted Ryes since they were early teeners and had spoken to him and Sabin about her for years.

"How about after dinner tonight, we pay a short visit to a hut near the river? After all, I do know the way, even in the dark." Maren asked them. Sabin and Garth immediately gave him handsigns in agreement.

"Sounds good to me," Torr agreed. Ardis and Shadd nodded their consents to go.

Maren smiled at this, seeing it was going to be a good gathering for a visit. He knew he had to ask his sister and mother a few questions about why they treated Ryes the way they usually did. Ryes deserved better treatment from her own family! Whenever there was need, they would send her out to gather the plants, roots or other things required, so they could make the medicines. She did her duties as quickly as possible, in all kinds of weather. Rarely did he remember them thanking her for her help. And he recalled on one stormy day when they didn't even invite her in to dry off or get warm, even though her teeth were clattering with a deep chill. Surely she was due some compassion and he was going to make sure it started now; even if he were the only one in the household to extend it to Ryes.

Matlowe Village with its mud-plastered brick huts always seemed to harbor a harsh life for the few people still living here. With the nearby densely wooded hills providing little open flat land to cultivate, the people learned to live off of the Village terraced gardens and the small livestock animals they raised. Life was always said to be short. Ryes lived by the river, but since the quickest way home was through the Village today, it was the way her feet took her. She rarely gave any of the buildings, or people, a glance, keeping her gaze to the ground before her flying feet.

"Ryes! Ryes!" She heard a high-pitched cry rise up from behind her, as she took the path toward home. So she stopped for them, with a smile upon her face, as she turned around to see them running towards her. These were the villagers she was happy to spend her time with most days. Several of the young cubs caught up to her quickly – an air of childish pride and delight about them.

"You really showed them how to hunt today? Didn't you?" Lixi asked breathlessly. The others chimed in their questions, wanting to be heard too. Ryes smiled down at her youthful enthusiasm.

"I tried to, Lixi. I hope they listened." She playfully ruffled the child's short honey-colored hair.

"I caught a fish today! It was this BIG!" Jons boasted, spacing her hands out to demonstrate how enormous it had been. "My mom was real proud and said I'll make a fine huntress one day. An' I did it, just like to you tol' me." There was pride in her eyes which couldn't be denied. Rand tugged on her arm, demanding attention as well.

"That's great news, Jons," Ryes agreed as she knelt down to hug them, laying her spear on the ground beside her. They crowded in close, trying to all hug her back at once. She laughed merrily at their antics and showered each with the attention he, or she, craved. Few villagers gave them such attention. The animals and gardens needed tending most of the day, as well as the other daily chores. So, this handful of cubs were the bright spot of her life. Ryes gladly showed them small things they could learn like fishing or gathering wild berries, tuber roots and other foods. This way they could feel like they were helping their families too. And if she had plenty to share out of her own hunts, she would give them food to munch on or take home. And she was teaching them how to read and write, to reinforce the lessons they were being given by the Village elders. These young ones had become the young siblings she would never know.

Then Sela's voice was heard calling out for Lixi. Ryes looked up and found herself caught up in a moment of uncertainty, noticing how many faces looked out from the huts at her and the cubs. She wasn't sure if there was approval, or not, on the faces nearby. She was afraid to look too closely.

"Better go home before you catch trouble," Ryes warned them all in a low voice with a gentle smile upon her lips. Uneasiness arose in her as she knelt by her spear and watched them run off, happily greeting their parents. The villagers rarely paid her much notice. This sudden attention caused the hair at the nape of her neck to rise.

"See you tomorrow," Rand promised as she hugged her one more time before running off. She veered towards the other hunters, who'd just entered the Village and appeared to be discussing something vigorously.

"That's a promise," Ryes shouted back. Rand gave her a glance and a raised hand before running up to the tallest hunter, Torr, asking to be picked up. Ryes chuckled as she picked up her spear, stood up, and pretended not to see the villagers as she continued on her path. The last several springs had seen the birth of many cubs. Their mothers were protective, but also accepted their friendship with her, as if she were their accepted day-time caretaker for the youngsters. She thought it was because she took every effort to keep the cubs safe while they tended the gardens, or cooked or cleaned. This sudden notice made her wonder and she turned back to see some villagers were still watching. As the voices of the hunting party were raised in greetings to their families, she turned away. At least they'd bring some good news tonight from a very successful hunt. The entire Village would be happier with full stomachs. She hoped...

As she resumed walking home, she passed the hut where her father, aunt and grandparents lived long ago. It'd been the place where her mother died too. It was dark, falling apart and very sad looking. She didn't dare set foot inside it now, as she'd be afraid the roof might fall in upon her. When she was young, she used to dream of coming back to repair it for when she was older and would want to establish her own home. Now she might have to come and pull it down so none of the young ones would get hurt exploring it. This one and several others nearby. There were plenty of homes in Matlowe, but with the population declining, more were being left uninhabited each year. There were all kinds of stories being told to explain why it was happening, but Ryes firmly blamed Korman and the way he strove to destroy families. He was the village curse.

Korman wanted all the women of Matlowe to answer his needs and his needs alone. And once he made the cubs, he refused to help nurture them. He seemed to believe it was the responsibility of the mothers to provide the food, too. With no true father to provide for the cubs, it usually fell to the siblings of the mothers to help out. But Ryes did note that few of the younger cubs bore the look of Korman. She bet several young couples managed to evade his notice and were getting away with it. She hoped it was true. She'd never allow him near her! She sighed as she thought of the young men who paid her such close attention today. If it hadn't been for her cousin at her side, she would've been too nervous to teach anyone any hunting skills.

There was still so much she needed to go over with all of them as she had barely covered a few of the basics today!

Distracted by her musings, she didn't see Old Korman standing in her way where the path narrowed going between two larger, crumbling buildings, until too late. Her nostrils flared and her eyes narrowed to slits, but she was determined to keep her temper under control this time. His heavy sour odor filled the small alleyway making her uneasy. Korman was known for his violent outbursts and fierce temper which had taken many lives of the villagers in the past. She noted his face was unreadable. There was an unspoken war between them. She feared the old murderer, but still held her ground. She was determined to never show her fear to him, which is why she continued on this path in spite of the danger. Her mother escaped him and publicly embarrassed him, with herself the lone, living proof. She would've given anything to ask her how she found the courage to do it all.

Ryes' anxiety grew as she approached his commanding bulk, but her own stubbornness kept her feet moving forward. She felt as if she were treading on a knife's edge. It was more than his size which disturbed her. He always watched her and usually turned up nearby to stare at her whenever she was in the Village. It annoyed her at the very least, but there was little she could do about it. She tried to duck past him, when his hand shot out and grabbed the top of her shoulder. His fingers and sharp claws dug in painfully, bringing a silent snarl to her face. Her rage was evident as she met his cold mad eyes.

"You time is near and I am ready," he growled out roughly, looking unimpressed. "You'll be mine and no others." His eyes pierced her with their cold insane light.

"I'm my mother's daughter and I choose my own mates," she hissed back; a chill rising within her to match her hot anger. Korman's own anger started to show on his face as he shook her violently against the wall of one of the buildings, digging his claws in cruelly.

"Then you'll suffer her fate!" he declared and suddenly threw her hard against the crumbling wall, releasing her. He stalked past Ryes, the incident settled in his mind. She was sure he was thinking it would only be a matter of time.

Ryes stood ridged, silently snarling at his retreating form. She gripped her spear in both hands, aching to hurl it after him, but she would never sink down to his level and be a cold murderer. Finally, she turned away and took a deep breath. A sudden shudder gave her body a little release from the tension. She shrugged her shoulders and winced as the heavy bag thumped against her back. The shoulder he gripped hurt sharply; even through the haze of her remaining rage. It would need tending, and with that would come the questions. It'd been such a wonderful day up to now.

Rowan was sitting outside his home next to the Yuri River, taking a break from his weaving. He thought about the lateness of the hour and there was still no sign of his granddaughter. There were times when she'd stay out to watch an insect weave a web, or a special flower slowly bloom, so there was nothing to worry about yet. She'd return soon and regale him with her new adventures. For now, it was good to sit outside, resting his back and letting his mind wander its many paths of thought.

Rowan knew he was getting old. He finally came to the point in his life where he could no longer deny it. It wasn't just the presence of a vigorous granddaughter to dote on him constantly, nor the scores of young cubs, who sought him out for his tales of old, while their mothers were busy with chores; it came from within. A knowing that no matter how warm the blankets, nor how bright the fire, there was a chill settling into his bones. If it weren't for Ryes and Tanns, he would've left with one of the caravans long ago to seek a quieter place to die – if such existed on Tayna. Or at least to finally meet the other peoples who lived upon Tayna, too. To be the explorer he had imagined himself to be in his youth! There were times when he so envied Darman and Rinna and the chances they had to explore the world.

A storm cloud's shadow passed across his thoughts and Rowan looked up in surprise. He immediately spied the cause of the thought-storm. Ryes was approaching with an obviously full hunting bag and an even more definite anger. He knew she had many of the Talents of the ancients, but no real power as they were said to have. Living with her from infancy had made him sensitive to her moods.

"Now what could've set her off?" he muttered to himself. He knew she usually had a tolerant nature, but was coming into her full maturity and was actually temperamental lately. He looked up again as she stopped in front of him. He was startled when he saw blood seeping through her tunic at the shoulder. This had been no ordinary hunt!

"Korman," Ryes answered the question in his eyes. "He let me know his plans for me." With these words, the last of her anger drained away. She finally let her shoulders droop as she ducked past Rowan into the house. He stood and followed her in. She heaved the heavy sack up on the table, and sat down in a chair abruptly, next to it. She grounded the butt of the spear into the rug and leaned her head heavily upon her one arm and the shaft of her spear. A small sob welled up as she fought back tears.

Rowan's surprise turned to a frown as he went to fetch their medicines and clean bandaging cloths from a wall cupboard. Picking up a small knife from his loom, a bottle of water and clay bowl from the sideboard, he finally felt ready to begin to unravel this newest problem Ryes brought him. He let go a long breath, as well as the last of his anger with her. What had she done to provoke him now? He set everything down on the table and sorted it out to begin.

"So, what did Korman say?" he asked, as he undid the lacing at the shoulder seem with his knife. Ryes sat up straight at his silent urging, so he could see her shoulder better.

"He told me that I'm to become one of his whores," she replied with a catch in her voice.

"And what did you say to that?" Rowan coaxed as he examined the claw marks. He knew Ryes well enough to know how she answered. He wanted to distract her as he washed out the painful gashes. Korman had been serious indeed!

"Owww!" Ryes exclaimed, pulling away, and then relaxed again as she caught her grandfather's glare and let him finish his ministrations. "I said the wrong thing. I reminded him I was Tyra's daughter," she breathed out. Rowan grimaced at that. He knew Korman wouldn't need to be reminded! Ryes was the mirror image of Tyra, in many ways. She only lacked Tyra's ages-weary depth in her eyes.

It hadn't been easy for either of them when both of Ryes' parents were killed and he was forced to care for and raise the tiny infant. Most men would've given the cub over to the nearest female relative, but Rowan had just lost his own wife, Jana, and needed Ryes' company as much as she needed him. And it didn't help that his only daughter, Tanns, had taken in Korman as her mate and he suspected that since he had killed Ryes' parents, he wouldn't hesitate to kill her, too, even if she was an infant. The other villagers were outraged at first. So, he relocated to an old home near the river bank. It was a home which used to belong to his own grandparents. The other nearby dwellings were well-kept but only used in the winter, when the caravaners stayed in Matlowe; away from the winter snows. And sometimes, on a moonlit night, he thought he could see Jana's face upon the river's water, smiling up at him. It brought him a feeling of peace and he felt closer to her here. Even if they lived mostly apart from the Village, it had been a good life for them both. He focused upon her torn shoulder and worked to stanch the bleeding.

"Maren! What's in your bag?" Tennan questioned as he came into the house and set his hunting bag down on the dinner table. He grinned widely in response; his eyes full of mischief.

"Something wonderful!" he replied, baiting his sister. She closed her mouth and glared at him for a moment before turning away.

"It's full of rocks again, isn't it?" she accused as she picked up their youngest sister, Rowis, and perch her on her hip, then turned back to her brother. Her fury melted to shock as Maren had pulled out roots, a large hunk of meat he had just unwrapped, and his bag still appeared to be almost three-quarters full. His grin broadened as he held the meat out to her.

"How do you want this cooked?" he teased with a merry light in his eyes. "Salted, smoked, or in a stew pot?"

"Ohhhhh Maren!" she breathed out, astonished, "How about all three? There's enough here to feed us well for a week!" She put down Rowis and pushed forward, to look closer. "Where did you get it all?"

"We were out hunting today. We came across a huge buck with an impressive rack and pulled it down pretty well," he boasted as he set it aside. Tennan snatched it up quickly and turned for the kitchen.

"Ryes took you out today, didn't she?" she quipped in return. She went for the big knife to pare out the portions for the meals she was already planning in her head.

"Tenn," Rowis protested, but was pushed aside by Karis as he crowded her with his arms filled with the tubers.

"Tars, would you please come and get Rowis?" she called out as she put down her knife and helped unload the tubers before Karis dropped them. "Thanks Karis," she said as she smiled, seeing the joy on his face. "Would you like some fried tubers tonight?" He nodded enthusiastically then ran back to the main room to see what else was being unpacked by his older brother.

"Yes, we were all out with Ryes today on the hunt," Maren stated as he walked in with a half dozen large eggs in his hands. "I finally got to know her a little for the first time in my life."

"And?" she replied as she took out a large bowl to contain the eggs. He saw she could feel he had more to say from the tone in his voice. He knew she was doubting him and not sure if this was a good thing, or not, coming from him.

"She's not a farga. She's a decent person and a bit shy around everyone, and she has a good heart," he told her, letting her take the eggs and place them safely into the bowl.

"All this from one day of hunting?" she replied with a bit of a bite in her tone. Maren struggled to keep a rein on his temper, but it was everything he had to not slam his fist down on the counter in response.

"Yes, all in one day. We need to start treating her as a member of our family, as she truly is after all. It's not her fault Korman's been stalking her practically her entire life. I think that's the reason mother hates her so much. We don't need to hate her, nor treat her as anything but our only cousin. She deserves better than that from all of us," he asserted in a controlled voice. He was NOT going to be like their father, he vowed to himself. Tennan stopped and stared at him, looking into his eyes.

"Why? Really, why?" she pressed, wanting to hear his truth. He let out a pent up breath, slowly.

"Because we can be better than our parents and see the world in a better light," he replied. He picked up Rowis as Tars and Karis stood listening to them now. "We don't need to be cruel to each other just because we can create some unreasonable scenarios in our heads. We need to live in the world around us and just get along better with each other."

"Why?" Rowis mimicked her older sister, giggling.

"Because we want a better future for all of us," he replied, finally smiling again. "And Ryes should be a part of our future, too." Tennan turned away from him again to work on the night's meal, but she seemed to be thinking over his words.

Later, feeling much better with her shoulder cleaned and bandaged and freshly washed with clean clothes on, Ryes sat over dinner telling her grandfather about the unusual time she'd had this day.

"I didn't know most of the people of the Village were going hungry," she stated, accusing him. Rowan met her eyes, which were filled with new interest. She noted his own bright amber eyes were filled with curiosity.

"What? You barely know the names of half of the people in the Village. Since when would you notice whether they were well fed, or not?" he demanded sharply in return. She squirmed uncomfortably under his glare. Then let out a long sigh.

It was true. She'd never shown much interest before. She went her own way, having her own ideas about hunting and nature. She rarely returned with an empty sack and didn't have to hunt as often as the others. She was different. She had no real family other than her grandfather and they lived far from the rest. Most left her alone now, which suited Ryes fine for she liked being alone with only her own thoughts to trouble her. And it kept her from being beaten for being different, as happened many times when she was small. At least the caravaners never treated her that way! When they were here for the winter months, it was a time of joy for her. It was as if her real village had returned. She was a part of their families with lots of siblings to talk to, play games with or learn new things. Exploring the world with them was always fun and filled with a sense of adventure. But they wouldn't be back until late in the fall. She missed them all so very much! Then she noted her grandfather was still waiting for her to continue.

"Today on my way out to hunt, I was stopped by some of the villagers," she began again, as she picked uneasily at her remaining food. "I just didn't know their hunts had been so poor lately. I'm sorry," she apologized, looking up at Rowan again. He nodded, seeming to accept her apology.

"What did they want from you?" he prompted, as he reached for his leather-covered mug. She knew he usually took a portion of her hunts and turned them over to Tanns for her family as well as others in need. The two of them could never eat all the food she gathered. Aside from putting some things by for the winter months, Rowan thought it was a good way to be sure the food was used before going bad. With this year's hunts turning out so poor and Ryes still finding plenty, Maren told her his mother had insisted they approach her and ask for her help. She saw it meant them swallowing their pride, but they seemed sincere so she decided to spend her day teaching them a few new things about hunting. Ryes smiled at the memory of her conversations with Maren earlier, when they were tracking, or taking a break.

"They wanted me to teach them my ways of hunting. It was such a surprise! And from the way they looked, how could I refuse?" Ryes paused thoughtfully, pain in her eyes at the memory. "They appeared so pitiful." Her eyes met Rowan's; sure he must've known about some of this already; he looked too smug. "I never realized how much you taught me, or how much I've learned since by watching the ways the plants and animals live," she continued. Rowan smiled gently at a memory of his own.

"Part of what I taught you came from what your mother taught me." He paused for a moment as he gave a small shake of his head. "Tyra taught us all many things." Ryes thought a moment on how much Tyra was esteemed by Rowan and her Aunt Tanns. All the things she knew and could do still haunted Ryes. She wanted to have a mother of her own for so long and found it difficult living with a ghost of the perfect one. She just wasn't her mother; nowhere as perfect as she'd been.

"Anyway," Ryes sighed with a smile. "Teaching that group today was an experience. It was like looking after a bunch of overgrown cubs! They did the craziest things! Stealth? A herd of moss eaters in mating season couldn't make more noise. Was I ever that bad?" Ryes asked, picking up the last piece of stew with her spoon. There was a glint of mischief in her eyes as she asked the question.

"Worse," he assured her with a chuckle.

"I think they accepted me as a part of their circle when we pulled down an old two-prong buck." Ryes lifted her mug to drain it, hesitating. She ventured thoughtfully, "I never realized there were so many bachelors here. There were a few who watched everything I did too closely. It was embarrassing!" Rowan threw back his head and roared with laughter. She looked at him with a lopsided grin.

"My little cubling has finally grown up. She's noticing the young men!" he declared. She blushed furiously as Rowan patted her good shoulder. "Don't fret. It was bound to happen to you someday," he assured her with a broad smile.

"How could I help but notice them? Some were practically trying to walk in my shoes with me! And some of the huntresses didn't appreciate the attention they gave me, either," she assured him. "They weren't so bad and I wish I could've spent some time with the women – away from the men. I have a thousand questions and I'd like a fresh point of view." Rowan closed his mouth in surprise, a shocked look in his eyes. Ryes realized that he probably thought they were closer than that, but she didn't know of a way to explain it all to him. Much less ask him things that she felt could only be voiced young woman to woman. And she wanted to talk with someone more her age, as opposed to Grandmother Rinna. None of the caravaner's younger women who were her age had been with the vans this year to winter in Matlowe. She'd felt so frustrated.

Just then there was a polite scratching at their doorpost. A frown flitted across both their faces as they looked to each other inquiringly. Few people came calling to their home this time of year. Most villagers stayed home indoors at night with their families. Ryes stood with her hand ready to her beltknife, as Rowan went to answer the door. They usually had the curtain across it on a nicer evening like tonight, only closing the door when they went to bed, so whoever was out there probably heard their discussion, too. Aunt Tanns or Maren sent out on an errand would've only come inside without any announcement, so this had to be someone else. Rowan pulled the curtain aside.

Tale Weaving

"Come in... come in," Rowan invited, as he nodded toward Ryes, across the room. He had an odd smile upon his face as their visitors came into the light of the room. It was Garth and some of the hunters who'd been in the hunt earlier today. They looked a little uncertain as they surveyed the neat, spacious room, bunching up near the doorway.

To the left of the door was the workroom containing Rowan's loom, with the new blanket he was weaving still upon it. The blanket was very colorful with lots of blues, greens, yellows and whites making a playful pattern across the weave. Beside the loom was a large window with real glass, tightly shuttered against the dark of the night. Beside the workroom door was a door to the hallway leading to their sleeping rooms. Across to the right was a large trestle table set up with the leftovers of dinner still upon it on one end. It was large enough to accommodate a very big family. And a circle of a half-dozen stuffed chairs was grouped near another large, shuttered window. There were paintings upon the walls, brightly woven rugs upon the floors and decorative oil lamps on the walls and small tables in the room, giving it plenty of light. And two shelves crammed with real books upon them. To the back was the kitchen, an actual separate room with a colorfully woven curtain to separate the rooms. And right before them was a fireplace with a friendly fire, crackling in warm invitation. They seemed entranced for several moments by the clean, simple elegance of their home.

Half in panic, Ryes scooped up the dishes and started to take them to the kitchen, but Garth, upon seeing her, strode up to her with a smile on his face. He saw the fear in her eyes. He knew few villagers ever visited them and it was amusing to see the calm, confident huntress undone by their simple visit. He recalled, with a twinge, that some of this fear could stem from several incidents long ago. She stopped in her tracks, barely breathing, nor daring to move, like a small surprised bounder.

"We didn't get to thank you properly, before you left today," Garth said gently. "You've been the one who has opened our eyes to the greater world, and we felt we should give you something in return." He extended a package bound with cords, just noticing she already had her hands full of their empty dinner dishes.

"Sit down and share a drink with us," Rowan invited with a chuckle, gesturing the others toward the table. As they moved to comply, he stepped over and took the dishes from Ryes' still hands. She seemed to thaw again. He gave her a wink as he disappeared into the kitchen for a few moments, then returned shortly with a tray holding a large flask of mead and six more leather-wrapped mugs, setting it down upon the table for their guests. He began to pour the drink into the mugs and handed them out as the others took seats and got comfortable.

Garth gave Ryes the package, then helped her to her own seat as he took the chair next to hers, watching her intently as she looked up at him, then finally, carefully undid the cords at his obvious urging. A look of wonder swept across her face as she saw what it contained. There was a cape of white marl fur, a rare and dangerous beast found only in the high mountains. Also a newly-made beltknife set with small blue gemstones in the hilt. She looked up in awe and puzzlement to Garth and the others around the table. The fur was an obvious treasure, but the beltknife was beyond any reasonable value by the look in her eyes.

"This really is too much," she began, her eyes full of questions as she appeared clearly uncomfortable with the gifts. "It was just one hunting trip and I truly didn't get to teach you very much, yet." There was pain in her eyes and Ardis nodded her own understanding.

"No, it's not! Today's hunt saved lives," Garth assured her, Sabin nodding in agreement as he spoke. "My older sister, Karr, has two young cubs to feed. I help her as I can, but I'm nowhere as good as you are out in the forest. Torr has a mother who's ill and desperately needed the medicines you showed him how to gather today. Sabin, Ardis and Shadd also have sisters with cubs to feed. And you know that Maren is the only hunter for his mother and your younger cousins. The extra food was distributed to other families, who also were desperate for the food we provided today. You made a difference in a lot of lives, Huntress, and we want to keep learning from you, so that we don't 'spoil the land,' but reap the harvests, as you scolded us about today." He practically chuckled as her mouth dropped open in surprise.

"You were listening," she breathed in return with almost a smile playing about her lips.

"It's all Korman's fault! All he wants is to get the women with cubs and to the four winds for providing food for any of them!" Maren burst out angrily, his fist slamming the table top. Ryes practically jumped out of her seat in surprise, but Garth's smile seemed to calm her and she forced herself to relax a little. Sabin squeezed Maren's shoulder in understanding. Rowan poured the rest of the drinks, handing them out and nodding in sympathy then settled into another chair, as Garth had taken is own.

"He's upset the natural order of things," Sabin stated. "Brothers shouldn't have to provide for their sisters. They should have mates of their own providing for them!"

"It just isn't right," Maren said, "how will I ever have cubs of my own?" He looked to Garth, who shook his head, not knowing any real answers. "All I'm going to get out of life is to scrape together a meager existence for my mother and siblings. When will the Village unite and cast Korman out?"

"I don't know if we'll ever see that day," Ardis spoke up, looking down into her mug as if she could divine their future from it. "Not with his brother being the head Village elder." She shook her head, barely suppressing a shudder, as if a cold wind had danced around the room. Shadd appeared to be enjoying the taste of her mead; her eyes shut with a smile of delight upon her face. Garth knew they had all hashed this out fruitlessly before. They still had no real answers, nor ideas of how to get the rest of the elders to listen to them.

"Because of Korman, Ryes never knew her own mother, father, or siblings," Rowan added, looking at Ryes, as if daring her to forbid him to tell the tale. She grimaced, but glancing up into Garth's eyes again, sighed and settled back as if knowing this was something she could not simply escape from tonight. He wondered how many times she had been forced to sit through the telling of this tale? It was probably a well-known story for her. Garth wondered if it was painful because of her great loss, or because it was told so often she never wanted to hear it again?

"How did it happen?" Torr asked in a low voice, also noting Ryes' look of discomfort. "We've heard so many different tellings of it that it's hard to know where the truth lies." Rowan nodded his head at this as he cleared his throat. He sat back in his chair and looked down into his mug, as if contemplating the hazy images from the past. Ryes fidgeted uncomfortably, slowly running her fingers through the marl fur. Rowan looked up to see the pain in her emerald green eyes. He knew the distortions the other villagers threw into the story either intentionally or through ignorance, so here was a good chance to set the record straight with her new friends.

"To tell this tale well," his voice ground out, suddenly sounding very old indeed. "I must go back to tell you of my own true-mate, Jana. I was still young, about your age, but Jana was almost beyond cub bearing years when we discovered each other." The others shuffled and mumbled softly among themselves in shock.

True-mate vows were almost unknown. It bound the two souls together even beyond life! Most men lived with a woman for a time, to help when their cubs were young, if the woman permitted it. Traditionally no man would tie himself to only one woman, and rare was the woman who tolerated any one man for any longer length of time in her home. Unattached bachelors usually lived with their mothers or sisters, until they could find a mate of their own. Rowan knew the young men and women sitting at his table were all exceptions. They had moved out of their family homes to live in two group homes, next to each other in the Village. The women lived in one dwelling and the men in the other. They supported each other and their siblings and were the talk of the Village for months two years ago when they made their moves out of their family homes. He had found them a curious group, but had never seen any harm in their living the way they chose. And Ryes was an exception in her own way by choosing to remain with him here in this home. He cleared his throat and they settled back to a listening mode again.

"The only cubs we managed to have were one birthing of three. A son and two daughters," Rowan continued, starting out again.

"Three cubs? In one birth?" Sabin questioned abruptly, his eyes appeared doubtful at this news. But both Rowan's glare and Maren's nod silenced him. He picked up his mug and appeared to mull it over as he settled back in his chair ready to listen again.

"We lost Ranna to a fever when she was still an infant," Rowan added, looking to the others with a steady light in his eyes. "The other two grew up to be sturdy and bold. They may have had their mother's looks, but unfortunately inherited my temper." Maren rolled his eyes, nodding in agreement. But there was pride in Rowan's voice as he gave his grandson a merry wink. They were still his cubs and his cubs' cubs.

"Jana wasn't one to stay at home, either. She journeyed often in the woods and hills, looking for something she couldn't name. Sometimes she let me go with her, but other times she just wanted to venture out alone. I let her go because I loved her. Then one day, when Ronn and Tanns were fifteen summers old, she didn't return home. I searched all the night and found no trace of her passage. For almost a month she remained away. We exhausted ourselves from our searching and grieving and couldn't believe our eyes when we found her in the kitchen preparing breakfast one morning. She acted as if she'd done no more than spend a night out in the woods. She had also brought home a stranger."

"The stranger turned out to be a young woman named Tyra of House Li, who spoke with such a heavy accent and in a strange way that it was hard to understand what she was saying at times. She was shy, oddly dressed and seemed no older than our own cubs until you looked into her eyes. Her eyes were the holders of the ages. I recall feeling like the youngster when I beheld her eyes. And she had the most beautiful, long flaming-red hair. It wasn't too long after that I had noticed Ronn had taken to her. I wasn't unhappy with this because she seemed like a good, caring person. Jana treated her as a daughter, while Tanns accepted her as a sister, replacing the one she'd lost, in many ways. We were a mended family and lived quite happily."

"About a year after Tyra had settled in with us, Korman started to realize his greater size gave him certain advantages over most of the men in the Village. He was beginning the rampage which would continue to this day, over twenty years," he related. His eyes were bright with the pain the memories opened afresh in his heart, as he looked at them all, sitting around the table. The young men and women stirred restlessly as his pain swept them all deeper into his story. Ryes lowered her eyes, seeming to feel his pain within, too.

"Was that when he killed them?" Torr questioned in a low voice, sounding worried. Rowan glanced at him, then smiled and chuckled, breaking the suspense in the room.

"Then Ryes would've never been born," he chided. Bemused, Garth cuffed Torr lightly on the shoulder, and turned smiling back to Ryes, seeing her blush.

"Well, Great Storyteller, what did happen?" he asked. Rowan saw where his true interest lay and smiled to himself. Garth looked as if he wanted to reach out and touch Ryes, but hesitated. He obviously didn't to look to rush things between them, yet. Rowan wondered if after all this time, it might be the best for them both? He realized he could be patient too.

"Ronn and Tyra ran away to escape Korman's interference, when he started to show an interest in her too. They journeyed many long days to the ancient ruins on the far northern horizon with our mixed blessings. There they made whatever life they managed to gain, before Korman finally found them. The only reason I can think of was he was so deeply insulted by the incident which happened when they left, as they humiliated him before the whole village, that he felt he had to track them down and finish things the way he thought it should have gone. I will never speak to the man after all the horror he's inflicted upon Matlowe and my family through the years, even to find out. All I know is that it'd been about a year and a half since Ronn and Tyra left when one morning I came out to find Tyra on the doorstep, drenched in her own blood. I brought her in and tried to clean and bandage her wounds, but she was horribly torn up. I'd never seen someone so savaged. The only thing I could do was make her comfortable as she insisted on telling me all that happened. In a small pack she carried on her chest was a tiny, snarling she-cub. With her last breaths she gave me their tale and Ryes' life into my hands." Rowan noted everyone was still again, rooted by the images in their minds his words wove for them. He took in a deep breath, still seeing her blood staining his hands. After a moment, he was ready to continue.

"She said they lived happily in their chosen isolation, near the destroyed city." Rowan stopped, to muse a moment. "She never called them 'the ruins,' it was always 'the destroyed city, or Hailys.'" He shook his head and puzzled it a moment, then continued, "Anyway, the gods blessed them with a fine litter of cubs, four in all."

"Four?" Torr whispered in disbelief. The others shook their heads in wonder or looked surprise. Rowan cleared his throat noisily, glaring them back to silence. He knew the truth in this matter himself and would never tolerate their doubt. They saw this and granted him their silent acceptance.

"One morning, as she was out hunting, since she and Ronn took turns with their daily chores, Tyra heard a strange cry. Fearing the worst, she ran back to Ronn, who stayed with the cubs that day. She burst into the clearing near their shelter to find Korman over the bodies of her new family. Ronn lay across the clearing in a pool of his own blood."

"'You're mine and I've come for you!' Korman had cried out in his blood lust. Rage overcame Tyra, so she showed him her answer in action. She charged him with her hunting spear and drove him away."

"Her spear?" Maren blurted out in shock, "But that's against all laws and custom!" His outrage showed plainly in his young face. A hunting spear was to be used for hunting animals only. By long tradition women were forbidden to ever take up arms against a man. For Tyra to use her spear against Korman was to declare her life forfeit.

"I'm not defending her," Rowan replied reasonably, "I'm merely telling it as she told me." Even though the tale was old, he still felt the sting of his grandson's cry. His heart ached for those he loved, whose deeds were far beyond recall.

"Someone who was desperate, or shocked at the sudden carnage of her loved ones wouldn't be thinking of custom; only of defense, or revenge. Since she merely drove him off, she wasn't too far out of line," Garth offered in a low voice. Ryes, who had been acutely embarrassed at the anger over her mother's actions, looked up startled at his quiet statement. Their eyes locked and everyone else could see the sympathy he'd given on her behalf was gratefully recognized by Ryes. The intensity of their apparent emotions caused Ardis to look away for a moment.

"I don't think it sounded too unreasonable, given what he'd done," Shadd said into the following silence. "Who kills babies like that?" she asked, sounding horrified. She frowned and blushed, but stood by her words. Ardis met her eyes and smiled, nodding her support.

"Only a heartless monster," Ardis added.

"That could well be a very justified reaction," Sabin voiced his support of Garth and Shadd's observations. He looked meaningfully at Maren, who seemed to get his hint and settled back again. "So Rowan, we know she didn't kill Korman, or Tyra would be here to tell us this tale, herself," he prompted.

"She would've saved the Village a lot of pain and lives IF she had been able to kill him then," Torr remarked with a twisted grimace. This earned him both agreement and disapproval from the others around the table.

Taking another pull off his mug and clearing his throat once again, Rowan regained some perspective. When Tyra had given him the accounting of what had occurred, she had given it to him directly mind-to-mind. It was the one reason he knew it all so well, having her own memories of the time. He knew it was something he could never forget. It was the one detail he'd never spoken of to anyone, as no one would believe a woman having so strong a Talent. Having given him the clear details, so he could stand for her in the Village Council yet shielding him from her intense pain had spoken to him of how great a Talent she'd actually been. It was why, he was sure, he was so in tune with Ryes even to this day.

"No, she merely drove him away. She returned to give her family as good a burial as she could, when she discovered one small daughter still survived. Putting the remaining bodies of her children with that of Ronn, she built a cairn of stones, which she gathered from the ruins nearby. Knowing there was little protection for her out there, now that Korman found them, Tyra set out for the Village. True to his nature, Korman tracked her and attacked her twice more before she could get back to me. They were savage, brutal attacks filled with unreasoning hate." Rowan looked up to the other faces around the table, his eyes returning to the present. "I tried to present Tyra's story in a Village Council meeting, but they did not believe me and Elders Kornn and Roul forbid me to ever speak of it again in a council meeting. They banned me from the council for years afterwards." His deep betrayal was clear in his voice and eyes. "She never received the justice she deserved," he added, then took a deep breath and let it out. It did not do him, nor Tyra, any good to get so upset any more.

"Later, when things around here had calmed down a bit, I left Ryes with Tara of House Itten, one of the caravaners whose own first cub was due soon, and journeyed to the ruins myself. Korman had gone on a journey to Toulton with his father, so I knew she'd be safe while I was gone. Tara and the other caravaners would make sure she was protected. It's not that I doubted Tyra's story, but rather I wanted to see the last resting place of Jana's and my only son."

"Why couldn't Jana take care of Ryes?" Shadd asked, frowning.

"She'd died a month before Tyra returned. She slipped and fell while fishing and hit her head, drowning before Grandfather could reach her," Maren supplied, seeing the instant pain in Rowan's eyes that the question brought out.

"So you found it? What was it like?" Torr asked in his straightforward manner, bringing them all back from that other old tragedy.

"Yes, I found it very quickly since she had described it so well. Tyra had used the rock from the ruins to good advantage. It was beautifully done. I didn't disturb a stone of it." Rowan's eyes misted up for a moment, recalling a scene only he had seen. Maren nodded, understanding.

"Life is short enough without Korman to add more troubles," he stated, meeting his grandfather's eyes. There was a small moment of quiet, as if to honor those who died so violently... so young.

"Well, the 'snarling she-cub' sure grew up to be one fine huntress," Garth spoke up, breaking the silence. Smiles broke out around the table. Rowan looked across to Ryes and nodded.

"I really didn't have to teach her too much, there. She took to the woods, as a bird to the air. There was a time when Ryes was three years old and we..."

And so the tales of the harrowing hunts began. Rhys sat and half-listened, fingering the fine white fur in her lap. She was thinking for the first time on how the young men here were quietly competing

for her approval. It was an entirely new thing for her. She didn't
know how to react. She'd never been close to any of them.
Whenever other villagers called upon Rowan, she'd either watch
quietly where she couldn't be seen, or retreat to the river bank, or
forest for the peace of nature. Rowan never forced her attendance.
This was the closest she'd ever come to sitting near Maren at a table!

It was different with the caravaners. They were her extended
family and more like cousins to her than potential mates. This just
seemed so unnatural.

She was examining the beltknife and noted the same design
and stones decorated the one Garth wore on his belt. She closed her
eyes for a brief moment, wondering what it was like to have family;
cubs and a man to care for. Tyra and Ronn had seemed to have it all,
until Korman showed up and took their lives. When she opened them,
Garth eyes sought hers with a strange warmth in their depths. Her
breath caught in her throat for a moment, as her heart hammered in
her chest. Why had he given her the knife? It looked well-made and
the gemstones had been faceted with great skill and care. Was he
thinking of mating her, when the time came? If so, she'd have to
warn him of the danger with Korman watching her so closely! She'd
never let him get hurt, if she could help it. What could she do to
protect him, or the others here, if they chose to try to stand against
Korman? She didn't think she was worth the price they'd pay for such
arrogance.

"Don't you like the knife?" Garth finally asked her in a low
voice, as the others were loudly arguing over some niggling point of
an old village legend. "I finished it last winter and wanted to give it to
someone special. With the way you've taken us under your wing to
teach us all to become better hunters and providers, I thought you
deserved it more than anyone else I know."

"Something like this should go to your first mate," she quietly
protested with an embarrassed smile quirking the corners of her
mouth. "Not someone like me."

"What's wrong with you?" he asked, a look of concern upon
his face, "And what makes you think I wouldn't ask for the privilege of
being your first?" She blushed darkly at this, her eyes shadowed.

"Korman," she said in a low voice, barely above a whisper,
looking down at her lap and avoiding his eyes. "Let me know his
plans for me earlier this evening. I'd rather die," she admitted. Her
shoulder twinged in pain, in reaction.

Garth was shocked. The laughter around them only added to
the unreality of what he just heard. He wondered what she planned
to do? He could understand Korman wanting to force himself on her,

most especially to prove he could take Tyra's daughter as his ultimate victory, but thought they could find a way to hide the signs of it being her time from him. Then he, Garth, could take her to wife and get her pregnant with his cub instead. It was a simple plan and one that could work. But he couldn't see her as trying to kill herself to keep out of Korman's claws. Did she plan upon running away, as her mother and father did before? Did he want her badly enough to leave Matlowe with her? All his friends and family were here. What truly lay beyond Matlowe?

"There are other ways," he tried to encourage her. She looked up, her green eyes held his in question. Yes, he thought, it was those beautiful green eyes which held his heart captive! As a child, he couldn't believe how different they were, and that as he helped to hold her down for the others to strike her, he found himself caught up in her eyes. It wasn't witchcraft; it was a glimpse into her soul which caught at him. There was kindness, gentleness and caring, yet a rock core to solidly center herself upon. He could see it all and wanted her more than ever.

"What other ways?" she asked, glad for answers from someone. There was no derision here. He meant it.

"Free mating will sometimes catch you earlier, than waiting for your regular, full season to come. That's how Glyn managed to father Karr's two cubs. We could also try to hide the signs when your time comes, so Korman wouldn't know," he offered with a confident smile.

Her heart caught in her throat a moment, as she thought on what he was offering her. Freedom to mate as she willed? No wonder few of the cubs looked to be Korman's! The villagers were outwitting him! And no wonder Karr allowed Glyn to live in her home, after the shaking fever left him almost crippled last winter. He was the father of her cubs! He was skilled in making creative pieces out of metal, but not good at more than simple chores or watching the village herd beasts, when it came to providing food for the cubs. Once the Caravans reached the village this winter, things would be easier for him. For Darman, the Caravan leader, loved his creations, fetching a good price for them in the other villages and towns, and would reward him well for his craft and skilled imagination.

"But he watches me all the time," she protested in a small voice, as hoped dawned in her eyes. "I'll have to think on this," she finally stated. So many possibilities now opened at her feet, making her feel giddy. Free mating? It was the love play between those in love; an imitation of the real mating which promised to come later. It could cause a pregnancy before it was the proper time? This was news, indeed! And since Korman can't be everywhere at once... She wanted to jump up and hug Garth in joy. It was all she could do to hold herself still, as she wasn't sure how he'd react to such a display of emotion. And not to mention how the others in the room with them would act.

"I'll be waiting for your yes," he promised. She blushed once more. She recalled Ardis casting her a look which promised a fight, while out on the hunt. Did she consider Garth her mate? Were they already free mating? Still, he looked at her and her alone, all day. She realized she needed to know the truth about it, one way or the other.

"What about Ardis? Aren't you two..." she realized she couldn't even finish her question, as their eyes met.

"No," he chuckled merrily in a low voice. "She wishes, but since we've been cubs, there's been no one but you. You recall that rainy day?" he asked, knowing he was damming himself. She nodded her head, her eyes shadowed for a moment.

"You held me down," she agreed, "but you never hit me, even when the others were telling you to do it. I didn't know why, but was very glad when you let me go." A smile teased at the corner of her lips, tantalizing him. "You're very strong."

"I now know that what we all did that day and at other times was wrong. I'd take away those memories from you, if I could. But when your eyes looked into mine, I knew then that I had to win you for my own someday. I just never thought I'd get the chance," he admitted.

"What does everyone do to an outcast? To someone who's different? I managed to get through it and put it well into the past, where it belongs. I never thought of myself as a prize for anyone to pursue; that you would ever want me..." she admitted, as she smiled for him. She wondered if this was some kind of twisted joke? She saw Sabin and Ardis noting their quite discussion, but they were more involved in what the rest were talking about. Could Garth really mean all he said? His apology sounded true to her ears and the pounding of her heart betrayed her own interest in him... But, why now? When Korman threatened to rip everything she valued apart?

"Give me a chance and I'll show you how very special you are to me," he promised, glad she'd seem to have let go of the pains they had caused her long ago.

"All right," she agreed, "I'll give you a chance." She was blushing once more and very unsure what to do now that she'd agreed. She wished Rinna was here so they could talk about it all. She briefly met Rowan's eyes and saw he looked to be keeping an eye on them, too. He gave her a heartfelt smile of encouragement, which reached within and gave her courage. "We probably should join in on the amazing hunting accounts the others are talking about for now," she suggested with a smile. His face looked as if he were so terribly pleased as a huge smile lit up, dazzling her again.

"That's probably a good idea," he agreed, shifting closer to her and looking up to get a nod of approval from Sabin. He felt he didn't need wings as he was already soaring.

Finally, after several more hours of jokes and stories and odd Village history shared, Torr put his hands up in surrender.

"Hold!" he declared, then stretched and shook his head. "The hour must be getting late!" He threw in a huge yawn. Ryes cracked a smile to see so great a yawn. "It's about time for us to crawl back to our old hole." He stood up, knocking his chair to the floor accidently. He grinned as he bent down to pick it back up, setting it into place. The others started standing up, stretching and nodding in agreement.

"Please," Rowan said, standing up too. "You can stay the night here. The fireplace is built to warm this room and the sleeping chambers. It's very comfortable with the spring chill still in the air. The old fathers of my family really knew how to build a home." There was a measure of pride in the old man's voice.

"Hey, you can see into the back rooms through here," Sabin declared as he stood next to the fireplace. Rhys was staring at Rowan in shock. He'd never asked any of the villagers to stay over before, and it was almost a month since Darman and Rinna left for their annual rounds of the more established villages and towns for trading, entertaining and doing their parts in helping to keep order among the Kingdoms. She had neatened their room and made sure their things were safely stored and ready for their return later in the year. So they did have their expansive bed for a couple of the men to use, as well as her own. The women would have to use the bunks up in the loft, as she would have to tonight. Now she was glad she had cleaned and freshened up the loft beds last week.

She smiled and blushed as she set aside her gifts, then stood and walked over to the chest near the door to their sleeping rooms. The rest watched as she fetched extra blankets to keep them warm.

"Here you go," Rhys said playfully as she loaded Torr down with an armload of bedding. He smiled in surprise and grunted in exaggeration at the weight she'd dropped into his arms.

"Let me help with your load," Maren laughed as he joined them in the fun and took one of the blankets. Rhys laughed with the others at their antics, as she gathered more for her and the ladies then closed the chest.

"You men get to sleep in the rooms down here while the ladies and I get to sleep upstairs," she told them with a smile; her eyes meeting Garth's once again as she gave him a big smile. Ardis and Shadd appeared relieved at hearing this news. Rhys stepped over to the stairs leading up, at the end of the room to show them the way.

"Then we'll bid you a goodnight, Torr Strong-arm," Shadd teased as she turned with a laugh, following Ryes. The men's laughter followed the three up the loft.

"You do have a large home," Ardis commented, looking around the neat loft and the beds against the far wall. There were chests to store clothes and paintings as well as shelves on the walls. There were even tables, and a writing desk. The chimney of the fireplace radiated enough heat to keep them warm, too. She was amazed.

"In the winter months our friends, the caravaners, live in the homes around us, but sometimes they bring extra folk along with them. So, it's better to have the room, if needed, than not to have it and everyone uncomfortable and over-crowded," she explained with a smile. She went to one chest and pulled out night tunics for all three of them, guessing their sizes, then tossed one to each of them and stepped behind the one drape to change. Ardis let out a low whistle.

"All the comforts of home," she sighed as she picked out the bed she wanted to use for the night, sitting down upon it and feeling how thick and comfortable it was just to sit upon. And it smelled fresh up here in the loft, as if it was cleaned and cared for regularly.

"I think we all need to move out this way," Shadd suggested. "It must be a lot of fun to be a part of life out here in the winter." She held up the gown Ryes had thrown her way and was feeling the smoothness of the fabric, as she marveled at the pattern woven into it. Ryes stepped out from behind the drape with a big smile.

"It's the best time of the year," she told her, "Go ahead and change. There's a dirty laundry basket in there to use for your soiled clothes, too," she offered.

"Do all the houses have bathing rooms and waste chairs like yours?" Ardis asked, having marveled at those luxuries earlier this evening. Those rooms were off the kitchen and just a wonderful idea.

"All the ones I've been in have them," she replied, taking out her braid and brushing out her hair as she sat down on one of the beds. It was very long, curling and a dark red. "I thought Aunt Tanns' house had them, too?"

"Very few in Old Matlowe do," Shadd replied as she appeared wearing the night tunic and smiling as she twirled in front of a mirror she discovered hanging near a corner. Then she started fussing with her blonde-kissed light brown hair, pulling it back from her face and smiling at herself. Ardis smiled to see her friend so happy. She was fingering a brush she'd found on another nearby table. Ryes didn't object to her using it, either.

"It's something to think about," Ardis agreed. "Would you want us out here near you, Ryes?" she suddenly asked. She turned to see Ryes smiling, her eyes lighting up with humor.

"Why not? I think it would be fun to finally have some real friends year round and close by," she returned. Then she looked surprised and stood back up from the bed she was sitting on. "I forgot something downstairs. I'll be right back!" She tossed the brush to Shadd as she peeked to see if the men had left the main room. Ardis laughed as she realized what it had to be. Shadd appeared puzzled.

"Her package," she mouthed in a low whisper. Shadd nodded catching on. She used the brush as Ardis stepped back to change, too. She admired the intricate carving in the wooden back of it and sighed. Yes, she could get used to this too quickly.

Rowan had extinguished the oil lamps, closed the front door and ushered the young men through to the sleeping rooms. They quickly picked from the two rooms offered and Garth was cozying down in the warm, soft bed he had once slept in long ago, his eyes turned to the slowly dying fire. Sleep refused to come to him right away. His mind wandered upon the day's events and that Ryes had finally accepted him into her life. How they would go about it from here would be something they would have to figure out, but he had finally won the chance to win her heart. He remembered Korman had let all the men in Matlowe know that she was his and his only. Still, today he had won and he would do everything he could to keep her safe. She was a mate worth having! She was smart, a fearless huntress, had a kind heart and kept a neat home. Her laughter was musical and her eyes magical.

As his thoughts drifted towards sleep, Garth was startled as he saw a lithe form slip quietly across the main room, as he was looking through the flames. It was Ryes and he almost chuckled aloud as he saw her returning to the stairs with a bundle in her arms. Rowan had put it on a cupboard in his weaving room and she couldn't sleep until she was sure it was safe. He wanted to go to her and hold her in his arms, but knew this was not the time, yet. Maren was sleeping soundly against his back already, so he nudged him away and settled down to sleep again. With a sigh of regret, he surrendered to his body's fatigue as a smile still played upon his lips.

Near the Yuri

Ryes awoke early and wondered for a moment why she wasn't in her own bed, then saw her new friends soundly sleeping in beds next to hers. She smiled as she remembered she had plenty of company to feed this morning, realizing it was akin to having her caravaner family back. She dug into a chest she kept some extra clothes in and came up with something suitable for each of them, then taking her own choice, went downstairs to the bathing room and started filling the tub and putting on some fresh wood to warm the water. Then she started to see to things in the kitchen, since it would take several minutes for the water to get warm enough to bathe.

Garth awoke, hearing water flowing nearby, and then recalled he was staying in a house right next to the Yuri River! He smiled to himself as he realized he needed to use the waste chair. Whatever it was they were drinking last night was easy on his body, since he didn't have the headache, or nausea, he would've had with his own home brew. He eased away from Maren, shoving the blanket he'd been wrapped up in against his back, so he wouldn't wake right away. It was still early light and the birds were just starting their morning songs. He saw the fireplace embers were banked, but still radiating their residual heat. He walked into the kitchen, noting the oven was going with fresh wood and he thought there was dough rising in a large bowl on a table next to the oven. Curious, he peered into the bathing room and saw Ryes immersed in a tub of warm water, quietly humming to herself with her eyes closed in pleasure.

"Good morning," he said, in a low voice as he stepped into the room. "I was just going to use your waste chair. Do you mind if I take a bath too?" he asked. Her eyes flew open and focused on him in surprise.

"No, I don't mind," she replied with a smile alighting upon her lips. Garth disappeared for a few moments, then she heard the flush and he returned and finished stripping down, piling his clothes atop a basket near the curtain with his back to her. He pulled the curtain closed with a grin, turned and stepped over to the tub. She looked surprised as she saw he meant to bathe with her. She blushed and appeared flustered, but seemed to steel her courage.

He grinned mischievously. Good. She wasn't going to retract her offer, as he feared. He thought this was a good test to start things off with for them both. He saw she saw his arousal and she averted her eyes from his body as she moved over to make room for him next to her, blushing furiously. There was plenty of room for them both here. He reveled in the warm water as he climbed in then wrapped his arms about her, holding her against his body. She was tense, but then finally relaxed after a few moments and looked up to him, smiling.

"I've wanted you in my life forever," he admitted in a husky whisper, realizing they were both trembling.

"I used to wonder why you liked to try to follow me at times. I remember telling Tara about it and she laughed and told me you'd never harm me, but I had no way of knowing for sure. So, I became one with the forest to get away."

"So you became a better huntress because of me?" he huffed out a laugh as she nodded. "I was only trying to get to a chance to talk with you alone… to get to know you better," he assured her with a grin, holding her closer. He could feel her heart beat faster.

"I know. I think I've known it for a long time, but never really believed it until now," she replied breathlessly, as she looked into his eyes. He smiled as he bent down to kiss her and teased her until he got her to relax fully. He realized this was the way he wanted to start every morning for the rest of his life.

"Oh, that smells good!" Maren exclaimed as he appeared in the kitchen. Ryes grinned at this and playfully swatted at his hand as he tried to snatch a cooking meat strip.

"Not yet," she scolded him, still smiling. "I put fresh water in the bathtub, if you want to take a bath," she offered as a distraction, "It should be ready by now."

"Ah, it's been at least a year since I got to use your bathtub," he sighed with pleasure at the memory. "But I don't have anything clean to wear," he protested, wanting to be fully clean.

"I put some of Ronn's old things in there for all of you to use. They're clean and might even fit." Garth came in from outside, looking happy. He was wearing a fresh tunic with a hunting bird in flight stitched into the left breast. He remembered seeing it before, folded up in a chest upstairs.

"I hope you're right," Maren told her with a shake of his head. "I recall messing with Ronn's things once when I was little and the scolding Rowan gave me then. I had nightmares for a week!"

"Maren, he's softened up through time. Ronn is gone and I'm sure will not have minded you using his clothes. Don't worry! Now scoot!" She ordered, giving him an impish smile. He nodded and went through the curtain quickly. She heard his sigh of pleasure as he climbed into the water.

"Oh there you are," Sabin said as he entered the kitchen shortly thereafter. Ryes was handing Garth a mug of hot tea. He looked up and smiled at his friend, as if he were extremely pleased with himself. Sabin gave him a nod, guessing what it might imply. "Where's Maren?" he asked, knowing he'd get the tale later.

"In taking a bath," Ryes told him as she handed him a mug, too. He caught the rich aroma of the tea and closed his eyes for a moment, enjoying it. Then his eyes opened with a puzzled look.

"Taking a bath?" he questioned. She pointed towards the curtained doorway opposite the kitchen hearth. "I have to see this! This had to be what you and the women were fussing over last night!" He set down the mug, crossed the room in two strides to pull open the curtain and look inside. Maren was practically submersed in the water with his eyes closed in pleasure.

"You're letting in a cold draft," they heard Maren protest. Sabin laughed as he went into the small room to stand next to the tub. His eyes held wonder at such an extravagance!

"You'd better hurry! I want a bath, too," he demanded. Then left to go use the waste chair, he'd been introduced to the night before. They had a bug-filled outhouse at their home, which they shared with the ladies. This was a whole world better! He had to know if any of the other houses out here were also this well-equipped!

"Maren comes here with Tanns from time-to-time, so knows how to use the old-style things we have. Aunt Tanns doesn't like me much, so I never stick around when they're visiting. That's why I'm only starting to get to know him now," she explained to Garth as they sat at the kitchen table.

"Why doesn't she like you?" he asked, puzzled.

"Rowan said he thought it was because I looked too much like Tyra and she mourned her death for a long time. I guess they were very close and I remind her of what she lost. Other than that, I don't know," she told him. She looked a little lost. His heart went out to her. To live in the shadow of all her mother was and could do and to be rejected because she wasn't her mother. It had to have been hard for her.

"That doesn't make it right," he stressed. There was a loud splash from the bathing room and Ryes shook her head with a smile and sigh. Sabin had decided he was going to bathe with Maren as he did not want to wait. They sounded more like children than young men.

"It might not be right, but it is the way things are," she returned. "I quit trying to get her to like me and just have gone on with my life. She doesn't want to change and I don't want to make her change, anymore. Tara used to always tell me it was what was best for me and as I've gotten older, I realized she was right."

"But anytime anyone's sick, I've seen her send you out for the plants she needs to make the medicines. You let her order you about all the time."

"I know where to find them and know what it's like to be sick. So, I don't mind doing it for her. She tries to help everyone else as best she can. The only thing I never understood is her attachment to Korman. I guess that makes him my uncle!" She made a disgusted face as this thought occurred to her.

"How can she hold dear Tyra's murderer, if she loved Tyra so much?" Garth questioned, puzzled even more. He wondered if Maren would have any insights to make matters more clear? Understanding this may provide him with a key to dealing with Korman.

"Ryes, your grandfather's still asleep," Torr told her, as he stepped into the kitchen. She nodded her head in understanding.

"It's getting harder and harder to get him up and moving in the mornings. He's aging, but no matter how I try to get him to see he still has plenty of years ahead, he won't listen. I think he's starting to see himself as a burden to me. But he's never been that – ever!" she declared with a heartfelt sigh.

"He only needs new challenges to find the drive again," Garth told her with a gentle nudge. She looked up at him, meeting his eyes.

"Like new cubs to help take care of?" she queried with a blush. He nodded his head with a big smile, as he winked at her in agreement.

"That might do," Torr agreed with a surprised smile. Garth appeared to have finally managed to get past her shyness. They both looked too happy this morning! And they were sitting close together and very relaxed. Rhys glanced up at him and gave her head a small shake as she laughed.

"Is nothing around here sacred?" she questioned, teasing them both.

"No. Nothing," Garth assured her laughing, too.

"Where have Maren and Sabin gone off to?" Torr asked, thinking they might have already gone home. Still, it smelled too wonderful in here with all the baking and food preparation, so knew they wouldn't have gone far.

"In taking a bath," Ryes informed him, indicating the curtained doorway across the room.

"A bath?" he asked, astonished.

"Why not? It feels great!" Garth stated merrily. This was all Torr needed as he turned and strode quickly for the indicated doorway.

"I don't know if three of them will fit," Ryes commented with a chuckle and a shake of her head.

"Let them settle it," Garth said as he put his arm about her. She started to pull away, then relaxed against him with a sigh, as they snuggled together.

"This is going to take a lot of getting used to," she warned him.

"For both of us, I think," he assured her, feeling ever so content in this moment, as he nuzzled her ear in affection.

Rowan watched them for a few moments from the doorway, trying not to be seen. He slowly backed away with a quiet sigh. His plan had worked far better than he ever dreamed. He had seen him draw her out last night and his heart had been filled with hope. The only surprise was Garth dressed in one of Ronn's old tunics. It called to mind seeing Ronn and Tyra together, so long ago. He realized it was time to let his son's ghost go. It was only right for Ryes to use her father's things as she felt best. Maybe he could now find the courage to let a few other ghosts go onto their final rest? He hoped so... He retreated to his room to give them a little time together.

"I don't know about this," Shadd commented as she pulled down her night tunic, still smoothing the fabric against her body in pleasure. "This had to have been the best night's sleep I've ever had in my whole life! Can you imagine sleeping in a bed like this every night?" Ardis scrunched up her nose and then tossed her pillow at her friend's head. Shadd ducked and laughed.

"It was my best, too," she admitted. "I don't recall ever sleeping in this late, before. And the mouthwatering odors from below are like a dream in their own right. Still..." she started, but couldn't finish her sentence.   She bent down to finish making the bed, determined to make hers as neatly as Ryes had made the bed she'd slept in last night. How had she done it all with them sleeping in the same room?

"Are you sure it's not just jealousy? After all, Garth's never been interested in you. He treats us both like sisters, no different than the way he treats Mitt!" Ardis stopped to glare at her, but Shadd met her glare with the truth in her steady gaze. "I thought we were looking for a good, new friend. And I think we've actually found one in Ryes. Let the fantasy of him go, and give her a chance," she suggested, trying to get her to see reason.

"I don't know if I can. It's like I can't help myself," Ardis admitted. Shadd laughed lightly at this, stepping close to her friend, putting her hands upon her shoulders. Then she brushed some of Ardis' curling dark hair away from her face.

"You're so pretty, you could have just about any man in Matlowe you wanted! He's the one who will lose out. Let him go. Ryes has a lot to offer us if we have the courage to accept her friendship," she pressed, gripping Ardis' shoulder. She finally relaxed, closing her eyes as she sighed and nodded, trying to re-center herself and find sanity. She opened them a few moments later, a smile blossoming upon her lips once again.

"Hmmm.... Maybe Torr, Kovan or Sabin would be better choices?" she teased in return, pulling away as she laughed.

"Hey, watch it! I'm after Torr for myself," she returned, as she laughed merrily. "Let's go see about a bath first then some breakfast?" Shadd suggested. Ardis scooped up the clothes Ryes left for her atop the chest at the foot of the bed she used. The tunic looked her size and the stitching was so pretty.

"Why not? I was dreaming of a hot bath last night! Time to make that dream come true," she agreed, smiling.

"Mind if we take that bath together? That way we can get a share of that food that much sooner," Shadd suggested, as she was looking at the tunic Ryes had left out for her, too. It looked like it was a good fit. They hadn't bathed together since they were kids, but the tub had looked plenty big enough to accommodate them both.

"Now that's something I haven't heard from you in a lot of years! It'll be fun! Yes, let's go and bathe together," Ardis agreed with a laugh, snagging one of the brushes as well as her borrowed clean clothes.

"Should we go down dressed as we are now? Won't the men get ideas, seeing us in night clothes?"

"Let's see if they get the hint!" she teasingly returned, feeling daring this fine morning. "It'll be fun to see their jaws drop open!" Both women laughed as they headed for the stairs down.

"Now you two look just so cozy!" Shadd commented as she and Ardis came down to the inviting aromas in the kitchen. Ryes turned around from putting the last of the sweet bread into the oven, as Garth looked up from where he was mixing some honey butter in a bowl, as he'd been asked to do for her. The women were still dressed in their night tunics, carrying the clean clothes Ryes had set out for them earlier. She gave them a warm, inviting smile as she gestured to the bathing room. Maren emerged from it and pulled the curtain aside for them, seeing they had arrived.

"I cleaned and filled it with fresh water which is just about the right temperature now," he told them, as if expecting the women. Sabin and Torr were eyeing their friends in amazement, as they sat at the table with mugs of tea in their hands. "Enjoy it, ladies!"

"I'm sure we will," Ardis replied, noting the reaction they were getting out of the other two men at the table. She smiled in a teasing manner as she stepped inside after Shadd and pulled the curtain closed. Maren shrugged and went over to the wash sink, starting to fill it up so he could get started on washing the dirty clothes.

"Oh Maren, you don't have to do that," Ryes started to scold him, realizing what he was doing. "I'll take care of it, honestly." He grinned at her with a shake of his head in denial.

"I'm all grown up now and can do this by myself," he declared. "And, you have to finish breakfast. I'm starving!" Garth finished with the honeyed-butter and put the bowl into the cool box, as she'd asked him earlier. Then he went outside to get some firewood for the oven and cooking stove. Ryes didn't know what to say about all this help, much less what to do about it. She kept having the cross the kitchen back and forth as she forgot things she needed, as she was finishing her preparations. Torr gave Sabin a nudge and smile as they watched her trying to ignore them.

"This is tea!" Sabin declared as he finally put down his mug, feeling very satisfied. Torr chuckled and agreed.

"Are you sure you don't need us helping you?" Torr asked Ryes. She stopped and shook her head.

"Even if I could find something for you to do, there's simply no room, Torr. But thank you for the offer," she replied with a chuckle. She surveyed the room again, trying to see what needed to be done next. So she grabbed a large pot and went over to the sink to fill it. Next she took it over to the stove and put it on to let it heat up. After a while, the women emerged from the bathing room as the water was boiling, looking refreshed and practically glowing.

"That was amazing!" Shadd stated as she crossed the room. She threw her arms about Ryes, giving her a hug in gratitude. "Thank you! And you get to take a bath like that every day?" she asked, as she pulled away.

"Pretty much," she replied with a light laugh and a merry smile in her eyes. "Did you like the soaps? I make them myself."

"They're much better than the ones we have," Ardis said, grinning as she took a mug of tea Sabin was handing her. "You're going to have to show us how to make them."

"Why don't you make them and sell them to the rest of the Village? You could make some real money pretty quick as I'm sure everyone would love them," Shadd asked. Ryes offered her a mug of tea as she shook her head and laughed.

"That might be, but when would I get time to hunt, if I have to mind a shop? I make my soaps in the winter when the caravaners are making theirs. But we'll set aside a few days to do it, so I can teach you how, if you wish to do that for yourself," she offered, smiling. Shadd's eyes glittered with plans in the making.

"Good morning," Rowan happily greeted them as he stepped into the kitchen. "I hope everyone slept well?"

"Very comfortably, Elder Rowan," Sabin assured him, with a small bow of his head. "Are the rest of the houses out here this well-equipped?" he asked, curious. "Bathing rooms and waste chairs, soft beds and amazing kitchens, all with running water! It would make living out here more than worth it all."

"There are about twenty-eight or so homes which the caravaners use and have sealed up until their return this winter," Rowan replied, "but the rest of the houses do have plumbing and other comforts. They only need to be cleaned and some repairs done to make them usable again." Torr and Sabin's eyes met, looking like their plans were already forming with this news. It might be outside the regular, settled area of Matlowe Village, but it was a far better home than the ones they used now.

"It'd be better if I moved out near you, Grandfather, so I can help you, too," Maren stated as he now had their soiled clothes soaking in the sink with some of the soap shavings he recalled Rowan using once, a couple of years ago. "Ummm... sorry about this. I'm washing my own clothes, so I can change right away," he added in apology as he tugged on the fabric of Ronn's tunic. Rowan chuckled at this with a shake of his head.

"Maren, you can keep those clothes. I'm sure your wearing them is an honor to your uncle's memory." Garth emerged from the bathing room and smiled at this statement. He gave Rowan a nod of his head in agreement.

"Your bath's ready," he informed him. This surprised the old man, so he gave him a small bow in thanks.

"I should hurry then, so we can all eat breakfast. Thank you," he replied, meaning it, as he met Garth's eyes. Garth stepped aside letting him into the room, then letting the curtain drop again. He saw the surprised expression upon Maren's face as he stood in the middle of the room.

"What's the matter, Maren?" he asked. Ryes looked over as she put down her pot of cooked grains on the work table. She frowned, appearing to wonder.

"He's letting me keep this?" Maren finally spoke up, finding his voice.

"Why not?" Ryes questioned. "Ronn's well past being able to use it," she scolded. "And the blue looks very good on you, too." He turned at her compliment, a happy smile on his face. He stepped over, grabbed her hands and spun her around in a circle, in a happy dance. Amazed, Ryes laughed with him joyfully. It reminded her of Winterfest Day and as if they were dancing around a Winterfest Tree!

"He didn't yell at me!" he declared, finally letting her go amid the laughter sounding from the table.

"Of course not," she replied with warmth in her eyes. "Do you really mean to move all the way out here? Would your mother let you?" she asked, looking hopeful.

"I moved out last year," he told her with a smile, "she has no say about where I choose to live. And as long as I provide her with food, what can she complain about?" Ryes nodded her head in agreement, smiling as she returned to her last few tasks.

"The color does look good on you, Maren," Shadd told him as he returned to the table, still grinning happily. He gave her a nod of agreement as he picked up his mug, still feeling extremely pleased. Then there was the sound of scratching at the back door. A puzzled look was exchanged among the others in the kitchen, then Shadd's face broke out in a huge smile.

"What?" Torr asked her, frowning. She shook her head, hoarding her suspicion. Rhys started for the door, but Garth beat her to it. He let out a laugh as he swung it open wider.

"Mitt!" he declared, as he stepped aside and gestured her to enter the warm, inviting room.

"None of you came home last night and I was worried," she tried to scold as she came into the home. The bright, colorful rug below her sandals caught her eyes for a moment; then she tried to take in the whole room and the merry gathering of people in it. It was a spacious kitchen. Bigger than any she'd ever seen in her whole life! She froze, not sure of herself any more. Garth caught her up in a hug and pulled her away from the door with a laugh, closing it once again.

"We were invited to spend the night," Shadd told her. "You really should've come out with us, too." Mitt let go of her brother and nodded her head in agreement. Garth took her spear and put it into the stand next to the door where Ryes' were stored. Ryes offered her a mug of tea and gestured towards the table, around which everyone else was sitting.

"Sit down and make yourself at home. Breakfast is almost ready," she offered, smiling warmly. Numbly Mitt took the offered cup and sat down on a chair next to where she was sure Garth was sitting. Maren took the chair next to hers. He was grinning happily as he sipped his tea.

"That's a new tunic," Mitt stated, her eyes were wide as she noticed everyone was wearing new clothes. And they all looked clean, too! The women even had damp hair. "Did you all bathe in the river this morning?" she added. There was laughter from everyone in the kitchen.

"Well, we did take turns but we all took baths," Garth admitted, sitting down at the bench across from her.

"It was amazing! I have never felt so refreshed!" Shadd declared.

"We decided to look for a new house out here as our own," Ardis told her. "Would you like a room of your own?"

"Isn't this a bit far from everything and everyone?" she returned. She sipped from the mug in her hand and took a moment to look at it as the rich flavor lingered in her mouth. She sniffed it and closed her eyes in enjoyment.

"I'm moving out here," Maren assured her, smiling to see her expression.

"It'll sure be different having you about the house every day," Ryes confessed as she finished pulling the loaves of bread out of their pans. She reached up for a platter on a shelf overhead, so Maren jumped up and fetched it down for her, realizing what she needed. She laughed at this, speechless, and then hugged him.

"He won't be the only one here," Garth reminded her with a grin. Ryes nodded and blushed. He turned back and winked at Mitt. Mitt raised an eyebrow as she struggled with digesting it all.

"I'm surprised that none of the young men from the Caravan decided to stay with you this year?" Sabin pressed, baiting Garth. Ryes was just finishing slicing one of the loaves of bread and looked up to see the tension in Garth's back and shoulders. She blushed and shook her head in denial. Sabin was chuckling, seeing he'd scored.

"Darman's been promoting his one grandson, but Shams is out helping his mother on one of their southern routes. I've never truly been that interested in any of them that way. They're more like my brothers and cousins than ever a mating interest," she told him truthfully. "They're fond of being rootless and I don't think that's the life I want." She took out a clean cloth to wrap around her bread to keep it warm as she started on the other loaf. The others fell to chattering at the table while her own mind was still whirring. She wanted to escape the Village, but not her grandfather, nor the cubs she dearly loved. She saw Maren sneak a couple of slices of the fresh bread, sharing one with the others while he munched on the other.

"You just can't wait, can you?" she questioned merrily, as she realized in just over a day he had worked his way into her heart too and was another one she'd stay to protect. He shook his head no at this, enjoying his game. The others were laughing.

"Good Morning, Mitt," Rowan greeted her as he emerged from the bath room, joining the gathering.

"Good Morning Elder Rowan," she replied, smiling.

"In my own home, Rowan will do," he assured her, smiling in return. "I cleaned out the bathtub, so if you would like a bath, you are very welcome to take one after breakfast," he added in offer.

"Thank you, ...Rowan. That'd be wonderful," she stammered out, blushing. Rowan moved to the head of the table and took the chair on the other side of Mitt. Ryes had taken his appearance as a queue and started bringing over the platters and bowls of food to the table. Maren and Garth jumped up to lend her a hand in moving things to the table. Last came the honeyed butter and a few other bowls from the cool box. She finally took her seat on the bench, next to Garth and Rowan's chair.

Rowan noticed Ryes had gone all out in her preparations. There was a platter of tender, hot meat strips, a basketful of warm, nut biscuits, a large bowl of soft yellow cheese, a crock of sweet berry preserves and one of fresh honey-butter; a bowl of freshly boiled eggs, a very large bowl of sweetened cooked grains, two sliced loaves of sweet-seeded bread and finally two large pitchers of hot herbal tea with a jar of honey set between them for sweetening. The hungry young men and women dug in with sounds of delight. Ryes ate slowly, wondering when their last meal had been. They ate as if famished! Soon all the plates and bowls were cleared to the last crumb. They all relaxed around the table, drinking mugs of tea and appearing sated.

"That was delicious!" Sabin declared, patting his stomach. Ryes smiled in return, just finishing her last mouthful. It was what the Caravaners often told her, too. She looked around and saw happy smiles about her and was pleased. If she closed her eyes it was as if her dear friends from the caravans were around her. There was laughter and happy chatter and a warm feeling of belonging. She opened her eyes and smiled again; then sighed as she stood up and started collecting the platters and bowls that were emptied out. Garth's hand shot our and gently grabbed her wrist, startling her.

"No, Sweet One, let us take care of that chore. You've done quite a lot this morning already for us." There was a slight emphasis on the "sweet one" and she looked at him puzzled. He smiled expansively. "This is our way of repaying your kindness." Torr look at Garth in rebellion, Sabin nodded his agreement, while Maren laughed and started gathering up the empty plates within his reach.

"True Garth," Sabin agreed, "but the honor of scrubbing goes to you." Garth laughed as he took the dishes from Ryes' hands. She stood with a puzzled frown. Ardis laughed, seeing her uncertainty.

"Will I have any dishes left when you're done?" she teased, smiling now.

"We'll watch and make sure they do a good job," Mitt offered with a grin, joining the game.

"Let me get you some fresh clothes, too," Ryes offered, remembering she still had a guest needing a bath. She went into the bathing room to start the water then off to her chest upstairs to find something for her to wear. She returned and set it up for her, showing her the tunic. "Do you like it?" she asked, holding it up.

"Yes!" She stood up to take the offered clothing.

"Come on, let me show you the bathing room." Ryes led her into the room and closed the drape behind them. She emerged a few moments later.

"I do have a few other things to take care of," Ryes said to the rest, smiling again. She stopped at the laundry sink and gave the clothes a good stir then added a few more soap flakes and a few more dirty clothes. Then went off to check on the other rooms of the house, and opening windows and shutters to let in light and air. She noted their guests had been neat and folded and stacked the blankets used from last night. She would air them out later, so put them aside and went to attend her other chores.

"She sure is quiet," Torr commented as he returned to the kitchen table, having secured a fresh pot of tea. He sat down once again. Ardis got up and left the room, appearing as if she'd forgotten something. Shadd followed.

"Ah, that is mostly my own fault for letting her do as she wished for too many years. If any villagers came to visit, she'd take off to the woods. But it's another thing entirely when the Caravans arrive in the late fall. She's always right here in the thick of things, wanting to know the latest news of the happenings out in the greater world," Rowan admitted with a hearty sigh.

"Maybe because the caravaners never passed any judgments against her for things she had no control over?" he asked, seeming concerned. "How can we help her come to accept us more?"

"If we move into some of the empty houses out here, she'll have to get used to having villagers around all the time," Maren put in, having finished drying the pots, putting them away. He seemed to know where everything belonged in the kitchen.

"That might be the only way. If she's forced to live day-to-day with all of you and your families who come to visit, she'll have to get used to dealing with everyone normally. This truly is a good start," Rowan agreed. "Garth just put that bowl in the cool box. We can use the rest of it later," he directed, pointing.

"Let me," Maren offered, taking the bowl and putting a flat cover over it, then placed it in the cool box and secured the door again. Sabin and Torr stepped over and pulled the door open to look inside. A cool waft of air blew in their faces. There were shelves within which held fruits, herbs, cloth-wrapped meats, eggs and other, covered bowls and dishes. Maren closed the door again. Garth smiled, having marveled at it earlier.

"It's to keep foods cooler so they don't spoil too fast," Rowan explained, coming over to join them. "Of course it doesn't work as well in the summer months as in the winter."

"Now that's clever," Sabin stated as he looked, still appearing to think on it. He opened it again and found the small pipes which ran inside along the back and sides. He could hear the water gurgling as it flowed through them. With the thick walls to insulate it, the air inside was much cooler than outside. Another marvel lost in the march of time! He closed it again and secured it.

"You realize more and more of all the wonders we've left behind us, as we've forgotten how to make or repair so many useful things," Garth commented. Rowan chuckled.

"And this one was considered to be very primitive," he merrily related. "My grandparents' grandparents had ones which used the sun to power it and it wasn't water cooled. I recall my grandfather saying how you could keep food for months in the 'freezer.'"

"If people with a mind, a heart and hands like ours could build these things in the first place, then we can find a way to either do it all again, or repair what they left behind," Garth asserted, holding out his hands in emphasis.

"But where do we find any books or scrolls which they might have written about it all now?" Torr asked, wondering. Garth looked them each in the eye, already knowing the answer to his question.

"In the destroyed city," he told them, sure this was where they needed to begin their quest. Sabin gave him a strange look at this and he suddenly wondered if he'd had a Vision he hadn't shared with him yet?

"Darman has many contraptions that are supposed to be very old, but I don't think they could date back to then," Rowan said, not seeing the surprise in Garth's eyes. "Maybe in one of the bigger cities someone's figured out how to make them already?"

Garth recalled the toy flyer Ryes had as a child. It drifted upon the winds as the aircraft of the ancients were said to have flown. Who'd made it and could they make a larger one, he wondered?

"Korman told me yesterday, on my way home, what he has planned for me," Ryes told Ardis as they were straightening up the loft room. They sat down on some chairs nearby. The shutters were open and sunlight came streaming in through the actual glass window panes.

"You're making a joke?" Shadd asked, but saw the agony in her green eyes. There were no defenses in their emerald depths, just open trustfulness. Now she could understand why Garth had set his heart on her years ago.

"I can't see Garth getting hurt over this. And other than running off to the horizon, I've no idea what to do. There's no way I'd ever become one of Korman's whores!" The vehemence in her voice caught at her own heart. Ardis nodded her agreement too.

"Have you and Garth already..." Shadd suddenly prompted, hinting at what she wanted to voice with a crude gesture. Ryes blushed darkly and averted her eyes. She nodded her head in answer. She never saw the spark of fury alight in Ardis' eyes but Shadd did and elbowed her in the side – hard.

"What was it like?" she pressed with an eager look in her eyes. Ryes turned to face them again, looking a little uncertain.

"It was far more than I ever imagined. Most of the caravaner girls our age have been teasing me forever, saying I'm going to die an old, sterile maid. They've been free-making at least a year now."

"Well," Ardis began, clearing her throat as she shifted closer to her, "free-mating can sometimes catch you early before your season, but it doesn't always work," she admitted. Ryes gave her a nod, glad to hear the news confirmed.

"Wasn't that how Glyn fathered Karr's two cubs?" she asked, blushing. Ardis and Shadd laughed, nodding their heads.

"And Sela's two and quite a few others. But it's supposed to be harder with the first one. Korman's getting lazy. He may not bother you. Maybe he only wants to terrorize you into thinking you have no choice?"

"He watches me all the time. I think he's wanting to get back at my mother still, through me." Ryes then dropped her tunic off her shoulder to show her the gash marks, just scabbed over this morning. When Garth asked her about them, he was very upset. "He did this to me yesterday."

Ardis was shocked. Seeing the depth and length of the cuts in her shoulder kept her rooted for the moment. Korman was very serious indeed! It unnerved her as she planned on avoiding him when her time came – sometime before the end of the summer per her mother. This was proof his streak of cruelty still ran very deep!

"Maybe a few months in the woods would be the best idea after all?" Shadd finally advised. "With your woodcraft skills, I'm sure he'd never be able to track you down." Ryes sighed as she pulled her tunic back up into place. She looked so hopeless!

"He found my parents. It took him well over a year, but he hated Tyra that much for something she did to him," she stated. "Even if I can get through my first season out and away from Matlowe, I still think he'll try to do something to my grandfather before I could return. Revenge is his favorite thing, after all. Korman has no honor. If I do leave Matlowe, I'll have to find a good enough place to move Rowan in with me, to keep him safe. I just don't know where to go."

"You must have maps here. Have the caravaners given you any ideas?" Ardis asked. Ryes barked out a short laugh.

"Yes, I have maps but Darman only tells me where I shouldn't go," she replied, smiling at a memory. "I think I'll have to go exploring on my own to see."

Suddenly voices were raised in anger and yowling cries could be heard coming from outside. Ryes jumped up, surprise and panic in her eyes. She turned to see a steely look in Ardis' eyes as they both realized who it had to be at the same time. Shadd face held panic.

"We have to get out there now!" she stated, angry now.

"Korman," Ryes breathed as they all pelted for the stairs and the front door.

Confrontations

He awoke early in the morning, before Tanns and the cubs; still bothered by that little shibler's attitude, yesterday. He thought sure she was going to run her spear through him when he turned his back on her in the alleyway. A memory of Tyra charging with her hunting spear briefly passed before his eyes, reminding him of their similarities, again. Tanns was unhappy over his interest in Ryes, but after all these years, he wasn't going to let Tyra win again!

It was as clear to him now as the day it happened, twenty years ago... As Tyra and Ronn were leaving Matlowe, wearing their backpacks and laughing, he stood to block their path out of the Village. Ronn may have been of a smaller stature, but he was very strong; maybe the strongest in the Village. He looked forward to this day, when he could publicly take possession of the most beautiful woman in all Tayna. But, just as he was about to issue his challenge, Tyra saw him and ran forward, hunting spear held before her as a staff, shoving him into the great well in the middle of the Village. She took him totally by surprise! And, as he floundered in the cold water sputtering, they laughed at him! The whole Village joined them in their mirth! Then, Ronn and Tyra turned and went their own way, leaving Matlowe behind. It took over a year for him to find them, and then he waited for the right moment to get things settled properly. Now, he wanted to seal his vengeance by making Ryes mate with him, but the farga was no better than her mother. He'd wipe that look of defiance from her eyes once and for all time!

"Korman?" Tanns sleepily quested after his warmth, as he rolled away from her.

"I can't sleep. You rest before the cubs awaken," he told her with a gentleness Ryes would've been stunned to hear coming from him. He loved Tanns and was proud of their cubs, but this problem with Tyra ran deeper. And even if she already threatened to throw him out of their home if he didn't stop, he knew he had to do this one last act, or he felt his soul would never be at peace. Tanns shifted and replied to him sleepily as she drifted off, once more. He pulled the blanket up over her shoulder and got up.

Korman got dressed, grabbed a bowl of leftover stew, and then went outside to eat his breakfast in peace. Maren had done very well on the hunts this week and they were eating well off his work. He knew he didn't like him, but it was well past the point where he cared if his son would ever understand him. Maren was honorable in his support of his family at least, but he knew that when he finally settled with a woman of his own, he'd be too busy to help them much. In a way, it was too bad Ryes was Tyra's daughter, because as a Huntress supporting her family, she was superb. He was still undecided if he would let her live after the mating. Killing her meant he'd actually have to take up his own spear and start hunting once more; something he hadn't done in years.

Korman saw one of the young huntresses dressed and heading toward the river. She was carrying a spear, but not a load of laundry to wash. She was looking around as if searching for signs of something, as she went. She appeared concerned. Perhaps, she was heading out for an early morning swim? She was the youngest one of the women living in that separate house. He was sure the others living there were due for their firsts later this year, but was stirring up enough trouble with Tanns over Ryes. He knew she wouldn't tolerate much more. They weren't important to him. Tyra's daughter was the only one who mattered! Still, as he finished his stew, he found he was curious as to what she was up to. So, he decided to follow, but not too closely...

"This is the main inflow pipe for the house. The river's current keeps the pressure mostly constant, so we don't have too many problems with it. The pressure is actually higher in the early spring with the snow melts up north. We have a valve we can adjust to make sure we're not flooded out then. If you were to wade out a bit from the shore, you'd see where the intake lies, deep underwater, but anchored well up away from the silty bottom and it's braced with large stone blocks. There's three grades of metal mesh over the intake, to keep small animals, debris and trash out of our water," Rowan explained, happy to have such keen interest in these old engineering concepts. "We have to replace the meshes every few years, and our supply's running low now. Darman'll bring us more in the fall. We clean them out every day when the spring floods hit and sometimes more than once a day. That's what that harnesses are for, so the currents don't carry us away." He pointed to three stout ropes with leather harnesses tied to them and secured to a very sturdy post.

"And this one's the outflow?" Sabin asked as he pointed to the larger pipe, which took a strange turn from running near the inflow tube, as if going its own direction.

"Yes, it is. Since the houses here, and the rest of Matlowe, get fresh water supplies from upstream, the outflow pipes from these houses join up and dump back into the Yuri River further downstream. That way our water stays clean. Each house has vent pipes too which also need care, but we have them covered with the meshes too. We care for the pipes most of the year, with the caravan people helping during the winter months, when they're living here. They're very easy to maintain and take up little time, for all we save in using them."

"They sure do," Torr agreed with a nod of his head.

"Do the flood waters ever reach your homes? Or have you ever been flooded out?" Sabin queried. It was an important point with living very near the flowing waters.

"Not since the days my father was a child," he replied with a chuckle, understanding their trying to cover the possible situations! "The chance exists and the waters will rise up to the top of the bank with the spring thaws and rains, which is another reason to get used to the river's `voice;' to know how the Yuri's feeling. It takes time, but you'll know when things aren't right, and can prepare for it. I think that's why all these houses have snug, well-built lofts - in case the waters ever invade the lower levels. And there's at least one roof door set to give access up top, some homes have two. It was another precaution the old ones took, because of the dangers in living next to the river. And a small boat is stored in the lofts of most of the homes, again, just in case."

"So, which houses have the caravaners set aside for their own use?" Garth asked, surveying the area. A small, open meadow lay between the houses and the bank of the river. There were some docks out into the water but no boats were present. The land down to the river was lush with grasses and other small plants. He saw Ryes had a small, kitchen garden planted, which looked to be thriving.

"The three right here next to ours, then there are six of the ones lying behind those three. There are three more beyond those and I think about eight on the side away from the river, from us. The rest are empty and need repair to be more comfortable," he told him. Garth saw which ones he indicated, noting the Caravaner's mark above each of their doors. It made it easier for them to pick and choose which houses they could take for their own use. As soon as the huntresses were finished, they'd start giving them a serious evaluation, to see which ones were best.

"Which would you suggest?" Sabin asked, wondering how much work would be needed to get them in shape for living? It may only be spring, but it always paid to plan ahead. And it was a good thing there were many hands to help with this project!

"Any of those three, downstream from us. A caravan lost a wagon and two families two years ago to a forest fire. They're in

pretty good shape, even for sitting abandoned for that long." Then
Rowan stopped, spotting Korman nearby watching them. The young
hunters saw him too and the smiles melted from their faces as a
grimness settled within their eyes. This was trouble!

"We could set one of the houses up for Shadd, Ardis and Mitt
to use, if they want to move out here, too," Maren continued, turning
his back on his father and continuing their conversation with his
grandfather. He already knew Korman's opinion of him, and didn't
care. He knew if he took up an active interest in any of the women in
Matlowe, Korman would probably do his best to take her before him.
Just to prove that he could. So, he gave him as little time or attention
as he could, knowing in this he truly was behaving recklessly. He'd
felt his claws before.

"Yes, you could," Rowan agreed, not taking his eyes off the
old murderer. Korman saw he had their attention, with the one
exception, so leaned casually against a tree, checking his claws for
dirt. Rowan strode forward several paces and stopped.

"Enough is enough! What do you want here, Korman? You're
trespassing!" he demanded outright, his anger flashing in his amber
eyes.

"You know what I want," he replied, paying him little, real
attention. "You can't protect her forever, old man."

"She's not yours," Garth stated in a quiet voice, as he
stepped up next to Rowan, recalling the gashes on Ryes' shoulder.
Korman's eyes took on a deadly glint as he stepped away from the
tree. He looked incensed that one of the young men dared to deny
him what he wanted.

"Then who do you think she belongs to?" he demanded,
taking a step closer to the group. Garth's heart hammered in his
chest. If he couldn't protect her from someone like Korman, what
right did he have to take her as his own, he wondered? He came to
his decision.

"Me," he stated, flat out, his eyes never leaving Korman's as
he spoke. He suddenly yowled out his very first, real challenge cry,
with Korman answering it with his own. Rowan and the others were
startled to hear this coming from Garth. He was always so laid back
and easy going, that none ever considered him a fighter before. But,
before either of them could do anything else, Ryes ran around from
the front of the house, throwing herself at Korman's bulk in a wild
fury, hitting him with her balled fists. Maren, Sabin and Torr were
astounded, watching as Korman roughly grabbed her flailing arms,
turning to deal with her. He pinned her arms against her sides and
lifted her into the air.

"You don't own me! I belong to myself!" Ryes screamed out hotly. She was trying to twist and kick him, as well. She scored a glancing kick to his face. Growling, Korman shook her harshly and threw her to the ground. Ryes rolled away, scrambling to get back on her feet. Garth was incensed, his blood boiling. How dare Korman put his hands on her like that! Before he knew what he was doing, he ran across, placing himself solidly between the both of them, his fury plain in his eyes.

Ryes was getting up to attack again, but froze in her steps as she saw Garth protecting her. A wave of cold sanity washed through her. She wanted to protect him, not be the cause for him to be hurt, or killed! How could this have gone so wrong? No, she thought, he'll tear you apart! Garth glanced briefly at her, as if he heard her thoughts, but wouldn't be swayed now! She was worth all this to him, and much more...

"You have to throw women about to prove you're tough," he taunted, "Afraid to take on someone more your own size?"

"I'm not afraid of the likes of you, cub," he returned. Korman's face was fierce with delight. It'd been a very long time since he was last challenged and it looked like he was ready to show these young upstarts he was the leader in the Village!

Garth and Korman began to strip to the waist. Garth handed his things to Ryes, without looking at her. They both knew that Korman would fight underhanded; he had before. It was best to keep an eye on him, at all times. Ryes paused long enough to give Garth a quick touch on his cheek, surprising him, and then backed out of the way. Her small show of support helped ease the cold dread in his stomach. And no matter what the outcome, he'd been her first after all, and Korman could never take that away from them! Rowan and the others stepped closer to watch. Shadd and Ardis appeared and hurried straight over, concern reflected in their eyes.

"They're not really going to fight?" Shadd whispered to Torr, suddenly appearing afraid for Garth.

"Yes, they are," he breathed in return, "should outdated traditions still hold so much power?" He saw this challenge had her shaken. She was such a kind soul, which was one of the things he loved best about her. He extended his hand and took one of hers, giving it a gentle squeeze, to let her know it'd be all right. If worse came to worse, he'd step in and make sure Garth wouldn't be killed. She smiled up at him, throwing an arm around him and hugging herself to his side, appreciating his strength. She looked happy about her choice expressed so simply! Surprised by this action, he put his arm around her shoulders, hugging her back. Yes, he realized, there were some things well worth fighting for...

"Old traditions shouldn't," she breathed in return.

Ardis saw this and smiled to herself. Sabin caught her eye, and her smile grew as she stepped over to him and put an arm around him, leaning her head against his strong shoulder, as he put an arm around her, too. Why not? After all the talk about free-mating, why not give it a real try, instead of relying upon the stories her mother, sister and other women told her? She was old enough now, after all! She saw Ryes looking so alone and scared, holding Garth's things. Her eyes were glued to the two men circling each other, not seeing anything else. It was plain he truly mattered to her. Possibly, as much as he claimed to want her through the years?

"Maybe if Korman tries to cross the line, we should all step in and break it up? After all, he couldn't stand against all of us at once," Ardis suggested in a low voice. She glanced at Sabin's face, seeing he looked ready to do so. She was relieved. Sanity might prevail, after all.

"That's the plan," he replied. Torr and Maren gave him a nod in agreement. Mitt ran up and joined the others, seeing her brother and Korman facing each other off. Her mouth was open but no sound came out. Rowan patted her shoulder in reassurance.

"We won't let this go too far," he let her know in a low voice. She nodded numbly, appearing worried.

Maren noted the pairing off, wondering. The women had NEVER done such a thing, before. And Ardis? She'd pursued Garth since he told her he was in love with Ryes, when they were ten years old. Had she decided Sabin would do, after all? And would he ever find a woman of his own? With his mother acknowledging Korman as his father, few of the young women wanted anything to do with him. They were afraid of his father having free access to their homes! He would do his best to keep him out, but wasn't sure if he could best him in a fight. Maybe his leaving Matlowe might be the only chance he'd ever have for happiness, after all? Tyra and Ronn might've had the right of things at that. He'd just had to find a place his father would never think of to look for...then, he might have a chance.

Garth and Korman started circling each other warily. Ryes thought he looked smaller, but then Korman was much older. Garth's muscles rippled under his golden-tanned skin, while Korman's barrel chest displayed little. With youthful vigor against long experience, it'd be difficult to guess the outcome of this match. She suddenly recalled Rowan's lecture about believing in people and realized she needed to let go of her fears for Garth, if she wanted him to win. He could only prevail, if he knew she believed he would win this fight. Somehow, she HAD to believe it and let him see it in her!

Garth feinted, but Korman wouldn't be drawn out, yet. His cold, brown eyes were narrowed to slits, studying his every move. Then he crouched, but Garth wouldn't charge. He, too, was studying Korman and using his head, as he knew this was the only way to win. With a jump, Korman suddenly launched himself straight at him. Garth quickly jumped high, twisting toward the right, aiming a kick at Korman's lowered head. Korman swerved, but was grazed by the kick; hit in the same spot Ryes kicked before. He turned and ran after Garth, pinning him from behind in a tight bear hug. But he'd only pinned one of his arms. With his free fist, Garth pounded Korman's head; the same spot he just kicked. Korman let out a yowl, but wouldn't let go, intending to squeeze the life out of his opponent, now. Garth gasped, struggling for air, his rising panic giving him the determination to claw apart as much of Korman's face, as he could reach with his one free arm. He knew he'd be finished if he fainted for lack of air! He managed to hook his claws into his brow and tore it open. Korman growled and released him, stepping back as he had a hand to his face.

Garth staggered forward a few steps, fresh air once again flooding his aching lungs, almost making him feel giddy. His eyes momentarily caught Ryes' emerald ones and saw she believed in him! She thought he could win! How could he lose her now? He spun on the ball of his foot, remembering where he was, to see blood flowing down into Korman's left eye, as he swiped at it to see better. Garth charged, aiming a quick kick at Korman's groin, but he twisted out of the way, trying to wrap his arms around him, again. He swiftly jumped back out of reach, looking for another opening. Garth realized Korman was older and slower after all! If he used his head, he could win this one; he knew it! Korman leapt toward him, grazing his ribs with his claws, as he sprang back to avoid another grab. Both opponents now stood in a ready crouch, panting, sizing up each other once more. Bright red blood welled up from the scratches on Garth's ribs, as blood still flowed freely from the scratches over Korman's left eye.

Korman angrily wiped the blood from his face and charged again. As Garth twisted aside to avoid the rush, he tripped over a rock and fell to the ground with a hard thump; shock in his eyes. Korman, half-blinded with his own blood, and going too fast to correct his charge, tripped over Garth. He tumbled down the bank and fell head first into the icy, cold river. In a daze, Garth started to get to his feet, while Korman floundered in the river bank mud. He stood unsteadily and then climbed up the bank to face him once more. Both were now exhausted, but determined. Unexpectedly, Rowan stepped up to stand between them to intervene.

"It's a draw, Korman," Rowan stated, as he signaled the young men to back him. They did so with a confidence Ryes was surprised to see. "You can finish this up later, both of you." There was a sternness in Rowan's voice which Ryes hadn't heard from him in years! Korman shook himself, but didn't answer. He saw the other young men backing his decision and wasn't up to fighting the whole lot at once, so he scooped up his things and turned for his own home. As he passed Ryes, he saw the same defiant stance the mother had once taken in his presence. Well, this one would learn to accept him, or she could join her long-dead mother. This challenge was far from over, in his mind.

Ryes was immediately by Garth's side with a happy warmth in her eyes, her heart beating strongly with relief. He was a far better fighter than she had ever thought. If the fight had played to its conclusion, he would've actually won!

"Guess we'll have to throw you back into the bath tub," she teased him with a smile. He huffed out a laugh as he scooped her up into his arms; his prize. She was as light as a feather!

"Hurray for Garth!" Maren shouted, hoping his father heard him, "the best fighter in the Village!" He thumped his shoulder in pride. The others were laughing as they gathered closer, offering their congratulations, too. Mitt was practically jumping up and down now in joy.

"We really need to take care of those scratches," Ryes suggested. He was laughing and feeling on top of the world, but she knew he'd start feeling every inch of those gashes, very soon.

"Give yourself a few days to heal, and then go for it again. I know you'll win," Sabin advised, having had an instant's glimpse where he saw into the mists of the future with his Vision Talent. He saw Garth standing over Korman, who lay upon the forest floor at his feet, bleeding and beaten.

"I will," he promised. "It's time to take this old murderer down and free our women!" he agreed.

"Let's see about getting you cleaned up, then having a look at those houses," Torr supplied. It didn't look like Garth was going to let go of Ryes, now.

"Come along..." Rowan urged them all back to his home. Matlowe Village had a new champion, after all. He suddenly felt sorrier for Tanns, than anyone else. She loved Korman deeply and would fear for him, now. And her fears might be for good reason.

"I'll be right back. I need to do something first," Mitt said, veering off towards the Village.

"You're missing out," Maren warned her, but she had already trotted off. He shrugged his shoulders and followed the rest back inside.

"Tanns!" she heard her husband shout out, as he stood blocking the light streaming in the doorway. "I need your help, please." There was a note she'd never heard in his voice, as she finished binding a poultice over a burn Marla had gotten this morning.

"Come in, sit down and give me a few moments," Tanns urged, sure he'd done something stupid again. She focused upon her patient. "Now here's what's left of the poultice. Just keep it from drying out and put on a fresh dressing before going to bed tonight, Marla," she instructed as she met her eyes. "And return the bowl tomorrow. We'll both see that the burn will be well on its way to healing by then."

"Thank you, Tanns. I will," she replied with a happier smile than when she started the treatment. She pressed a few coins into her hand in gratitude. "You're bleeding," she commented to Korman, who sat behind Tanns. He was stripped down to the waist and had blood streaming down from his forehead.

"Get out of my house!" he snapped, pointing toward the open door. Marla jumped up and quickly scrambled for the door, barely dodging Rowis as she ran outside, clutching the precious bowl. She was all too familiar with Korman's brutality through the years and didn't want to stay a moment longer.

"Korman!" she heard Tanns shouting at him, her disgust plain in her voice.

"Father, you're hurt," she heard Rowis declaring.

"Mother?" Marla heard as she gained the pathway heading home, again. Mitt ran and caught up to her. She stopped and leaned against a wall panting heavily as she tried to catch her breath. "Are you all right?" Mitt pressed, appearing wary.

"I'll be fine, Honey-sweet," she replied as she calmed down. "Where did you get that tunic? It looks beautiful on you," she observed. Mitt waved her off, appearing as if she had something else on her mind.

"I've got to find Gann. I've got some important news for him," she told her. Marla's eyes widened as she connected Korman's injuries and Garth's absence.

"He's over at Karr's helping Glynn with something today. If that man is like that, is Garth still alive?" she demanded suddenly panicked. "He was off with that outcast again, wasn't he?"

"She's not a bad person, and only seems very shy. And Garth's fine except for a few scratches," she replied. "The challenge was called a draw and I want to make sure Gann knows about it, too."

"So, where did this change of heart come from for the outcast?" she returned, plucking at one of the sleeves of the new tunic. Mitt looked annoyed and brushed her mother's hand away.

"Not because of gifts," she returned a little disgusted. "Get to know her, Mother, and you'll see it too." With this she rushed off, looking for her other older brother, not seeing the look of surprise on her mother's face.

"Ah, I remember Tara," Ryes told the others in a low voice, as they walked through her "mother's" former home. In her mind's eye she could hear her calling out, asking her to watch the little ones while she finished baking the bread. She smiled to herself at this recollection, but in her heart she missed her all the more. "She taught me how to walk a taunt rope suspended high over everyone's head without fear, how to cook, and several different ways to tan hides." She sighed as she picked up a brush she was sure belonged to Tara. "She called me her `Wild Child,'" she added, smiling at the memory.

"She's one of the ones who died?" Shadd asked as they walked through the house, now feeling as if she might be disturbing ghosts. Ryes chuckled merrily, seeing fear in her eyes.

"Yes, but there's never anything to ever be afraid of her, here. She was a warm, wise woman who'd be sad if her old home never knew laughter, or warmth, again. She had five cubs, with Tarn, her oldest, being the one she wanted me to..." She found she couldn't even voice it.

"Oh," Torr replied, surprised, but Ryes shook her head, blushing at his implication. She recalled Darman and Rinna wanted her to mate their other grandson, Shams, instead. And she had no idea what he was like, nor was interested in either of them. Garth's eyes meeting hers briefly gave her to know that she'd found the one and only man for her!

"No. He's not my type, at all! He's more interested in how much money he can make from telling others their fortunes. Ironic, but his sweet mother and siblings died, while he survived!"

"It happens far too often," Ardis agreed, smiling. "I kinda like this one," she commented, looking to Shadd for her opinion.

"Well, the plumbing's still working, except for the cold box, which we can fix. Just a little cleaning up and patching and it should be cozy for the winter," Sabin agreed.

"I still don't know... What about having cubs this close to the river?" Shadd asked, concerned. Ryes chuckled at this.

"How many of you know I've already taught most of the younger cubs how to swim? I've shown them what dangers to watch for in the water and how to avoid them. I want them to be able to fish with some measure of safety. If you never teach your cubs to swim, then they'll only end up in trouble," she related. "I knew how to swim, long before I was out of diapers!"

"Lixi knows how to swim?" Sabin asked, surprised. "She never told me anything!"

"I asked them to keep quiet about it, because I didn't want their mothers upset with me. Why do you think she and Jons are so good at fishing?" she reminded them. They'd already forgotten her status with most of the other villagers. How quickly they accepted her! She couldn't believe it! Garth looked surprised, then laughed as he shook his head, amazed!

"She's been keeping the cubs busy, and teaching them little things, all along. Things which could someday save their lives!" he commented to the others.

"Now, you're going to have to teach me," Ardis told her, smiling at this news, "since we're going to be neighbors." Ryes smiled as she gave her a nod of her head.

"It's not a problem, believe me," she assured her.

"Ah, hot baths every day," Shadd sighed, as they stepped into the kitchen. This house was arranged a little differently from Ryes', with a door giving access to the bath room from the bedrooms and the kitchen, as well. "Yes, I think this is the one I like best, too," she agreed with her best friend.

"I'll go up and check the tiles on the roof. They looked fine from below, but I want to make sure there's no leaks, nor storm damage," Torr volunteered, recalling the bad one from this last winter.

"Thanks," Shadd told him as she met his eyes smiling. She went back to check on the bath tub. She filled it earlier, wanting to make sure there were no leaks, nor cracks. It was holding up, just fine. "The waste chair works, as do the sinks in the kitchen. This is a dream come true! No more hauling water from the central plaza!"

"Come on Maren, let's go have a look upstairs," Torr urged, no longer sure his feet truly touched the ground anymore. Garth chuckled at this, giving them a nod as they left the room, heading for the loft stairs.

"What do you say if we go straight home and start getting our things packed, now?" Ardis suggested, wanting to move out by tonight.

"That's a lot to get moved quickly," Shadd cautioned her.

"I have a windracer mare I could halter. If you can find the use of a cart, that is," Ryes suggested, thinking this would be the best idea she could think of for moving their things, if they were serious about it. Shadd looked at her in surprise.

"Where do you keep her?" she questioned, not having heard of her around here, before. "You OWN a windracer?"

"Honey was given to me three years ago by Darman, since I helped him in her birthing. Rowan got tired of trying to keep her out of the garden when I went out hunting, so I keep her in the field the caravaners use, when they winter here. I go riding every other day and sometimes give the cubs rides, too. She won't mind it, if I handle her," she offered.

"Lixi knows how to ride a windracer, too?" Sabin questioned, as Ardis and Garth were laughing at the expression on his face. "You didn't happen to teach the cubs how to fly too, did you?" he teased. He bet his sister, Sela, would be surprised to hear of all the things her small daughter could do on her own!

"No. I haven't quite figured that one out, yet," Ryes returned, laughing with the others in relief, as she blushed. Thank the gods, they didn't seem upset at all, she thought!

"We never appreciated how much you've done for us, in teaching the cubs so much," Garth admitted, as he hugged her close to his side. "Well, I know where there's a cart to use. I know my

Uncle Aric will let me use his, so let's get your fine mare and see how much we can still accomplish, today." Ryes smiled up at him, trying to get used to all this attention.

"That's the plan," she agreed.

"Let's get Kovin and Teris to help with the bundling and hauling," Ardis suggested, thinking they needed more hands to get this done quickly.

"I'll help you pack, but they can come out here and get this place swept out, at least," Sabin countered, feeling a little uncomfortable with Kovin hanging around her. He was starting to think he had a real chance now that Garth was firmly attached to Ryes, and he didn't want any interference from someone like Kovin! Ardis chuckled in answer, as Ryes led them out, catching his eye as the two of them lagged behind. She understood only too well what she saw there.

"If you insist," she agreed, as Shadd laughed merrily, stepping out behind them, having rejoined them.

"What's wrong with Kovin helping?" Ryes whispered in question to Garth, recalling who Kovin might be from their earlier hunt. He chuckled as he draped an arm over her shoulders.

"Sabin wants Ardis for himself and doesn't want Kovin to interfere," he replied in a low voice. She HAD been outside of Village life, too long! It wasn't that she wasn't bright, but she just didn't know any of the villagers!

"Garth! What're you doing way out here?" Karr demanded, finding him in Ryes' company. She stood holding Jons' hand, glad her daughter knew where this outcast lived; Mitt refused to show her the way. She'd been so mad when she heard he fought Korman. He didn't look injured and she noted that, as Ryes tried to step back from her wrath, he held her firmly beside him.

"We're moving out here," Ardis stated, hating the way she tried to constantly run Garth, Gann and Mitt's lives! Just because she was their older sister, didn't mean she could tell them the way they should do everything! She saw Ryes wanted to retreat, but Garth wasn't going to let her. She smiled, as she realized there were a few things they needed to teach her, too. How to stand up for herself, for starters! She wondered if she was this way around the caravaners?

"Yeah, hot baths every morning are more than I can stand missing, anymore," Shadd bragged, smiling merrily. Torr and Maren came out behind them, so she snatched up Torr's hand, as if she'd already moved him in with her. "And they're so much fun together," she openly baited her. Karr went several shades darker, as she struggled to find the words, which stuck in her throat. Wait until she told Rein about this! She'd never allow her son to live out here with such a slut!

"I'm moving out here, too," Garth told her in a level voice.

"But it's too far! How can you hunt?" she demanded. Ryes frowned, then raised an arm and silently pointed to a lush meadow about two hundred yards away, with the forest springing up behind it.

"It's actually a lot closer to the better hunting areas," she informed her. From the way the other young huntresses were acting, and Garth holding her next to his side, firm but gentle, this had to be some kind of challenge for her to face off. If she wanted to keep him in her bed, she had to let Karr know she wouldn't let her push him around, anymore. Karr let go of Jons and stepped up to Ryes, coming almost nose-to-nose.

"He's not for you, you whore," she threatened in a low voice, dripping with venom. This took the others aback, as Ryes stood her ground and met her stare with an icy coldness in her emerald eyes.

"Who Garth chooses to be with is NOT up to YOU. He's got more courage than most men in the Village, and I think anyone who can face off Korman, can decide things for himself. He's not a cub, Karr, and I'm not a whore." She kept her voice level, recalling a time she saw Tara facing off another caravan woman over something she hadn't understood at the time... now she thought she knew why. Garth pushed them apart, looking exasperated.

"Go home, Karr," he told her, then saw Gann, Mitt and Glyn approaching. "Do you think you can talk some sense into her?" he asked, hoping he had his brother's support, at least.

"What's this about you fighting Korman?" Gann asked, surprised to find him very much alive and looking far better than Old Korman!

"It was declared a draw, but next time," he promised, as Sabin nodded his head in agreement.

"A draw?" Gann questioned astonished, as Glyn picked up Jons, balancing her with his infant cub, he held in his arms, too.

"Rowan decided they already proved enough to each other. I think he's more worried about my mother losing her bedmate," Maren told them, grinning proudly.

"You witch! You're going to get Garth killed for nothing!" Karr declared as she dodged around Garth, throwing herself at Ryes. Ryes grabbed her wrists as they went down in a tangle of arms and legs. At least she couldn't get her claws into her, as she concentrated upon keeping a hold of her wrists. She knew she was taking a beating, as Karr was far heavier than she, but there was little she could do about it, as she hit her with her elbows and knees. They struggled for several long seconds before Garth and Gann pulled Karr off. Ryes stood up, brushing some of the leaves and sticks off her tunic, trying to think of how to defuse this situation.

"She didn't start anything," Ardis shouted at Karr, getting mad with her behavior. "She was in the loft talking with Shadd and I."

"Ryes tried to drive Korman off herself, when she came out and saw him here," Torr told her in a calmer voice.

"Garth's the one who issued the challenge," Maren told them, shocking his siblings anew.

"I couldn't stand the thought of Garth being hurt by Korman," Ryes assured her. "I'd rather..." she started, then saw the warning look in Garth's eyes. "...hoped we were more civilized than this," she finished, blushing as she lowered her eyes. Shadd stepped over to her side, subtlety blocking her from walking off, as she suspected she was about to do.

"Don't go. Garth needs you," she whispered. "You're right," she spoke up loudly. "We should all be more civilized than this! It's not Ryes' fault Korman hates her mother so much, that he wants to carry out his revenge upon her. It's about time the Village brought some justice to Tyra's ghost and either banish Korman, or hang him for her murder."

"He's getting old and is mostly harmless," Glyn protested, letting a squirming Jons back down.

"That's not what we saw earlier this morning!" Sabin swore. "If he decides to take an interest in Ardis too, I'm going to have a real fight on my hands! He hasn't changed, and as long as we allow him to do as he sees fit, none of our women are safe."

"We need this debated and put to a vote before the whole Village, but right now we need to catch Honey and get our things moved. I'm not going to miss out on a hot bath in the morning because you can't accept Garth finding someone you can't control, Karr." Shadd boldly told her, taking Ryes' arm and turning her toward the meadow. She saw the mare standing near a gate waiting, almost as if she knew. Ryes smiled, giving her a nod of her head, readily letting her lead her away from this insanity! Even the caravaners at their worst, never treated others as this sister of Garth's. It gave her second thoughts about their budding relationship, even after all she hoped lay between already. Could she truly learn to live with such hatred around her, all the time?

"What do you mean a hot bath in the morning?" Glyn asked, starting to follow the two women, wanting answers.

"Many of the houses here still have working plumbing and bath tubs. There's running water in the kitchen and even a waste chair, instead of using a community well, or any outhouses," Ardis told him grinning, as she saw the looks of astonishment on his and Gann's faces. It looked like Karr just heard her for the first time, too.

"I don't believe it," Glyn declared, stopping and turning to face her. Torr invited him into the home Ardis and Shadd just decided to keep as their own.

"This one now belongs to the ladies, but I'm sure they won't mind if you see it for yourselves," he invited. Garth realized Karr was relaxing and he exchanged glances with Gann. It was probably safe to let her go, for now.

"What's a waste chair?" she asked as Jons giggled.

"It's what we use when we come out for Old Rowan's stories," she told her mother. "I gotta go, mommy," she insisted, dancing on her toes. Garth smiled at this display. She had a way of controlling Karr too, he thought, as she turned from watching Ryes' back, to her daughter's compelling need.

"Is it all right, Ardis, if she uses your waste chair?" she asked with a sigh, taking Jons' hand.

"Yes, it is," she invited, gesturing towards her new home and laughing at this display. "Cubs had their own priorities, after all."

"Now, are you going to move into one of these houses with the rest of your friends, or are you moving in with Ryes and her grandfather?" Gann questioned his littermate, in a low voice.

"Ryes is already my free-mate," he told him grinning, as he straightened up his stance proudly, "you guess. Karr's going to have to get used to it!"

"No wonder Korman challenged you! You look as if you're not in pain. Are you all right?" he pressed.

"Actually, I challenged him, just as Maren told you. I got a few scratches, which Ryes already took care of for me. In a few days, if Korman hasn't been banished from Matlowe, I'll challenge him again and finish it well. Sabin said he saw me winning our next match and you know he's never been wrong, yet."

"It's more peaceful out here," he commented, looking back to the flowing river, appearing disturbed with the thought of his brother issuing a challenge. "Is this where the caravaners winter?" he questioned, still struggling within.

"Yes. You can see their marks over the doors to the houses they use. Rowan said any of the others are free for the rest of us," he informed him, grinning. It was obvious what he was thinking. Running water indoors was heaven sent; a great gift from the gods!

"But the river and the cubs," he protested.

"Jons already knows how to swim," he returned. The shock in his eyes was amusing to see.

"When and where could she?" he started, then saw Ryes leading a windracer mare by a rope, talking with Shadd as they approached. "She didn't, did she?" He suddenly saw what had to be the answer.

"She didn't want the cubs to get hurt, so taught them how to swim, as she taught them to fish. We all knew she taught them which berries are eatable and which herbs to gather, while she fed them for us. While we've been out hunting, or tending the gardens, or pens, she's been seeing to the welfare of the Village cubs. We owe her," he told him. Gann shook his head, full of doubt, but recalling Marla seemed to trust Jons' venturing all the way out to this place, to spend the day with the old storyteller and his outcast granddaughter.

"Mother's never worried about her being here, before." he offered, as Garth nodded his head, meeting his eyes squarely.

"Ryes has forgiven us for being so nasty to her through the years. Look at the way she just held Karr back, not fighting, nor trying to harm her. She's a Huntress and good at it. She could've easily killed Karr, but never extended a claw. I don't know of any fight between two women, that I've ever seen, where the one who could've easily won, didn't even try." Gann nodded his head, seeing what Garth was saying, knowing he was right.

"Honey! Honey!" Jons cried, as she ran out the door toward Ryes and Shadd. Ryes laughed as she scooped her up and put her upon the mare's back. Jons leaned forward, wrapping her small arms about the animal's neck, happily laughing as she hugged her. The animal remained calm.

"She knows how to ride, too," Garth added, smiling at this display. Karr now stood in the doorway, watching her daughter with this mystery woman. She'd just been verbally dressed down by Glyn and the others and was unsure of everything all over again. Ryes had never treated any of the Village cubs poorly. It was only that she still needed Garth's help, and if he left to move out here with her... She feared for him - greatly! Korman was too sneaking and violent.

"Let Jons show her mother what she can do," Garth called out, hoping Jons was a good enough rider. Ryes smiled at this, then passed the halter to the child. Jons, delighted, took it and sat up correctly. She nudged the mare gently in the sides with her knees and rode Honey in a tight circle, going from a walk, to a trot, and then reining back to a walk, again. Laughing, she stopped before her mother's shocked face. Garth and the others were cheering at her accomplishment, as she patted the mare's neck.

"Ryes taught me how to ride Honey, mommy," she declared proudly. Karr was torn between wanting to pull Jons off the beast to protect her, or hugging her in joy. She couldn't believe how well she actually controlled her!

"You learned it very well, cubling!" she agreed, giving in and hugging her, briefly.

"Let's go see to the packing," Glyn declared, happy with his daughter's newfound skills. He had to admit, running water, a cool box, waste chair and bath tub - all indoors - surely impressed him! He and Karr had to discuss this tonight, just between them!

Rowan, who'd taken a break from his loom, as he watched the whole thing, saw the crowd head toward the Village proper, in happier spirits. He was relieved. Ryes got along fine with the caravaners, but she needed this more, and the young women were defensive of her and willing to teach her how to deal with the rest. It'd soon get too noisy out here, like with the caravaners, only all the time. This made him feel good. It was time they both got back into life, in Matlowe. He turned for the house again, thinking he'd better make sure to shift things in Ryes' bedroom, so there'd be enough room for Garth's things, too. He chuckled as he thought of having new infant cubs in the house next year.

Murderer

"Ryyesss!" Rand and Aldin called out as they ran up to her, as she stood outside of Ardis and Shadd's home with Honey, waiting. She had the harness rigged and ready, but didn't want to burden Honey with the cart, until they were finished loading. It surely looked like they had a lot of things! She turned to happily greet the cubs, but saw they were crying and terrified.

"What's the problem?" she asked, going down on one knee, instantly concerned. There shouldn't be anything around here to scare them!

"Come, quick! He's got Lixi," Rand insisted, pulling her hand. "He's hurting her!"

"Who does?" she demanded, suddenly serious as she let them lead her off. "Who has Lixi?"

"A stranger! We never seen him a `fore. We were playing in our ol' house and he tried to grab Rand an' Lixi. I was hitting him and he let go of Rand. He still has Lixi!" Aldin told her. His eyes looked haunted that he couldn't protect both his friends. "We couldn't make him let her go!"

"I'll find her," Ryes promised, her stomach knotting as she wondered who'd do such a thing? They led her to a house and she saw their toys lay scattered within. It looked like some kind of struggle happened here. Some of their things were smashed, as if trodden upon. Ryes' stomach suddenly felt lead-weighted.

"Where did he go?" she pressed, very afraid for the cub.

"This way," Rand said, as she led her back out and down one of the unused paths. They stopped after a few feet, not knowing where to from there. Aldin started to cry.

"Shhhh," Ryes ordered as she was concentrating, kneeling down to examine the ground. She saw the scuff makes of the cub's feet as they must have tried to fight him. His traces lead off alone. "Go back and tell Sabin and the others," she whispered, "I'll find her," she promised. She saw their bruises clearly and gave each of them a quick kiss on top of their heads as she smiled for them. "Hurry," she urged. They ran off, still very frightened.

A cub stealer didn't deserve to live by their standards, here in Matlowe. The mortality rate was far too high with "regular" tragedies and inbreeding, which was starting to show with this fairly isolated group. The Huntress was ready to hunt one who should never exist. She drew an arrow in the dirt to indicate which way she went, hoping the others would be coming soon.

Ryes followed the trace, tracking the stranger, until she came to one of the more frequently used paths. She carefully left arrows to show her path to the followers. He could've gone any direction and she feared for the time lost in trying to pick up the trail again here. She closed her eyes and stood stock still, listening for several long, agonizing heartbeats. Finally, she thought she caught the sound of Lixi's voice coming from the empty dwellings, down a ways and on the other side of the path. She double checked for his trail, finding it once more. He surely wasn't a hunter, with such an obvious trace to follow! She left an obvious sign for the others to follow and then continued. She found the abandoned house and looked in a window. He had her pinned to the floor with his weight and was tearing off her clothes. Lixi struggled to breathe with his hand clamped over her lower face. Ryes' blood boiled as she leapt in through the missing window and charged. She kicked out, knocking him partly off the cub, surprising him.

"Run, Lixi!" she ordered with a shout, as she deployed her claws, savagely digging them into his back. He struggled to hold onto the cub. She pulled him back, away from her. Lixi quickly scrambled to her feet, running out the door, crying. With the child out of his reach, he turned his full attention to Ryes, twisting, trying to get to her. She hung onto his back with her claws still buried deep, avoiding his claws, as best she could.

"Your cub may have escaped, but you won't," he promised, as he threw his weight over, rolling so he was now on top of her, his back still to her.

His weight was crushing her, as Ryes let go and tried to get out from beneath this stinking man. The stench was amazing - as if he never bathed! She wondered how long he'd been lurking on the fringes of the Village? Everyone should've all noted him by the stench, alone! She tried to bunch up her legs to kick him off, when he rolled and jumped to his feet. She scrambled to her feet, facing him with a snarl upon her lips, realizing he cut her off from the door. She made a dash toward the window she used, but he charged to block her, swiping at her with his claws extended. She jumped back, coming up hard against a crumbling wall, blood now seeping through her tunic, as she tried to think of an escape. She darted back to the door, but he still blocked her escape. It was a vicious game to him!

"What do you gain from a cub's pain?" she demanded, still angry, utterly shocked to see he was naked from his waist down. What was he going to do to Lixi? She was merely a cub!

"Pleasure," he bragged, ready to take her out. "Pure pleasure!" Then, he found himself roughly grabbed from behind and pulled out the open doorway, not having heard anyone approaching!

"No one harms my mate," Garth growled, as he slammed the stranger up against the crumbling wall of another, empty house with all his strength. He knocked the wind out of him for a moment but then his eyes focused upon him with a snarl upon his face. Torr, Kovin and Maren were beside him, ready in case he should try to break and run. Sabin set Lixi down and stepped over, blocking Garth.

"This one's all mine," he rumbled out, growling deep in his throat. Ryes stepped out, putting a hand to her side as Lixi ran to her, throwing her arms about her legs, seeking protection with the Huntress. She smiled as she knelt down beside her, pulling her against her shoulder to comfort the cub's crying. Her clothing was in shreds.

"It's all right, Lixi," she crooned, holding her tight. She saw Shadd stepping over to them with shock in her eyes. "Let's get her away from this," Ryes suggested, knowing she didn't have the strength to do more to comfort her right now.

"Right. Lixi, dear, let's get you home to your mother," she suggested, as she crouched down next to them, stroking the cub's hair, gently. Lixi pulled back, sniffing and nodding her head to this. Shadd smiled as she picked her up. She frowned as she saw the blood on Ryes' tunic. "Are you all right?" she asked.

"I'll be fine," she assured her. "Could you get her back to Sela for me, please?" she asked, having never had to ask anything of any of the villagers, before. But, she knew she couldn't deal with Sela and the questions she'd ask now.

"It's not a problem. I'll take her right away," she agreed, seeing Sabin was holding the strange man pinned to the wall for a few moments, his eyes glazing, as he must be "seeing" something. She quickly stepped past the others, who were crowding this narrow path, heading for Sela's home. She didn't want to see what Sabin would do; she could guess it well enough. It was a good thing Ryes had sent the cubs back for them, seeing the way she'd been injured and the horrible bruises all over Lixi. Garth looked upset, while Sabin face was furious. His little niece being attacked was something he'd never tolerate!

As Sabin held the stranger pinned to the wall, a sudden vista opened up to him, from within through his Talent. He saw the faces and heard some of the names of the cubs and other people this vile animal had ravaged and killed through the years. He travelled from town to village, stealing, raping and killing his small victims. Every chance he got was an opportunity; even small, remote farms, where he was welcomed, then disappeared before the morning, having sated himself upon the children, both male and female. He knew he was hunted, but Matlowe seemed ideal with all the old abandoned houses to hide in; even if there were few cubs to whet his appetite. It was so strange that his ideal haunt was where he'd be finally cornered!

"Sabin, are you all right?" Ryes asked, stepping over and touching his shoulder. It was like they were locked in some kind of internal duel. In a flash, she saw everything he saw, and then staggered back, her face white as new-fallen snow. Garth wrapped his arms around her as he saw her face and the stricken horror in her eyes.

"What?" he demanded, knowing better than to ever disturb Sabin when he was having a Vision.

"He uses the cubs for his sexual desires, and then kills them. He's..." she couldn't even find the words, as she was utterly reviled. "An evil monster."

"He's going to pay for all of them, now," Sabin stated flatly, his face a terrible mask as he wrapped his hands around the man's throat and started to crush the life out of him. The stranger struggled, kicking and tearing at Sabin's chest and arms with his claws, but he wouldn't be distracted. It was over very quickly, as he released the body to drop to the ground; lifeless. Panting, he turned around and faced Ryes, as she clung to Garth, not watching him administer his justice.

"How did you do that?" he demanded, frowning. His Vision had clarified and become stronger, more so than ever before in his life, with her brief touch. As if she amplified his Talent.

"I've no idea," she assured him. "Rowan's often said I have Tyra's gifts, but no power. I've no idea what `gifts' she had."

"We need to form a burial detail," Torr commented, looking to his friend, concerned. "What was it you both saw?" he asked, needing this answered, at least.

"All the cubs he's taken through the years and what he did to them. He was a sick animal who deserved death, long ago," Sabin stated then finally cocked a smile as he looked to Ardis. "I think Ryes and I both need to get cleaned up, now." She laughed at this and stepped over to him, taking his arm.

"I'll take care of you," she assured him, smiling proudly.

"What's happened here?" Metta demanded, striding forward to see the body on the ground, and both Ryes and Sabin badly injured. He was taller than the young men, but stood stooped a bit as his silvery hair was bound back from his face with a filigreed copper band. He wore a loose, open robe over his fine shirt and neatly-kept breeches, all in earth tone colors. His face was seemed but his gold eyes were bright, holding intelligence.

"Destroying something purely evil," Sabin told him, not even trying at any show of respect for the Chief Village Elder. Sela appeared with Lixi in her arms, looking alarmed. "I'm all right, but you'd better get Lixi out of this," he advised his sister. "Let's go," he told Ardis in a low voice, as he led her off, heading back to her home. Sela watched them with questions in her eyes, unable to find her voice.

"We still have to finish the packing," Ryes reminded Garth in a low voice, wanting to keep as far away from Metta, as possible. She was sure she'd be blamed for this, somehow.

"We need to get those scratches washed out, first," he returned, scooping her up in his arms, surprising her.

"I didn't say anyone could leave," Metta declared loudly, irritated with their behavior. "Who is this man? Who killed him? And why?"

"He was Heda, once a leather craftsman of one of the plains tribes, and he was going to rape and kill Lixi, and as many of the cubs in Matlowe he could catch." Ryes told him, since Sabin and Ardis had left; weaving their way through the growing crowd, and Garth hesitated as Sela unknowingly blocked their escape.

"How do you know this?" he demanded, stepping closer.

"Not now," Garth replied for her. "She's bleeding and needs to be treated."

"We'll hold a Village meeting tonight and you'll all attend," he ordered. He looked Garth in the eyes, getting a nod from him, at last. He was the unspoken leader of these younger men, after all.

"We'll be there," he promised. Then he pressed past the other villagers, weaving his way through the crowd, with Maren, Torr and

Kovin following in his wake. There were questions being asked by the other villagers, but Garth only shook his head in response.

"It's going to be interesting, tonight," Torr commented to Maren, as they cleared the crowd. Shadd was waiting for them and rushed to his side, her smile lighting up her eyes.

"When I saw Sabin..." she started. He laughed in response.

"He kept all the glory to himself," he returned. "Metta's declared a Village meeting to discuss what happened, and I'm sure to `punish' Sabin for the murder."

"Then he'd better punish his own brother first, if he wants to start eliminating murderers in Matlowe," she declared, still mad at seeing Lixi so fearful. Then Sela had the lack of wits to carry the cub back to where the body of her attacker lay! She was outraged, but helpless in this situation.

"I wonder what Tyra's gifts were?" Kovin asked, frowning as he looked to Maren for answers, having fallen in with them.

"I've no idea. All I recall is Grandfather saying she was strongly Talented, more than my grandmother Jana," he replied. "It's lunch time, let's see about getting something to eat, first," he urged then, as a distraction. He didn't want to discuss family issues in front of everyone else. He had some ideas where Tyra's Talents lay from overhearing his mother and Rowan talking through the years, but wanted to talk with Ryes alone about it, first.

"Those are DEEP," Shadd commented, as she helped Garth wash out Ryes' wounds. Ryes lay upon the table, in her old home. She wasn't sure how much they'd get accomplished today, but hoped to be able to sleep in their new home tonight. Kovin and Teris had returned, saying it was all ready and kept marveling at all the wonderful features that were in the houses out by the river. And sweet Honey still stood waiting, munching on the grass shoots growing around the house.

"He didn't mean for me to survive. I guess I was rudely interrupting his sport," she replied, as Garth frowned.

"And what's this?" Maren demanded, seeing the newly scabbed scratches upon her shoulder, as he returned from his errand.

"A present from your father, from yesterday," Ryes sighed in response. "It's funny how things change, yet never change. The only thing I'm worried about is how dirty Heda's claws were. At least Korman bathes regularly!" She huffed a laugh at this, but saw Garth didn't look amused.

"You got to Lixi in time," Maren scolded her, noting Garth wasn't pleased. "Here's a jar of that ointment you made last month," he said, as he handed it over to Shadd.

"Thanks, Maren. You didn't get into trouble with Tanns over borrowing it, did you?" she asked, worried.

"Nope. She's out watching the burial detail that's taking care of that maggot's body," he admitted, smiling. Korman had stopped him to ask what happened, and HE was amazed at the look in his father's eyes when he told him about the attack on Lixi and how upset he was over her abduction; how Ryes had saved her; and Sabin had meted out his punishment. The young cubs mattered to him most times, and watching them was about the only thing he really did, now. This stranger's presence deeply disturbed Korman. And Maren realized he'd never understand him, at all.

"Just put some into the scratches, then give the jar to Ardis, so she can get Sabin taken care of," Ryes suggested, meeting Garth's eyes, wanting to see his smile, once more. This really had him upset, even more than Korman's challenge earlier.

"Oh yeah, she's taking care of Sabin, just fine," Torr commented, as he sat and finished his lunch. It was his mother's cold, leftover stew, but was still good and filling. Maren sat down next to him, grinning and nodding his head, as he grabbed a bowl left sitting for him. Rein left off the stew a short time ago, worried for her son, and the rest of them.

"A hero deserves some special attention," he returned, teasing his friend. He could bet Torr'd be snuggled in with Shadd tonight, from the way she'd been behaving all day. Maybe it was that Garth and Ryes had finally gotten together, or the time they all spent together this week? But, it seemed to have sparked something in the other women. Kovin looked unhappy, but didn't dare say anything. It was Ardis' choice, after all.

"Look, what can they do? He had his breeches, undergarment and boots off. There's no mistaking what he intended to do to little Lixi," Teris supplied, still worried about the meeting.

"Letting one murderer live freely in the Village for years, doesn't mean they'll let another," Torr told him, his eyes grim. "What do you think, Garth?" he asked, seeing they were now wrapping Ryes' ribs in a clean cloth bandaging.

"It's going to depend upon if Metta accepts the Vision he had," he replied. "Fortunately, or maybe not, Ryes saw it too, and can back him up."

"He's been in Cootain and Berrals," she told them, recalling some of it - too clearly.

"How would you know, if you've never been there?" Maren demanded, sure on this score. Grandfather never let her leave with the caravaners in the spring.

"From the drawings and paintings Darman creates in the winter time. He paints beautiful scenes from all the towns and villages he visits. I've seen them and he showed me where they are on the maps, and has told me all about them. He's hung some up in his and Rinna's room at home and the others I hung up around the house. He has two of Matlowe; one showing a dreary, deserted, crumbling place and one from near the river with people laughing and dancing." She sighed as she remembered asking him for that one, once... and the way he merrily laughed, as he told her that she might get it, someday.

"Could you write down the names and places of the cubs that he's killed? If we could send runners to some of them, we might get proof that Sabin was justified in what he did," Garth suggested, finishing with securing the bandage. Ryes smiled up at him, feeling good that he needed her.

"It'll be no problem," she assured him. "Let's get Honey hitched up and what we can get loaded, over to the river. I can dig out my parchments and brushes and write out that list, while you men unload and set up the house," she suggested, teasing. She didn't feel up to hauling things around anymore, with her side still in pain. She could imagine what Garth felt like, now! And he hadn't stopped, all day!

"Great, because Sabin can't write and he's going to need every bit of help we can get him," Maren told her, gulping down the stew.

"Let's move, it's getting late," Garth scolded, smiling in agreement. He only suspected she could read and write, since she was talking about maps and books. He wondered what else she knew, or could do, besides "see" what Sabin was seeing? He gently picked her up and set her upon her feet, again. Ryes and Shadd laughed as he, Torr, Teris and Kovin picked up the table and headed for the door.

Maren finished his bowl of stew, and put it back into Rein's basket, with the other dirty bowls.

"I'd better wash these up, before we return this to Torr's mother," Ryes said as she stepped over to take up the basket, not wanting to be totally useless, but Maren snatched it off the shelf, along with the one holding what was left of the pot of stew.

"You're not going to be lifting ANYTHING, cousin," he ordered her, meeting her eyes. She blinked up at him in surprise, as Shadd laughed and headed back to her bedroom, to give Ardis the salve for Sabin.

"Okay, what do you have so far?" Sabin asked, his brows furrowed as he was concentrating on both what he was asking Ryes to read out and what his memory of his Vision showed him. It was still crystal clear – ever since Ryes' light touch.

"Oh my, that is just beautiful," Shadd commented looking down at the parchment on the table. "Sad that you have to write all this down for such a horrible man."

"I wish I could learn to write like that," Garth added, sitting across the table. Ryes smiled at him as she recited the listing to Sabin so he could compare it what he recalled.

"I wish I could learn to read," Ardis added, feeling so left out. She had never paid much attention to the lessons Elder Farra taught her when she was little. The flowing script on the paper looked enchanting.

"It looks like I'll have to set up some lessons in reading and writing soon," Ryes replied to the others, lightly laughing, after reading the list to Sabin again. They were filling in some small parts she had missed on the first time.

"Let me try something," Sabin suddenly stated, and reached over and grabbed Ryes' hand. He opened up to her from within, again. The Vison was stronger once more, as if fresh from the moment it happened. She shuddered but closed her eyes and looked at it all, once again. She tried to push aside her revulsion and concentrate upon the names, the places and when, as best she could. Somehow it was even more clear than the first time.

"See, you called this one Cootain," he prompted seeing she was setting aside her turbulent emotions and looking at everything

once again with him. "How can you be so sure?" he pressed.
Looking a little annoyed, Ardis lightly touched Ryes' shoulder and her
eyes grew wide as she was seeing it all, too. She quickly closed her
eyes, determined to see the whole thing. She heard their inner voices
as they discussed it calmly.

"Because of the towers above the docks. And look at that
building. It's exactly as Darman showed me in his books. There is a
look of them all together that says Cootain," she returned, opening up
fully from within now, for the first time in her life. She felt another,
but did not let her distract her now. "There is Fort and Berrals and
that one looks like a farm outside of the walls of Riverward, which I've
seen when I was a teener, travelling by riverboat with Rinna and Tara
and some others for a few days."

"Amazing that you're so sure," he returned. They finished the
rest, comparing it against her list, which was getting longer and
longer.

"I'll show you," she returned as she conjured up her memories
of the books and the things Darman said as he and Rinna told her
about some of the different places they had been in their travels.
"That is why I am sure. I've had these places shown to me all my life,
even if I've never set foot in any of them. You know, are you sure
you don't have Mind Voice too? You could have more than one
Talent," she pointed out. That seemed to surprise him and the other
one spying on them. She sighed as she let go from within and
without, gently. Ardis quickly snatched back her hand, taking a small
step back. Sabin opened his eyes, still frowning.

Ryes stood up and gestured to him as she grabbed one of her
oil lamps. She led them all into the great room and then showed
them each of the paintings and told them about them, so they could
get a better view of the world that has to this point been out of their
reach. Finally she led them to Darman and Rinna's room and showed
them the two paintings of Matlowe.

"I would love to see the main Village square cleaned up and
given some real life," she finished.

"Me, too," Garth replied, taking her hand and squeezing it.

"And after all that, I couldn't let him live to murder any more
cubs; ours or anyone else's," Sabin admitted, having been called forth
to tell his story. Metta held the list Ryes scribed earlier. It was long...
too long. Where she could, there were names listed, otherwise it was

descriptions of the cubs and where they lived, before this Heda got his claws on them.

"Murder is still murder," Rami spat out, speaking into the silence of the Village square which had held for several long minutes after Sabin finished his rendition. Her face was a mask in the firelight. "And all we have is your word that he's a cub killer."

"If Ryes hadn't gotten there in time, you'd probably have Lixi's body as proof, or would someone like you accept that, Rami?" Sabin snapped back, getting mad. "This whole thing is stupid! I took care of a very, dangerous killer, who threatened all of Matlowe with his presence!"

"That's right, Ryes was there. Let her tell her part in all this! Where did that list come from, anyway? How do we know you weren't out hunting him for some kind of sick fun of your own?" Spann demanded. "Does it just take a bunch of the young hunters saying something was so, to justify what they do?" he voiced loudly. This had the others nearby making small comments with some few agreements.

"Ryes wouldn't do a thing like that!" Garth declared, standing up. "She wouldn't even use her claws against my sister, Karr when she attacked Ryes earlier today." There were voices raised in shock and disbelief at this. Mitt sat with calm knowledge in her eyes, nodding her agreement.

"He's right. Ryes only held me back from hurting her. She never tried to strike me, even if she could've easily done so." Karr shouted out, more in Garth's defense, but knowing it was right. Her mouth had a sour taste at having to accept he'd openly taken up with the outcast. He kept her close to his side, even here!

"Ryes? You'll take the Circle," Metta ordered, looking directly at her. "Your reputation as a Huntress is already well known. Do you have an answer to Spann's accusations?" Ryes stood and went toward the Circle, as Sabin gave her a wink in encouragement. She tried to quirk a smile, as he strode over to his place on the bench. She KNEW she'd be called! Her hands were shaking. She'd never been in the Circle before, in her whole life! It seemed huge with the Elder's stand at one end and the rows of seats for the villagers set on the far side, but stretching a third of the way around the circle.

"Sir," she began, hearing a small quaver in her voice. She took in a deep breath and let it out slowly. It did them no good if she couldn't find the courage to speak, now! She could brave many things in the forest, this was no different. "I was helping Shadd and Ardis move. As I was standing outside, keeping my windracer calm, Rand and Aldin came running to me. They were terrified and crying, and I'd never seen them so upset," she told them in a stronger voice, as a low muttering started up from the gathering behind her. She didn't turn around, but kept her eyes steady upon Metta's and the other elders sitting before her. Rowan was there, sitting in a chair he rarely sat upon, but unable to say anything, since she now stood in the Circle and was his granddaughter. At least he could give his vote on Sabin's testimony.

"And?" Metta asked, coaxing it out of her. He knew Rowan had kept her out of things far too long, so understood this was hard on Ryes. Still, they needed the truth of the matter.

"They told me a stranger had grabbed both Rand and Lixi, but Aldin helped Rand escape. They took me to where it happened and I found their toys inside an old abandoned house, where they usually played, and the trail of this stranger, who still held Lixi. I told them to go back and tell the others," she related, recalling every detail with too much clarity, even yet.

"What others?" Spann demanded, standing up. Ryes blushed, not turning around and not sure if she was only supposed to answer Metta, or just anyone.

"What others did you mean, cub," Metta asked, signaling for Spann to sit back down. He did so reluctantly.

"Garth, Torr, Sabin, Ardis and Shadd. I'd taken off without letting them know why, but felt they should alert the rest of the Village - just in case," she told him. "I followed his trail, losing it when it crossed the path to the East Gardens. I heard Lixi's voice and started toward it, when I found his tracks again. I found the house he had her in and saw him holding her down on the floor. He was wearing nothing from his waist down and was busy tearing off Lixi's clothing." A sudden increase in raised voices was now loud enough to panic her. Ryes turned and saw the angry villagers behind her, incensed by her testimony. Some were agreeing with her, having seen the body shortly after Sabin killed him. She was ready to bolt, but caught Garth's eyes and saw his approval. He looked quite calm with the others raging around him. It was a little surreal. It took everything she had to force herself to stay put and turn back to face the elders, again. Her hands were shaking, as she ignored the growls and shouts, but was sure Garth wouldn't let her come to harm here.

"Silence!" Metta bellowed, causing Ryes to flinch. Then, as order was restored, he turned his attention back to her. "Go on," he urged. He almost smiled to himself. He expected they would've had to send Rowan out to bring her back!

"I jumped in a window and shoved him off her. I told Lixi to run, as I pulled him away. She ran out the door. Then he then tried to take his anger out on me for interrupting his fun. It was a good thing the other hunters arrived in time to save me from him, too," she finished.

"And how did you come to know this list?" Metta demanded, holding it up for her and the rest of the gathering to see.

"Sabin was holding this stranger, Heda, against a wall, but neither of them was moving. I stepped over to see if he was all right and touched his shoulder," her voice failed for a few seconds. "I never felt, or saw anything like that - ever! Heda was absolutely EVIL! The things he'd done to the cubs through the years..." her voice trailed off, as her tears flowed.

"You've never touched Sabin when he was having a Vision, before?" Metta questioned sharply.

"I never even knew he could see things that way. I didn't know anything about it!" she swore. "I would've NEVER touched him, if I'd known!" Metta turned and looked at Rowan for an answer.

"When they were small cubs, they beat her up several times, so she never went near any of them as they grew older. I never told her about Sabin, because I didn't think she'd be interested in knowing," Rowan admitted to him and the other elders. There were nods as they did remember and understand.

"So, how was it she could share what Sabin's Vision revealed to him?"

"I'm not sure, but I think she's a Catalyst. One of the caravaners told me that she touched her son and it brought out his Talent. Ryes didn't really understand what had happened then, since she was an early teener. And I don't know of any way to prove, or disprove it here. But I know it was one of her mother's gifts," he said, thinking it was the most innocuous of the Talents Tyra had and could be shared.

"If she is, then I might have a way," Rebin spoke up into the silence. "Come here, Riss," she urged her youngest son toward the Circle. He was about four years younger than Ryes. "I think he's another Visionary, but other than intensely bad dreams from time to time, nothing's manifested yet. If she's a Catalyst, and he truly carries a Talent, then she should be able to activate it. He's at the right age for it, now."

"Does anyone know how a Catalyst's Talent is supposed to work?" Metta asked the assemblage. There was some stirring, but no one came forth. "Even stories?" Still silence reigned and the villagers looked to each other for answers. Talents were known, but Matlowe had few people who actually had Talents, so knowledge of Talents not normally occurring in the Village was pretty thin. The Caravaner Catalyst rarely came to Matlowe as he usually went to the southern continent during the winter months.

"Ryes," Rowan spoke up. "Put everything here from your mind and heart, then take Riss' hand and close your eyes. Look for his truth, within," he urged, seeing she was still afraid. She gave him a nod and a shy smile, then closed her eyes and tried to put this whole meeting from her thoughts. This was no easy task! She tried to imagine she was sitting beside one of her favorite springs, with the voices behind her blending in with the water cascading down the rocks. She felt someone take her hand, so now she turned from her quiet retreat to look at another, as she never imagined in her whole life before. There was resistance, as he tried to hide from her probing. She backed off, unsure if she should do this against his will. It was like he was trying to hide behind some gray and white veils.

"Why?" she questioned, without using her voice, pushing the thought before him, as she and Sabin had communicated earlier.

"The dreams are bad enough," he replied. Then suddenly there was another presence, startling them both. But Ryes realized this one was now a very familiar spirit in her life.

"The dreams hold no power. How can you help others, if you don't open up and let it flow from within?" Sabin questioned boldly, feeling the resistance and understanding it. Ryes was relieved he was here to help! His inner voice was strong here tonight. Why?

"Through both your Talent and my own," he replied to her question. "Reach through to his core, while I try to explain things to Riss in a way you can't." In essence, he showed him some of the most beautiful visions he'd seen in the years since his own Talent awoke. He recalled his struggle with his budding Talent and well understood this cub's reluctance. He never had anyone to guide him and it'd been a living hell when his Talent awakened. He'd vowed to help others get through this time, every chance he got.

As Sabin kept Riss busy, she dove further within, searching for what, she had no idea, but some feeling from within her guided her now. Ahead she saw a brightness coming from a sphere, deep within this youth and she knew this was it! She reached down and opened it up, bathed in the beauty and wild energy emanating from the sphere. Carefully, she backed out, letting its beauty and power fill Riss' being. Sabin was utterly amazed and proud that she'd done it. The both of them backed off, but stayed near, in case he needed their support. Riss struggled against it for several long moments, then turned and reluctantly embraced it, forcing it to his will and making it a part of him, forever. Ryes and Sabin both let go at the same time, opening their eyes.

Ryes came back to herself, realizing she now held onto Riss' hand, while tears were running down his cheeks. Sabin was standing there with them now, an arm thrown over hers and Riss' shoulders.

"Are you all right?" she asked the youth. He opened his eyes and smiled.

"It feels strange," he told her. "When will I start seeing things?" he questioned. Ryes laughed, shaking her head.

"Sabin's the one you should ask, not me!" she admitted. Sabin laughed and hugged both Ryes and Riss to him, fiercely.

"We did it!" he shouted, happy as he released them. There was cheering from the other villagers now. Riss began to laugh, feeling better about the whole thing. "I'll talk with you about it, tomorrow," he promised him in a low voice, "so, you'll know what to expect." He turned to the elders, "Yes, she's a Catalyst."

"Thank you, Sabin. You and Riss may now take your seats," Metta instructed. Rebin was all smiles; proud to have it proved that her son truly did have Talent. Metta had been upset when Sabin stood and joined them in their inner commune, but it looked to have worked out best, all around. He pulled back to confer with the other elders, sitting in judgment, then they all took their seats again.

"We need you to make more copies of this list, so we can have runners go to these cities, to prove these cubs died, as you say," he ordered Ryes. She gave him a nod of her head, glad she had plenty of the waterproof ink. "Sabin," Metta called out. He stood and stepped forward.

"Yes?" he asked, as he joined Ryes in the Circle, once more.

"You'll be banished from Matlowe for six months. If we have received word of these other murders, then you'll be cleared of all charges of murder. But, if it proves otherwise, you'll be banished for life," Metta pronounced his sentence. "You'll have until noon tomorrow to leave Matlowe."

"Then, if I'm banished for committing a murder, what of Korman? He murdered Tyra all those years ago!" Sabin demanded, feeling this was only fair, and it was about time it be brought out into the open. Ryes blushed darkly, hearing the voices raised in protest behind them, her stomach tied up in knots again.

"There were no witnesses, nor proof that it was him," Metta defended his youngest brother, recalling the grounds his father used to have the hearing dismissed, so long ago. Korman stood up and left the Village square, no longer interested in the proceedings.

"There was Tyra's story, before she died," Ryes now spoke out, suddenly insulted by his answer. "Or don't the final words of a dying WOMAN count?" she demanded in outrage. Metta turned to glare at Rowan, as if he was supposed to have Ryes under control. He shifted, suddenly uncomfortable, but realized they were right.

"I spoke before a Village meeting over seventeen years ago, telling the whole story. Your father wouldn't hear it, Metta. Do YOU know how to listen?" he questioned.

"Storyteller, it's just another tale you weave to keep the cubs amused, like the one of the Great One, who's supposed to save all the Star People with his vast Talents, alone," he replied, feeling his temper coming out now. Rowan stood up, stepped off the elder's platform and went to stand in the Circle with the cubs.

"What I speak about Tyra Li is TRUTH. What you choose to hear, is a matter of conjecture," Rowan declared. "Will you hear the full tale, or not? The cubs are right. There's no difference if justice isn't applied to all equally!" he challenged.

"ENOUGH!" Metta ordered, standing up and leaving the platform, too. He left the square, heading for his own home. As his father before him, he refused to give the tale any credence. He knew what his brother told their sire the last time it was brought up in a Village meeting. The other elders sat in shock, not knowing what to believe. Having never seen them behave this way before.

"Then JUSTICE doesn't truly exist in Matlowe," Rowan shouted, as he turned to return home, too. His eyes met Ryes' and saw her sympathy and understanding.

"You tried," she comforted him, as they turned to face the disquieted, arguing villagers.

Partings

"I thought Old Metta was going to swallow his tongue, he was so mad!" Torr laughed out as he sat at the table in the great room in Ryes' home. The other villagers seated at the table laughed with him, adding in their own comments in most cases, too. A round of old jokes and stories started up with a few of the less favored Village elders taking part in the exchanges. There were more than just the young hunters at the table tonight; many other villagers were here still debating today's events and their final outcome.

Originally, they were all outside with a far larger crowd demanding Rowan tell the whole story of Tyra Li. He gathered everyone around the Caravaner's big firepit and settled them down as best he could, then he complied with their wishes. He included several things he left out of his telling of the night before, giving far more detail than the young hunters had heard. Once the story was told in its entirety and quite a few questions answered, about a half the gathering left to discuss it in their own homes, leaving this smaller crowd of villagers to continue debating what should be done, if anything could be done this long afterwards. Some were out at the firepit; some were inside at the long table in the great room. Rowan had shared out the lesser quality ale with their guests, but they drank it and behaved as if they had been everyday visitors to their home.

"I'm not letting you go alone," Garth quietly told his blood-brother, as they were helping Ryes and Ardis in the kitchen.

"Yes you are," he replied, not budging on this issue. There was no reason for him to come along, with Ryes and her willingness to carry his cub. "I need you to look after Sela, Lixi, Sana and Fane. I'm COUNTING on you to take care of them!" Garth met his eyes, his own stubbornness coming to the fore.

"Hey, hey," Ardis said, nudging her way in-between them. "If you're going to be arguing, then you're not helping, and can go back out into the other room with the rest of the pandemonium," she ordered, a smile in her eyes.

"If you go, then I'm going, too," Ryes told Garth, as she dried her hands upon a towel. She met his eyes, seeing his reluctance to take her into unknown dangers. "Do either of you two even know how to read a map, or are able to read at all?" she demanded, realizing they might both be pretty helpless, journeying out into the world.

"Someone has to keep you two out of trouble!" Ardis stood shocked, seeing Ryes meant every word.

"No, you're staying here with Garth," Sabin stated, flat out.

"I'm Tyra Li's daughter. I'll go where I want. And I know how to read a compass, at least. Do you?" she questioned, seeing the answer in his eyes. Did he even know what one was? "Just a minute. I'll be right back," she told them, putting down her towel and scooping up a tray of meat rolls they just finished baking, leaving the room.

"She can't be serious?" Ardis questioned them, wondering.

"She was on the verge of leaving, herself," Garth informed her with a heavy sigh. "She told me she didn't know if it was to escape Matlowe, or just to find out more of the world she's only learned through books, maps, pictures and stories. Either way, she intends to find her own place out there, then come back to bring Rowan out to live with her. She only worried about what might happen to him while she was gone."

"Does she hate it here, so much?" she asked, sitting down. The men took seats, too.

"Look at what she's had to deal with all these years," Sabin reminded her. "It's only been the last few days that everything's been different. I don't blame her," he stated. The kitchen curtain parted and Maren came in.

"What's going on?" he questioned, seeing the long faces.

"Trying to figure out who's going to take care of those we leave behind, here in Matlowe," Garth told him.

"Well, you're not leaving me behind!" he declared, as he came over to sit at the table with them. He grabbed the pitcher of hot, honeyed tea and poured himself a mug. This tasted far better to him, than the ale they were drinking in the other room.

"We kinda figured that," Ardis agreed with a smile.

"Now, listen. I told all of you that I'm going ALONE!" Sabin repeated, as Ryes returned with her arms full of rolls of parchments.

"And we're just going to keep on ignoring you," she assured him, smiling. She sat the maps down on the table, and sorted through them. She pulled one out and unrolled it, so the rest could see it. As Garth and Maren held it open for her, she fetched her favorite map reading lanterns, placing them upon each of the corners, then lit them. Now, they could see the details. She took her compass out of her pocket and placed it atop the map.

"What's this?" Garth asked, picking up the compass. It had a slightly, wavering needle within, with a black painted point and a red one. It looked curious and as he shifted it to examined it, he noticed the needle continued to only point one direction, no matter which way he turned it to try to change its direction.

"That's a compass. It can help you keep your bearings, so you'll know where you're at and hopefully find your way with fewer problems. The red end of the needle always points toward the north, but since it's not true north, as Darman calls it, there're adjustments you must make, to know where you are. He says from the ancient books, the mapmakers called it magnetic north. These long lines on the map help you figure out your adjustments." She was pointing to the latitude and longitude lines with the numbers printed along the bottom and side edges of the map. These maps were very special to her. They were copies from ancient maps etched into the great walls in Berrals. A gift from Darman several Winterfests ago.

"Wait a minute, what's all this?" Sabin asked, "I don't need it to find my way anywhere."

"It did take me years to learn to read them correctly," Ryes admitted with a smile, ignoring his protest. "And I'm not even going to bring out the star maps that I have. I can use another instrument at night to determine where we are by using the stars. But, you need these maps to base everything upon. There're places where the animals are very dangerous and it's best to avoid them all together." She indicated a distinctive mark upon the map. "Darman showed me quite a few of them. The old legends said that the animals were kept for hunting; for those hunters who wanted to track something which could hunt them back," she related, as a shiver traveled up her spine as she described for them the head of one they had preserved and were bringing to Cootain. "The caravaners kept it covered and cool but even so, I saw it when Darman was showing it to some other caravaners passing through the area. Its teeth were longer than my arm! Now they roam free, but usually stay near their original areas because they still have plenty of the food they can eat there."

"Why would anyone want to hunt like that? Can you eat them, once you kill them?" Ardis questioned, frowning. There were lots of symbols on this map, and she didn't know any of them!

"For sport hunting, and no, you cannot eat their flesh. It's like with the other peoples. They live and work in some of the larger towns and even have towns of their own, but if you tried to eat their food or drink, it'll make you sick, and may even kill you. It's not on

purpose; it's that they're different people." She saw the curiosity
alight in Garth and Maren's eyes.

"What're they like?" Garth asked her. She smiled.

"I only know what I know through the years from the
caravaners. They really are peoples much like us. They may look
different, but there are good folks and bad ones – just as we Starmen.
One winter Darman brought a Ruskin girl named Fanya, whom he
promised her family to take to a Ruskin village on the other side of
the plains. Her parents were killed and she was being sent to her
mother's family. We played the whole winter and she was strange,
but still a lot of fun. It was curious the way she thought about some
of the things I usually took for granted. I know she didn't like the
forest at all. It scared her. And she could only eat the foods Darman
had brought for her. I once tried a piece of fruit she loved and was
sick for almost a week." She realized she hadn't thought of Fanya for
a very long time, and that she still cherished her memories of the time
they spent together. It'd been the best winter she had, in spite of the
time she spent sick in bed!

"I remember! You had mom scared that you were going to
die. She yelled at Rowan for ever letting you near that strange girl, at
all," Maren related, now recalling that winter and how he helped watch
over Ryes. He remembered seeing this girl once, when she came in to
see how Ryes was doing, but his mother ran her off before he could
talk with her. And his eyes met Garth's briefly and the secret they
held of that time, keeping it as he'd promised. He gave him a nod of
assurance.

"Then, where do they get their food?" Garth asked,
wondering.

"They grow it, or raise the animals they can eat," Ryes told
him with a laugh. "Darman once said that the people in Matlowe are
too sheltered and need a little shake up, every now and then." She
gestured toward the great room. "I think they're getting it, tonight."
This got laughs from all around the table.

"So, according to your map, where's Matlowe?" Sabin asked,
trying to figure it out as he looked down at it.

"Here," Ryes showed them. "And this is our river, the Yuri.
You can see where it starts high up in the mountains, and then
crosses the plains, runs past us, and finally dumps down into a delta
at the ocean, here," she pointed out the river's course. It was the
longest river on this continent!

"Gods, it's far longer than I ever thought!" Ardis breathed.
Shadd and Torr appeared at the doorway, and came straight over to

the table to see what they were looking at. Their eyes were shining with curiosity in their depths upon seeing the map.

"What's longer?" Torr questioned, frowning down at the parchment. He could read some, but this was something new to his eyes. Ryes smiled up at him, then pointed to a long, blue line on the parchment.

"The Yuri River," she told him.

"That river is so huge and very dangerous to cross, yet such a skinny line here!" Shadd gasped, surprised, seeing the reference point to scale on the parchment now.

"The world's a pretty big place and it's easy to get lost, or end up in a place where you can't eat the food, because it'll kill you," she told them. "That's why I'm going, too," she informed Sabin, meeting his eyes.

"Just show me where I can go for a few months, until we get word back from those other places," he pressed, not wanting to drag his friends off on this dangerous venture.

"The best would've been to set you up with one of the caravans and journey with them for a while," she sighed out, thinking. "And then return in the fall, when things should all be cleared up for you here. I don't know, perhaps we can catch up to some of the vans and see if they'll take you in? If so, then I would still best accompany you to make proper introductions."

"How about the `destroyed city'?" Garth questioned, diverting her. Ryes looked to him, startled. It was where she wanted to go, but alone.

"That's perfect!" Sabin agreed, smiling. "Where's it on this map?" he pressed, wanting to see how far it actually lay.

"Here," Ryes pointed it out. "It looks like this might be the best route." There was a charcoal-drawn line on the map and they noted it with sudden understanding.

"What does this symbol mean, that's drawn next the ruins?" Maren asked into the silence of the room as all eyes had been drawn to the map.

"That's it's deadly. It's an underground city and you cannot journey down inside, because the dust will kill you. It kills everyone, no matter what people they're from and has been that way for all the years since the attack. It's left over from what was used to kill everyone there, so many long years ago. It's supposed to be where the people of Matlowe originally came from - fleeing the destruction."

"Do you know who'd do such a thing, or how it was done?" Shadd questioned, a cold shiver traveling up her back.

"No. Only that tales say they came out of the darkness of the stars above and killed all the great cities on Tayna, for a reason only they knew. No one, who could ask, was left behind to do so," she spoke in a quiet voice. "And there's no record of this murdering enemy ever coming down to continue the battle on our lands. Then we might have been able to give them a little back for what they did to Tayna."

"Would they come back?" Maren voiced aloud his question.

"I don't know. Maybe, if more great cities sprang up, then they might, but I don't think anyone on Tayna really knows," Ryes sighed in reply.

"And you want to go there?" Shadd queried, looking to Sabin.

"I've always wanted to see where my father and siblings were buried," Ryes answered her, not looking at the rest of them anymore. She'd turned away and was trying to think of what to bring. Her side hurt; she worried about an infection, so it'd limit what she could carry. Maybe bringing Honey along, even if her presence might bring out more dangerous predators?

Sabin's eyes met Garth's as they both knew there was no talking her out of this now. It was the others, who truly didn't need to come, who were their main concern.

"You'd better finish those copies of the list," Maren advised her. "So, Sabin can be cleared of that murder charge soon and can return home."

Garth saw Sabin's eyes suddenly going glassy, once more. Two in one day? It was incredible! Ryes didn't know what was going on and turned around placing her hand upon his shoulder. She was going to tease him about his life being in her hands, but her eyes grew wide as she was swept up by what his Vision revealed to her, once more. She let go of him as if she were being burnt.

"Somebody warn me about this!" she declared, as she sat upon a small stool by the oven.

"Snooping again?" Sabin teased, looking back to see her sitting down, trying to catch her breath. "At least it was nothing like the last one," he commented.

"What?" Maren, Ardis, Torr and Garth demanded, feeling left out.

"That we'll never call Matlowe our home, again," Sabin told them with a gleam in his eyes.

"You mean, they won't clear you of that thing's murder?" Ardis demanded, frowning, not liking the sound of it.

"No, that's not it. We won't want to come back here, other than to visit, or fetch our families," Ryes said. "There's a far better place out there and we're just going to have to find it." She stood up and wrapped her arms about Garth, a happiness showing in her whole being.

"No, WE WILL FIND IT," Sabin corrected her. She smiled lopsided, nodding her head in agreement.

"Yes, we will," she agreed.

"What's it like?" Garth pressed, frowning. "For us to leave Matlowe behind us forever, it must be a truly good home."

"It's different... truly amazing and I don't think I really understood a lot of what was happening, but the feelings were intense. It was HOME," Ryes said, as a sparkle in her eyes lit up at the memory of it.

"That's enough! Let's keep the rest unsaid. We want to find it and be surprised and amazed," Sabin ordered, laughing. Suddenly he appeared light-hearted as he jumped up, scooped up Ardis and twirled her about in his arms. She laughed out merrily, her own eyes shining now. The rest joined them with their laughter and clapping hands. This turned into an impromptu celebration of their last night in Matlowe.

Sela peered in from the curtained doorway, at first puzzled, then a look of understand alit her eyes. She gave her younger brother a nod of her head then retreated, leaving them to their merriment. Kovin walked over, wanting to see too, but she put a hand upon his chest to stop him.

"Nothing you need is in there," she advised. His eyes held hers with curiosity in their depths.

"You think I cannot win her over?" he asked, "Are you so sure?" She nodded in return, then stepped away from the curtain as her hand drifted up and gave his strong shoulder a squeeze before stepping away.

He hesitated, then nudged the drape aside and looked. They were all laughing and dancing and having a merry time. Sabin did not appear upset over his banishment at all! It was like they were all happy about this drastic change! He could not help himself and found he had stepped into the room, stopping halfway to the gathered group.

"Kovin," Maren said, giving him a nod. There was a happy grin upon his face as he gestured to him to come join them. Teris came into the room behind him and laughed as he saw the happy gathering.

"You can't tell me you're celebrating being banished from Matlowe, Sabin?" he asked loudly, with a huge grin on his face now.

"It's the start of a new life for all of us," he returned as he set Ardis down. She grabbed his hand, her eyes still merry.

"It is," she agreed.

"They'll be there with us," Ryes whispered to Garth. He laughed at hearing it, nodding.

"We can't all go with Sabin," Garth stated with another laugh. "We need some good hunters here to help take care of everyone while we're gone." Mitt came in as he said it and there was surprise in her eyes as she appeared to realize what he said.

"You can't go, Garth," she asserted, looking panicked.

"He is going, I am going and so is everyone here," Maren replied, gesturing to the group around the table. "And we're learning how to read maps now!"

"Maps?" Teris and Kovin asked at the same time.

"Here, look!" Shadd invited, gesturing to the one lying on the table. They stepped over. She ran her finger down the line of the great river. "And this is the Yuri! Who knew how long it really was?" she asked, grinning.

"Where's Matlowe?" Teris asked, his eyes looking all along its impossibly long length.

"Here," she replied, pointing it out. They both leaned down closer to it, looking at it.

"It's so small," Mitt added in comment, looking around the men.

"The world is so big," Ryes assured her, laughing. She pulled out a larger rolled parchment and unrolled it for them all to see. "This is our world as seen if we flattened it out. Now see if you can spot the Yuri?" she teased. She held it up for the others. They all studied it for several long moments. Garth finally laughed and pointed it out.

"There," he assured them, smiling at Ryes. Her mouth dropped open as she tilted her head at him in wonder.

"Yes," she agreed. "How did you know?" He huffed out and grinned with pride.

"The shape of her. She's a fine river and very unique, even when seen this way," he returned. He got a round of laughs and a few thumps on his shoulder in pride. Ryes lowered the parchment and then Kovin put out his hand, as if to ask for it.

"May I?" he requested. She handed to him with a confidence Garth was sure she didn't feel. He gently took it and brought it over to the lamps, pushing the compass aside and placing it over the other map. "This is amazing," he breathed.

"It was copied from the walls of Berrals and was said to have been etched into the walls by the ancients before the attack upon Tayna," she explained. "The caravaners, sea captains and many others have proved their accuracy through the hundreds of years since."

"And Rowan lets you play with them?" Teris asked, amazed. She frowned at this. They heard a chuckle at the doorway.

"She lets me play with them every now and then," Rowan assured them with a laugh as he came into the room. He was carrying a large tray with some mugs upon it. Spann, Rebin and Sonta followed him in, carrying various mugs and trays, appearing to be helping him. He placed his things on a counter next to the sink, and then turned to help unburden the others. Sonta stepped over to the map with interest on his face.

"Berrals, is this true?" he asked.

"Yes, it is," both Ryes and Rowan replied.

"It was a gift to me from Darman years ago. The maps were my reward for being such a good student," Ryes added.

"A rich reward indeed," he commented, "for one so young. So, where is Matlowe on this map of yours?" She pointed out a very small dot with "Matlowe" printed in tiny letters next to it. His breath caught for a moment as the perspective looked to hit him then.

"There is so much we don't know," he added after several long moments. The other younger men around the table had been silent as he spoke. He turned to look at Ryes. "Will you teach me about the world now?" he asked, smiling. She smiled in return.

"She can start classes in map reading and world history as soon as we get back," Garth promised, putting an arm around Ryes' shoulders. She blushed, but stayed where she was, snuggled in next to his side. "We're heading out with Sabin in the morning," he added at the surprise on Sonta's face. He gave him a nod in reply, understand more now.

"While she is gone, I can show you quite a few things, if she will leave her maps in my care," Rowan stated, stepping over.

"You would teach Metta's son, good elder?" he asked, his eyes bright with his challenge.

"I would. I think if I can help you see more of the world, you might make a better elder when it's your time," he replied with a broad smile.

"I would be proud to be your new student, Elder Rowan," he replied with a laugh as he offered him his hand, palm up. Rowan gave him a graceful bow of his head then crossed his palm with his own.

"There's hope for Matlowe, after all," Ardis whispered to Sabin, who nodded his agreement.

"We've got everything sorted and stored," Shadd told the others, as they joined them on the river bank. "It's a beautiful morning."

"It sure is," Torr agreed, taking her hand and smiling with a special look in his eyes for her. She smiled in return.

"I don't see how we're going to survive this, if the rest of you do nothing but look at each other that way," Maren spoke out, disgusted.

"You'll find the woman who's right for you and have plenty of cubs of your own someday, Maren," Garth assured him, lightly cuffing him on the shoulder. They had Honey laden with most of the heavier things they'd need, while they each wore backpacks with their personal items, and what they felt guilty about making the windracer mare carry for them.

Ryes had gone back in and did a more thorough search, to make sure she had everything she thought they'd need. It was hard for her to leave Rowan behind; even if it was in her cousin, Tennan's, care. She had barely spoken more than a handful of words to Ryes their whole lives! She was here last night and heard the full tale of Tyra Li's murder. She moved out of her mother's home, because she could no longer suffer Korman's presence and offered to take care of Rowan, while Ryes was gone. At least her tiny cub, Tian, would keep them both busy, she thought. Ryes had no idea who fathered her, only that it wasn't Korman. But, she suspected he picked the man for Tennan. That she was too young to have a cub had been a mystery to her, too.

She sighed. They had everything packed and ready. She and Garth moved their things up to the loft, securing it back and out of the way. She came down the stairs, picked up her pack and turned for the front door. As she faced the door, she saw a very familiar shadow walking toward the back of their home. Korman! There was no way she was going to let him spoil the start of their journey! A strong, sour odor pervaded the air. There was no doubt it was him, and he'd been drinking heavily from the smell, too. She ran after him, tossing her pack onto the ground, putting herself between him and the back of the house, where the others were waiting.

"Go away, Korman. You'll get nothing here!" In spite of her trembling, her voice was steady.

"You're not sneaking out with your young mate, this time. I claim you for myself," Korman's gruff voice growled out.

"Hah!" Ryes countered, holding her new walking staff in both her hands before her, not wanting him any closer. "You don't own me! I'll mate with whom I want." She balanced on the balls of her feet, ready for action. Korman stepped toward her.

"You break the same laws, as your mother. No spear can be used as a weapon!" Korman scoffed at her, his eyes narrowing to slits. Ryes could see he was poised for a charge. He was truly mad to fight a lowly female, even if she wasn't totally defenseless. She backed toward the river bank, slowly. At least she knew how to swim.

"Your eyes are bad, old man. This is a walking staff and I can use it, as I want," she returned with venom.

Korman charged her with a wild cry. Ryes easily ducked out of his grasp. As he turned, she came up with her staff and swung at his head. He threw up his arm to block it, but wasn't fast enough. It still connected with his forehead where Garth had scored yesterday. Korman yowled in anger and stepped back; a deadly glint came into his eyes. But, Ryes wouldn't back down. Not this time! There was

too much at stake! She charged him, with her staff held before her.
It caught him by surprise. The force of her charge carried the both of
them tumbling down the bank, and into the icy river with a great
splash.

Ryes was still half crouched for a few seconds and then sat
back in the water in a daze, amazed at what she dared.

Korman was sprawled upon his back, floundering in the
shallow water. He sat up, sputtering, with pieces of weeds and mud
hanging from his body. Suddenly, Ryes found release as she started
laughing at Korman. He looked so ridiculous, she couldn't help
herself. She didn't see menace here, only a pathetic old man. She
threw back her head, pointed at him and laughed with abandon. The
ringing laughter echoed the laughter of long ago; the laughter the
mother once started. The laughter, which echoed throughout
Matlowe, and had taken him years to erase.

Never again! Indignantly, Korman found his feet and stalked,
stiff-legged, up the bank; brushing off the weeds and mud, as he
could. He headed back to the Village, before anyone investigated the
noise by the river. But the young hunters, who'd come running at the
sounds of the fight, now stood astounded at what they saw. Their
laughter soon followed him too, as he stalked off.

Ryes finally got control of herself and climbed up the bank,
holding onto her staff. As she reached it, Garth wrapped his arms
around her in a warm hug.

"YOU defeated Korman, all by yourself," he told her, a soft
chuckle in his voice. "But what did you think you were doing, trying
to take him on all alone?" he asked, still worried for her.

"I wasn't going to let him spoil the start to our journey," she
apologized, seeing his concern.

"I've never seen father look so silly, nor so mad," Tennan
commented with a sigh. She had a big grin upon her face too. Maren
nodded his agreement, still chuckling.

"I don't think Korman will bother you again. Your laughter
will ring in his ears, each time he sees you," Ardis assured her. Ryes
relaxed against Garth, enjoying the embrace. She was trembling
again. Probably just the cold water, she thought.

"That may be true," she replied thoughtfully, "but, I'm still
going to leave. We have to find our new home!" She reluctantly drew
back from Garth and faced him in the morning light. "And, I'd like to
find out where my mother came from," she admitted. "I might have

more family out there, somewhere." Garth chuckled, and hugged her against his chest again.

"Then we'll find them together," he assured her. Ryes chuckled, as tears of joy filled her eyes. Their friends were gathered around, laughing with them too.

"Let's get you dried off and into some fresh, dry clothing, first," Ardis ordered with a happy smile. "We're in no rush, so if you want another bath, you can take one."

"All right," Ryes agreed, as Garth picked a soggy weed out of her hair. She swatted at him as he tried to tickle her, too. "I'm going!" she declared as she slipped out of his arms and trotted off for the front door. She grabbed her pack from where she'd dropped it and tossed it to Maren. "Be right back," she promised, then disappeared.

"She is a handful," Rowan cautioned Garth with a smile.

"I'm starting to realize that," he replied as he turned to face her grandfather. "How did you manage to raise her alone?"

"I truly don't know," he returned, chuckling. "Just keep her as safe as you can."

"I will," Garth promised.

As Ryes came out of the bathing room, she saw Maren was sitting at the kitchen table, a mug of tea sat before him with both his hands wrapped around it possessively. He looked up, smiling at her, but there was a serious frown which crossed his brow.

"Waiting for me?" she asked as she had just refreshed herself using their wash-up sink in the bathing room. She now wore another of her older tunics, but one that was still comfortable and sturdy.

"You're not going anywhere without one of us escorting you from now on. I don't want to see you getting hurt again. And why didn't you tell me what my father did to you?" She saw he was serious and sighed, wondering about his sudden interest in her safety? Was it because of his friendship with Garth? Or had he finally accepted her as a part of his family?

"We've been busy," she finally answered, smiling a little as she spoke. "The other night, how could I tell you? We had just spent

the day together for the first time in our lives. And yesterday was a
little madcap with everything happening so unexpectedly. Garth was
pretty upset about those scratches, too." He sighed as she set down
on the bench next to him, hugging her to his side, briefly.

"Look cousin, I've finally realized you're not the curse, nor
terror, my sister and mother seem to think you are. What happens to
you matters to me. If Korman wants to make a try for you, he'll have
to kill me, first," he told her, as he let her go to look into her green
eyes, again. She loved the warmth she saw in his brown eyes and
smiled, shaking her head at this. "It was everything I could do to not
jump in to help Garth yesterday morning. If anything ever happens to
Garth, I'll be there to protect you. You can depend upon that." She
sat perfectly still, not wanting him endangered upon her account
either.

"I don't want to ever see him hurt you," she replied. Maren
shook his head at this, smiling as he picked up her backpack and
handed it over to her.

"I didn't say I was stupid. I'll find a way, I assure you," he
told her, confidence in his bearing. She threw her arms about him,
giving him a happy hug in return, laughing. She quickly released him,
seeing he was embarrassed. She wasn't the only one who need time
to get used to the new order of things, she realized. But, at least they
were both willing to give each other a try.

"I believe you," she agreed, grinning. Then saw Sabin and
Ardis watching them from the nearby, open doorway.

"Don't worry; Garth will win his next challenge with Korman.
I saw him standing over Korman as the victor, in a forest clearing.
So, we'll all make sure it happens soon, so we can get on with our
lives," Sabin told them, smiling assurance. "Do you know what gifts
Tyra had? She had to have more than one Talent, for your
grandfather to speak of it in the plural. It fits, since it was more than
just you seeing what I saw, you strengthened my Vision so it was
clearer than I ever experienced in my whole life! Your Talents have to
be very strong!" Ryes shook her head at this, not knowing what
Talents she had. She always thought of it as only one. But it had
seemed to shift from time to time, so she'd never been sure.

"I bet you're coming onto your power," Maren added,
reminded that he wanted to talk with her about her Talents. "Our
grandmother had power. Maybe she was a Booster? We'll talk about
it later. Right now, we'd best get moving," he suggested, grinning.
Garth and the rest now stood in the doorway, having heard them at
the last. Garth grinned, wondering what Talents Ryes had, too?

"Come on you lazy bones, let's started walking!" he urged, laughing aloud. They filed out the door. Garth came over to Ryes, as Maren stood and put the empty mug in the sink then out the door. "Don't worry, we'll both get through this," he assured her, smiling. "All you have to do is try." She laughed her agreement.

As they walked through Matlowe, using the road the caravaners used weeks ago, the hunters were stopped and offered small gifts and were regaled with endless questions by many of the villagers.

"Ryes! Ryes!" Lixi shouted as she ran over to her and clung to her legs with a fierce determination. Tears were streaming down her face. "Don't go. I need you," she pleaded. Ryes knelt down next to her and gave her a tight hug. They seemed as if they didn't want to part ever. Finally, she let her go and held her at arm's length.

"I know you need me, Sweetling, but I have to go. Someone has to make sure Sabin doesn't get lost," she told her, teasing her gently. Her tears were finally drying up a bit, but her eyes were still red. "I'll be back soon," she promised. "You'll see." Aldin, Jons and three of the other cubs crowded in close now, too.

"I'll make sure Lixi's safe," Aldin declared.

"I'll help," Rand put in. Sabin stepped over and picked Lixi up, giving her a big kiss and then held her close to his heart.

"You know we'll be home to keep you safe, very soon, Li," he told her. He tickled her belly and got her laughing again.

"I'm counting on all of you cubs to stay safe. Don't play in the old houses any more. Right?" Ryes asked the others as they gathered around her, giving her a group hug. She kissed each of the cubs, holding back her own tears now. "We're going to tear them all down and build some new, strong homes for everyone, someday," she told them. Then she stopped as she realized her words sounded very true to her ears. A chill travelled up her back and she wondered if Sabin had awakened something in her, too?

"That's what we should be planning," Kovin agreed, having joined the other villagers around them. "We need to rebuild Matlowe to be safe and comfortable for everyone. Those paintings on the walls in your home give me hope that we can be as great as any of those other cities." Ryes laughed as she stood up.

"Then I leave that in your hands, O' Master Builder," she teased, grinning. He stood straighter and she saw a determination alight in his eyes. He smiled and gave her a bow. "There're some books in my loft which Rowan could show you that might help give you even more ideas," she offered. "They're there for you to study and return when you're satisfied."

"Thank you, Huntress," he replied, giving her a small bow.

Tanns was fussing at Maren, as he held tightly to Honey's halter. She wanted him to stay and help take care of his younger siblings. He insisted he needed to get out and away from his father. Finally, they embraced and whispered their goodbyes. She turned back for her own home, looking so very sad.

"We need to go, or Sabin will never get out of Matlowe in time and we'll have Metta growling at us all," Garth asserted. "Gann, take care of things for me while we're gone?" he requested.

"I will," he promised as he pulled Mitt over and put an arm over her shoulder to help contain her. "But you know our little sister is a handful!" They both laughed at this in full agreement. She made a face and twisted away. She threw her arms around Garth's neck and gave him a last hug and kiss.

"Keep him safe," she asked Ryes, giving her a hug too.

"That's a promise," she returned, hugging her back, surprised but happy to be so accepted. "You stay safe, too." Mitt smiled, her eyes lighting up with mischief.

"What's the fun if I can't give Gann headaches every now and then?" she returned with a laugh, then bounded off, running towards her parents. Garth shook his head as Gann laughed.

"She's all yours," he told his brother, who nodded, then hugged him farewell.

Shadd's sister was clinging to her, crying. She was begging her to stay. Torr's mother was happy for him, but still had tears in her eyes, which looked to be tearing at his heart. Still, both stuck to their decision to leave.

Ardis' sister and mother were there, too. They too were fussing over her and crying. But Ardis saw her mother was very proud of her choice in Sabin.

"He's a strong one who will protect you, Cubling," she told her when they were saying their final goodbyes. "Get far away from here and find a good, new life. You deserve so much more than you can ever have here."

"I'll find a new home and bring you out to stay with us," she told her, very surprised. "I love you, Mother." They hugged again and finally parted, tears were now in both their eyes.

Finally, they made it across the open plaza and headed on up the big road out of Matlowe. Some people just watched the crowd from their doorways, or from nearby. They stayed out of things, but couldn't help but want to be part of the excitement. Nothing this exciting had happened in Matlowe in several long years. Several villagers still followed the group for quite a while, but finally they did turn back for the Village. Ryes remembered the times she would follow the vans out of the Village most years and understood why the others behaved this way, too.

Gann lead off a party of hunters to go gather what they could before evening. They waved final farewells and shouted out their parting wishes for each other with the hunters. Then they disappeared into the surrounding forest.

"So, do you think they learned enough about hunting from you to keep everyone fed better?" Maren asked, once they left. Ryes grinned as she shook her head.

"It can only be hoped." Garth took her hand and turned her forward and back toward the road ahead.

"Where do we turn off the road?" he asked. She laughed in response.

"Soon," she replied, a smile lighting up her eyes from within. "Adventure lies ahead now. And I'm ready for it."

"Me, too," laughed out Garth.

"Me, too!" the rest chorused, then they all burst out laughing.

Journey's Beginning

"Oh my," Ardis declared. "What a feeling of freedom!" She turned back to look at the rise which lay between them and where Matlowe was located, falling behind them. They just emerged from the thick of the forest and mounted a tall hill to get a look of the land about them. They had been on the trail for hours and now the results could be seen. Sabin chuckled grandly, agreeing with her wholeheartedly.

"Come on, you can put that thing aside for a few moments," Maren teased Ryes, as she studied both her compass and smaller map, which she folded, so as to make carrying it easier. She had a small journal of just numbers and symbols she carried in a pocket which she sometimes consulted, too. She looked up to him smiling as she shook her head no. "You've got to see this! It's a great view!" he pleaded.

"But, I've seen it," she assured him as she focused upon his face. "This is as far as I dared go before. The last time I came out here, I barely made it home before bedtime. Rowan was very upset with me that night!"

"So, you're saying that you've been further out from Matlowe than any of the rest of us have been, already?" Garth asked, as he saw she had an impish gleam in her eyes.

"Not counting a few short trips with the caravaners, the first time I came out here was by accident. I was tracking a tusker and by the time I brought him down, and had the time to look at where I was, I was fairly shocked. Later, I came out here purposefully to see what was around. Some of the larger game animals can be found in this area. With the shelter of the forest nearby and the grasslands around them for food, they're abundant. If we want something fresh for dinner, this is the place to find it," she informed him with a knowing smile. Her own gather pouch was half full of berries, greens and tubers for their evening meal and for a few days to come, already.

"Look, you're right!" Torr told them as he pointed out a small herd of tuskers about a hundred yards ahead of them, crossing the trail. "Let's go get dinner," he suggested to Shadd, as he hefted his spear. She nodded as she got hers off Honey. She and Ryes had left their spears there in a special holder, until they needed them. Ryes put away her map and compass, as she chuckled at the happy look in Shadd's eyes. The two hunters bounded off together.

"Let's find a good campsite," Sabin suggested to his lady, as he hugged Ardis to his side. They headed downhill behind their friends, following more leisurely.

"One with some clear water flowing nearby," Maren called out to their backs. He shook his head and then turned for a last look in the direction of Matlowe. "We might as well enjoy our first night out," he said, "but I wonder how things went there today? Do you think Metta declared another Village meeting this evening? We're not there to back Rowan." He sounded worried.

"He'll be fine," Garth assured him, seeing the shadow fall across Ryes' eyes as she thought of him, too. This had to be the hardest part for her... to leave behind the only solidity in her life up to now. "Metta won't dare go after him with most of the Village standing against him. That crowd last night was outraged and maybe justice will be done for Tyra, after all?" He took up Honey's halter and put an arm around Ryes' shoulders. "Come on, let's go find that new home you and Sabin saw, so we can come back and bring our families out to a better life, too."

"I don't think it's near here," she replied, smiling once more. "But, we'll find it," she assured him.

"If it weren't that we're heading toward the ruins, I think we'd have a better time travelling the caravan road along the Yuri," Maren commented, following them down the trail. He had studied the maps closely last night, once introduced to them. It had been difficult at first to wrap his mind around the symbols, but once he grasped it, he found them amazing as the whole world had been opened up to him all at once. Ryes laughed as she realized she had just taught him how to read the maps last evening. Garth laughed, as he nodded agreement.

"Most probably, but who can resist the ancient city? I wonder how much of it is actually left? You're sure about that dust? Is it really that deadly? When was the last time anyone checked it?" Garth questioned Ryes, wanting to be sure. She sighed as she shook her head no.

"From the latest Darman had two or three years ago, and yes it's still deadly. The animals were all killed by it overnight, when their cages were suspended through some large opening. The cages were intact in the morning and the animals were not damaged or mauled, just dead. Darman said they just threw the cages and animals back in and cut the ropes. The men who brought the ropes up ended up very, very sick and two of them died, too. They at least accorded them with a proper funeral pyre instead of a burial. That's why the quarantine was renewed for that area. People going into it still die."

"Maybe we could devise some kind of masks to protect us?" Maren suggested, "some heavy cloth to filter it out possibly? And gloves to protect our hands? Like Aric wears when working the forges? I want to see what treasures lie down there! There must be a way to wash the dust off of us, once we come back out. Our ancestors survived it, after all!"

"Let's leave off with going underground," she insisted, "I wonder how much is left above ground? There are great buildings there, but still people are uneasy about being there and don't explore them very often. And what are those spires we see from Matlowe? Did people live in them? Their buildings must've been amazingly high! Those can't be illusions!" Garth chuckled at this as he nodded in agreement, hugging her tightly to his side, now.

"We'll see soon enough," he assured her, wondering too.

"Maybe they launched their fliers from them? Like those toys you used to have." Maren suggested. They all laughed as they wondered about it. The nearby tall trees cut off their view of the towers from where they stood. Still, they all turned toward them appearing thoughtful.

"You don't look so good, tonight," Shadd finally told Ryes, as they finished washing out the camp pots in the cold stream near their campsite after dinner.

"It's those scratches. I thought I was doing a good enough job to keep you from seeing it," she returned with a smile. "I'll wash them out shortly and apply some fresh salve. I should be better by morning. I usually heal up pretty quick."

"It's carrying that heavy backpack that's hindering your healing. That and starting out soaking wet and needing to wash up again," Shadd scolded her. "Let one of us carry your backpack tomorrow," she insisted, wondering at her insistence at bearing it, when she was obviously in pain?

"I can carry my own things. I'll be fine, truly," she insisted, as she blushed. "I can pull my own weight. I don't want anyone babying me."

"We're not babying you. We're just helping our brave
Huntress get better, faster, so she can teach us more of her hunting
skills," she teased. "Let us do our small things, in our small ways."

"It's just all new to me," Ryes finally admitted with a lop-sided
smile, then stood back up and bent to pick up the pots she had just
washed out and her bag of soap.

"For us all now, I think," she replied. They both laughed.

"It is a whole new world. It was only Rowan and I for so
long." Ryes straightened back up with a merry grin upon her face. A
heavy pendant necklace fell out of her tunic, unnoticed.

"What's that around your neck?" Shadd questioned, as she
was dazzled by it.

"It was in the pouch Rowan gave me before we left. I
remember him showing it to me before and telling me long ago that it
was my mother's," she replied, pulling it from her tunic fully so she
could show it off better.

It was an absolutely dazzling necklace with colorful, fiery
gemstones which held every color ever made in their milky-white
depths. These alternated with some brilliant-white, sparkling
gemstones, all bound along the length of the heavy white-metal chain.
Attached to the chain was a large, gold medallion with a symbol
painted upon it in a shiny black paint.

"I'm afraid of losing that small pouch out here, so I took it out
and decided to wear it for now, to keep it close to my heart," she
explained, as Shadd marveled at its beauty by the fading sunlight.
"In a way I feel like I'm keeping her close to my heart, too."

"This is something which speaks of wealth and a family of
some standing!" she scolded, awed by the beauty of the necklace.
The symbol on the medallion was curious, too. "Where did your
mother come from? And why didn't her family come to Matlowe to
find you at least, in all these years? You don't give a young woman
something like this without some love in your heart for her." She
reached out and touched it, cradling the pendant in the curve of her
palm as she admired it.

"I've no idea. She died when I was too little to ask," she
teased in return, getting Shadd to smile and blush. "Darman said he
found some books in Berrals, which show the family crests, so he
sketched it and he's going to look this one up for me this summer.
Hopefully we'll be all settled by this winter so when I make a quick trip
back to fetch Rowan, I can see if he has news of my mother's family?"
Shadd let the necklace go, loving its sparkling beauty in Shaysa's

bright moonlight, as the great moon was rising into the sky. Monrush was going down, setting the sky afire with its setting light.

"Maybe, if you find them, they'll come and demand some justice for Tyra Li's murder, too?" she suggested. Ryes huffed out a laugh at this and shook her head.

"I don't think anything will move Metta to act against his own brother. No, I only hope to bring them word of her fate, so if there's anyone still wondering about her, they can put their hearts to ease." She felt this would be enough. She tucked the necklace back within her tunic and gathered her pots again, as did Shadd. They stood up, but were suddenly confronted by a tall, dark shadow, surprising them. He chuckled at their shock.

"I thought you'd need this," Maren told Ryes with a smile, as he extended his burden to her. He was tickled that he caught them unawares. He'd been listening to their chatter and wondered too about the other side of Ryes' family. Why hadn't they come to claim her when she was little? "There's some obvious seepage," he warned.

"Thanks, cousin," she replied with a relieved sigh. They exchanged the pots for her pack, as Shadd giggled merrily; glad she hadn't been the only one to notice. "Okay, you can go on back, Maren. I'll take care of this, myself," she insisted, as he still stood next to her, as if waiting upon her.

"I'm going to watch your back. After all, we're still too close to Matlowe for comfort," he reminded her. She noted he held his spear in his other hand.

"You don't think?" Shadd started, then her brows furrowed as she realized it was a real possibility. "We weren't hiding our tracks," she added with a knowing sigh.

"No, we didn't consider doing that. And I've lived with that animal all my life. It's not beyond him," he asserted. "Go ahead, Ryes, take care of those scratches," he urged. Shadd took the pots from Maren's other hand, thinking he'd make a better guard if he were unburdened. She headed back to their campsite with a frown still upon her brow. She met Garth on the path, as he was headed toward the stream.

"She's washing out the scratches and Maren's watching her back," she assured him. The worried look on his face was replaced with one of relief.

"Mine are already scabbed over, even with all the activity of the last two days, but she hasn't looked too good this evening. I'll see if she needs a hand. Thanks, Shadd," he replied, then passed her and continued toward his mate. Shadd smiled to herself in relief as she walked back.

"Where is everyone?" Ardis asked, as she came back alone.

"Ryes is cleaning up her wounds and rewrapping them. Garth went to help her out and Maren is there to watch their backs," she recounted for her closest friend as she piled the pots in the place they designated for their cooking prep spot.

"She hasn't been as energetic today as she was before," Sabin added, hearing what the women were talking about.

"Actually, I was thinking she was looking a bit like Karr did last year," Ardis put in, looking thoughtful.

"What do you mean?" Torr asked, puzzled.

"Right before..." she started, trying to think of a way to put it gently.

"And now she has Kala, a sweet baby cub?" Sabin finished for her, laughing. "I think you're right, wonderful lady of mine!"

"Oh!" Torr exclaimed as he sat down, delighted surprise now upon his face.

"And we want it made very clear," Ardis spoke up suddenly standing and looking very serious indeed, "WE are not going to allow ANY challenges to determine WHOM WE MATE WITH from now on!" Torr and Sabin looked surprised while Shadd and Ardis appeared determined.

"That was never an issue with us," Sabin finally voiced into the following surprised silence, then cocked a smile. "We had already decided that, ourselves, years ago when we were teeners. I'll let Garth know what's going on when they get back."   The women appeared relieved at this news. "Let's pull out her maps and take a look. We'll have to figure out where to go so we can give them some time alone," he added in suggestion. Laughter erupted once again from everyone else gathered.

"So, we'll take Honey with us and leave a more obvious trail," Sabin suggested to Garth and Ryes after they and Maren rejoined them at the campfire.

"Then you two can slip off and see if what we think is happening, actually happens," Ardis added. "And we'll meet up near the southern end of the ruins in about a week, or so, at this lake, here. It looks like it's called Lake Ever." She indicated a spot of blue on the map.

"Odd name for a lake, but it sounds like a good plan," Garth replied, feeling elated as he formed further plans in his mind.

"Are you sure?" Ryes started, feeling a little shaky inside. She didn't know if it was excitement, or nervousness. Here was the event she'd awaited for years! And she was with the only man she could now imagine being at her side through this time!

"When I think on it, I'm very sure," Garth told her, hugging her closer to his side as he laughed merrily. "You do look exactly as Karr did then and it is the right time of the year for such things." A big smile blossomed upon her face as a merry light filled her eyes.

"We escaped Matlowe just in time," she teased in return. "But I'm not really happy with him tracking the rest of you, either."

"We'll be fine," Maren assured her. "The hard part will be convincing him both of you are still with us. He's always suspicious."

"We'll handle it," Sabin added, speaking to them all.

"Let's wait until it truly is more obvious her time has come," Garth finally declared. "It did take Karr a few weeks before she was ready. We'll then leave when Ryes is ready and that way we can find a good place that will be better for hiding our tracks as we leave. So, for now we'll stay all together. Agreed?" He got nods and agreements voiced from all the others gathered.

"Well," Ryes put in, standing up. "Tonight we should deal with other things, anyway. See those clouds crossing Shaysa's face and the way the wind has started to gust and blow? They tell me we'll have rain very soon, so we'll have to use the extra ground cloths I brought along, already." She strode over to where she had left the packs she'd taken off of Honey earlier and started going through them.

"There's no shelter here from the rain," Shadd stated, standing up to look at the clouds better. "It's going to be a cold, wet night." Ryes tossed Torr a coil of rope, since he was looking at her. He caught it deftly.

"We'll make our own shelters and we'll be fine," she assured her. Ardis stood and stepped forward and extended her hands to take some of the heavy tarps.

"What do we do first to create them?" she asked with a merry smile. Ryes smiled in return.

"Actually, it's not too hard," she started.

"The whole Village is restless today," Korman complained, as he came in the back door, making sure to close it securely behind him. Tanns washed her hands in her basin before she looked up to her husband with concern in her eyes.

"Old wounds have been opened. Ones that never truly healed," she replied with sadness in her whole demeanor. He crossed the room and put his arms around her, pulling her into the warmth of his chest and stroking her hair as he sought to offer his comfort. She sighed as she pushed him away. "I need to think... I need to breathe..." she told him, turning her back to him as tears threatened to start to flow once again.

"What is wrong?" he pressed, spreading his hands to show his helplessness.

"Why are you back so soon? I thought you were going fishing today?" she replied, looking annoyed as she turned back to him.

"Metta ordered me to remain in our house," he told her. "I thought I'd help you with the chores for a while."

"You truly killed her, didn't you?" she accused in a low voice, as tears started to flow again. "Of all the people on Tayna, you killed her. She used to truly make me feel loved... deeply loved... as if she were my own sister in truth. You took her from me!"

"Honestly?" he pressed, with his face now impassive, "How did you know that so well?"

"She was an amazing Talent. Mind-to-mind, heart-to-heart, we were sisters in truth," she finally admitted to him after all these years. "I don't know if I can ever forgive that being taken away from me, so cruelly."

"I cannot unmake the past," he finally admitted, breathing out a large puff of breath, not affirming his guilt even now. "She's gone. What would you have me do? Go gather my things and leave?"

"You can care for the young ones while I finish with the greens," she finally told him after a long, silent pause. She turned back to her work table; her face appeared seamed as her brow furrowed in thought. She did not heed her tears any more, even if they were still flowing.

"Stuffed greens?" Rowis exclaimed as she ran into the kitchen with a huge smile on her face and looking very excited. "Truly? Are we having stuffed greens?" Her voice hit a high pitch at the end as she grabbed onto her mother's tunic and laughing happily. It brought a smile to Tann's face once more. She wiped at her eyes with the back of her hand.

"Yes Sweetling, stuffed greens tonight," she promised. "The meat is almost ready, so I have to hurry here. Go show your father what you've been working on today," she encouraged to divert her. Rowis turned and grabbed his hand with both of her small ones.

"Come and see father! Jons taught me to make a fish net a 'so we can catch some fish together. I mostly got it right," she tugged on his hand. He couldn't help but laugh at her joyous energy, as he let her lead him out into their main room. It was the escape he needed as he couldn't face Tanns right now. His mind and heart were in turmoil again.

The Village Square was filled with almost all the villagers tonight. Discussions had been going on all day long in small gatherings of three or four or five villagers. The people were openly discussing the definitions of murder and how to rate these crimes and the punishments to be meted out. The Laws clearly defined the structures of the definitions and it was up to the Council of Elders to decide how and to whom they applied. Matlowe Village might have been small compared to most, but it had been a hub of order for the land, as decreed by the Chiefs of the Caravaners for centuries. There was a column upon which the Laws written by the Ancients had been inscribed by them, but it had been lost for some years, when it should've been on proud display in the Village Square. Its absence was felt strongly this evening.

"Order!" Sonta called out. He was standing in his father's stead this evening. The rest of the elders were in their seats and ready; even Rowan was present and appearing calm for all that his granddaughter had left with the others, who accompanied Sabin this morning into exile. "Order!" Finally the gathered villagers settled down, most finding seats as close as possible around the square.

"Where's Metta? He should be a part of this, too," Kalu demanded, standing up as the rest were settling down to their seats.

He looked determined. "He has some of this problem to answer to since it was his father, your grandfather Kornn who was Chief Village Elder at the time. His decisions have brought a smelly smear to tarnish Matlowe Village for well over a decade."

"I am here in both their steads and will help us all address these issues," Sonta affirmed. "Now sit down so we can get started." There was a note of solidity in his voice that could not be denied. Kalu sat, even if he did not appear satisfied. Sonta turned about making sure everyone was seated before he began.

"Metta was not feeling well enough after the stress of yesterday. And today has been a continuation of last evening. All day long. So, he never got enough rest to be able to carry out his duties as Chief Elder tonight." He paused, eyeing everyone sitting around the outside of the Circle with an accusing look upon his face. Some of the villagers shifted uncomfortably, some appeared defiant, some had doubt in their eyes, and some appeared to be thinking.

"He's getting old, Sonta. All I want to know is why he wouldn't let Rowan speak last night?" Spann asked, as he remained sitting and appearing agitated.

"What would it have hurt him to sit and hear the accounting in full, as his father should have done in his time as Chief Elder?" Allis asked as he sat near Spann. Other voices started asking questions about it, all around them, and even though they kept their seats to avoid being banned from the meetings for as long as the elders dictated, they wanted to be heard, too. Sonta let it play out for a few minutes then held up his hands, urging these friends and neighbors to calm down. They all settled back down to hear him, again.

"I don't know why my father would not simply listen to Rowan last night. I was too young to understand all that was happening at the time when he first attempted to tell what happened to Tyra in a Village gathering to my grandfather, or why he took me home and never stayed to listen to the whole story then," he stated, speaking out loudly as he turned and tried to meet as many eyes of the people as he could, as he spoke. They were clearly still very unsettled. He noted Korman was not here, but Tanns was with their children. She was upset and appeared to have been crying. She put up her hand, so to be called upon.

"Yes, Tanns?" he recognized her, since she had been the only one to raise a hand.

"Let Rowan tell it now. That way it won't get Metta upset with having to hear it, sense he's not here. And I want to let the full story be told so I can hear it with an open heart," she requested. She lowered her hand, as suddenly other hands sprang into the air all around the circle.

"How can I know that what Rowan says is the truth?" Rivo questioned, doubt filling her eyes, as well as fear. Rowan stood up at this one, looking ready to defend himself.

"We don't have anyone strong enough with Mind Voice to verify," Sonta intervened. "But we could wait for when the caravaners return to their winter camp, or send off to one of the larger cities for a real Talent to pay us a visit, but that's at a cost." His offer seemed to satisfy some while angering others.

"Rami has Mind Voice. Why can't she verify it for us? She can at least say what's true, or not," Aric stated, gesturing to his wife beside him. The Village smith was one of the few villagers no one bothered, not even Korman, because of his muscular body and sharp wits. Rami blushed but nodded her head in agreement. Sonta smiled at this, seeing an opportunity.

"Then we have a way of at least telling the truth of the matter," Sonta agreed, gesturing for Rami to stand up and come join him in the circle. Aric followed her over, carrying a chair for her to use as she was carrying his cub and he was very concerned about her standing for long periods of time. Rowan noted this, so picked up his own chair smiling at the idea. Rebin offered him a water skin, as he passed her. He smiled his surprise but accepted it gratefully.

"We don't want your throat getting too dry, Storyteller," she teased, smiling. He gave her a small bow of thanks.

"Thank you. I'll do my best to bring out the story in full," he promised her.

"As good at least, as last night," she breathed in response. He nodded, then stepped off the platform and headed towards Sonta and Rami. The other elders watched him keenly. Rowan placed his chair slightly in front of and to the right of Rami's chair. She settled into hers and he into his, setting the water skin across his lap.

"Please begin," Sonta urged, stepping away from them. A hush fell upon the Village Circle as everyone prepared for the story, each in their own way. Sonta returned to the Elder's Platform to allow them to tell it unhindered by his presence.

"Have you ever done this before?" Rami asked as she reached for his hand. Rowan chucked at this.

"Long ago for one who was dear to me, who wanted to see my truth within when I told her a story from my own youth. What you're going to see will be painful at times," he warned. She smiled in return and nodded, as she grasped his hand in her own, not truly believing him. She closed her eyes, as did Rowan, to help create their inner bond.

The shock that coursed through Rami's being as she caught glimpses of his memories of Tyra almost threw her out of the link, but she hung on, determined to see this through. She pulled back enough to just watch the flow of his tale, so she wouldn't burn out trying to know it all at once. She felt Rowan's amusement and understanding, as he had to make sense of it all long ago.

Finally, Rowan opened his eyes and began his story from the beginning when Tyra was brought home by Jana from an unknown place where she had been held captive. As it unraveled and became a new, rich tapestry, tears could be seen in Rami's eyes as she witnessed from within more than just what words could convey. And she realized that Tyra, even with her skills at a low ebb at the end, was far more powerful than she could ever hope to achieve with her own Talent. It awed her and she wished she'd known her better, before.

For his part, even if his eyes were open, Rowan saw things as they were when they happened. True, Tyra had been far more skilled in her Talents than Rami, but the birth of her cubs had robbed her of many of them and by the time she reached him, only Mind Voice had returned more fully. He told the tale as completely as he could, leaving out as little as possible. For some of it, there were no words and again his heart ached for all that he lost in this horrible violent act. When he finally reached the end of all he could tell, he found he could finally focus again upon the others before him. It had been hours, he was sure, but truly had no idea how long it had been.

Sonta strode back across to them with questions in his eyes. The villagers gathered around had moved closer to the pair, not wanting to miss any part of the telling, sitting on ground as close as they could. Rami opened her eyes and wiped at them with the back of her hand. Rowan uncapped the water skin and offered it to her first. She grasped it, met his eyes for a moment and then took it gratefully. It gave her something else to focus upon for a breath of time.

"Rami, was what Rowan told us the truth?" Sonta asked as she lowered the water skin and looked around. She huffed out a breath and nodded her head.

"Every word and then some," she replied. "There was no deceit, nor lies in anything he said. Matlowe lost a great treasure when we lost Tyra Li and her other three children," she stated. "I never knew..." but did not explain any further.

"How can you know so much about it, Rowan?" Sonta pressed, bewildered now in the face of the declared truth. It had been a very complete life's tale.

"Because Tyra gave him her memories directly," Rami told them all. "It was amazing what she could do! I learned a lot more of how to use my own Talent while watching and listening here tonight." Aric was beside her now, wrapping an arm around her shoulders and helping her to stand more steadily. She gave the water skin back to Rowan who smiled and gave her a nod before downing a good share of the healing water.

"I did give more of it today than last night, but then last night I was still very agitated over the things that happened then," Rowan admitted. "Now are you satisfied in knowing the full truth of the events of that time? And why I felt justice was never meted out, as it should have been before?" The people now standing around him were quiet as they tried to understand it all. Tanns and her children were now gathered next to Rowan as she grasped his hand, smiling.

"Thank you father, for telling me all the truth. I was finally able to say I was ready to hear it," she told him. He hugged her tightly, breathing a sigh of relief.

"I now understand many things and have more to think on," Sonta admitted. "We will discuss this in an Elder's only meeting tomorrow afternoon. And perhaps see what we can do now to repair what should have been done before. It's getting late and we should all be off to our beds," he stated, looking at the others gathered near him. They were far more subdued but he knew it would be all discussions again tomorrow. He smiled. Change was in the air.

"I don't know if I can sleep now," Rami told her husband. "I have so much going through my head." He grabbed her chair and chuckled as he turned them both towards home.

"Let's go try," he advised with a smile. She nodded her head as they threaded their way through the others gathered around.

"Mother," Mitt said in a low voice, tugging her hand, wanting to pull her away from the crowd gathering around Rowan. Marla finally relented and allowed her daughter to lead her a bit away from the rest.

"What do you need, Mitt?" she asked, puzzled.

"I want to go follow Garth and Ryes and the others," she told her.

"No. It's too dangerous. They're a bigger group and the larger predators will leave them alone. You're just one person and would be killed," she replied, appearing deeply concerned. "That would break all of our hearts."

"I'll be fine," she insisted, "I've learned a lot of how to get along in the woods."

"And how will you find them, cubling?" Garvin asked, joining them. "Do you really know how to follow such a trail?" She didn't immediately answer. He chuckled as he ruffled her hair. "Give yourself some time to grow older and learn more of your own mind, huh?"

"Oh father," she sighed out in return. "Please let me try?"

"Not now. I need you to wait and see," he urged, appearing more serious now. "I'm sure they won't stay out there for very long. They'll all be back soon and telling us all about their adventures."

"I don't want to be sitting around and listening to them, I want to be out there living the adventure, too," she insisted, frowning.

"I know, cubling, I know," Marla told her, pulling her close and giving her a hug. Garvin wrapped his arms around both of them, cherishing the moment.

Mitt realized that she needed to do this smarter. Some of the others from last night had had a better look at the maps. Perhaps she could find out more information so that when she was ready to leave, she would have a better chance of finding them quickly? And perhaps more practice in the woods would help her learn to live in it better? She was not giving up on her brother, yet.

Nightmares

Ryes stirred, uncomfortable in her sleep, deep in the throes of a disturbing, confusing dream...

A misty figure... female... dressed in a long, flowing, wispy robe gestured welcomingly to Ryes. She appeared young, but her cold, dark, greedy eyes echoed the centuries. She emerged from a bone-chilling darkness and an eerie, green light haloed her silhouette. Ryes felt fear rise up within her. A coldness deeper than death held her in its grip and it was inspired by the image before her! There was something about this woman's eyes! A dark madness dwelt there! She felt she was evil and wanted nothing to do with her! She tried to back away, but there was an incredible force pulling her closer against her will!

"Come, my daughter, here you'll find peace," she spoke in a lulling croon. The sound of her voice made chills run up Ryes' back. There was a deadness to it which leached the warmth of life from her very limbs! Fighting, Ryes turned her face away, and so managed to twist her body from her grasp as well. It was freeing her mind first from the stare which helped her finally break away fully. She ran far away from the woman. Then she was confronted by another ghostly female figure.

This was an older woman who was dressed in a very fancy, embroidered gown, fashioned of a pearlescent blue material. There was no madness in her eyes, just desperation and Ryes felt some strange kinship with this woman. There was a bearing about her which made Ryes take instant notice, as if she were used to commanding others. She was more ghostly than the first image and she called out to Ryes by name; her hands were outstretched, beseechingly, and a tall shadow stood behind her, watching them both. Yet Ryes realized she didn't fear this shadow and it was as if it were a part of this woman; that they BELONGED together. She reached out for her, feeling she needed her help, as she wondered who she was? But as she did, the lady faded into a vague, gray mist. Her cutoff, strangled cry as she disappeared, wrenched at Ryes' heart.

A last figure appeared, confidently walking through the thickening mist with grace and poise. She was dressed in a flowing gown which shimmered with a blue-white light radiating out from it. Ryes stood still as this one came to her. When they stood face-to-face, Ryes was shocked to find her own features clearly reflected in

this lady's face. Only their eyes were different. The lady's held all of
time in her eyes and they were a slightly deeper shade of green.
Ryes' heart beat a strong rhythm as she stood trembling before her,
with her own inner needs unvoiced. She HAD to be who she thought
she was... she was so very sure of it...

"Ryes, daughter of the House of Li, you are walking toward a
deadly danger," the hauntingly, beautiful lady before her warned.

"I have my spear and beltknife and I'm not unskilled in self-
defense," Ryes replied, as she suddenly found her own voice. She
hesitated a moment, then added, "Mother." The woman smiled at
this, giving her a nod of her head. Was it an acknowledgment of their
kinship?

"Yes," she answered vaguely, as if it were a game between
them. "But, the danger I warn you of cannot be fought by any
weapons you could make or hold with your hands, my daughter. This
danger will steal your very soul. The battleground lies not in the
world you know, but in another. One very much like this place."
Tyra's arm swept out, encompassing the gray vagueness around
them. Ryes wanted to reach out to her, but couldn't lift her arms.
They felt as if lead-weighted. This close to her and still she was out of
reach! Ryes felt her frustrations and anger come to the surface. She
needed to know the whys for so many things! And this image of her
mother stood before her smiling. She wasn't mocking her, but it was
as if she had no knowledge of her only living daughter's inner agony!

"Mother, what happened? Rowan told me his stories of you,
but that's still not enough. Where're your parents? Why have they
never searched for you? And why was I the only one to survive?" she
questioned, trying to reach out to her somehow. Tyra appeared
surprised at this, and then looked at Ryes as if seeing her truly for the
first time. A deep sorrow lay in her eyes as she still stood just barely
out of Ryes' reach. It appeared as if she were struggling for a way to
answer her, around her own inner agony.

Suddenly, around them arose a soaring, bustling city with
crowds of people going about their business. Ryes stood and
marveled at it. The buildings were enormous and so tall, and the
people were varied in race and appearance. There was so much to
see and it seemed everyone around them was in an unexplained
haste. Then a blast of brilliantly-bright, yellow-white light engulfed
them all. A wave of intense heat followed, as did a distinct rumbling,
which shook the ground beneath her feet. The very air buffeted her
and would have knocked her off her feet if she had truly been there.

"What's that? What's happening?" she demanded, turning her face away to shield her eyes from the intense brightness. A wild panic arose from within, urging her to flee.

"The destruction of the greatest city upon Tayna. Only ruins remain of a great city once called Hailys. It is where you were born," her mother answered calmly. Then she faded into a blue mist. Ryes began to feel the heat of the flames about her. She could see the forms of the people running - mad to escape the disaster. She tried to reach out, aching to run herself and...

...awoke suddenly. She gasped as she opened her eyes and coughed a couple of times, as if to clear her lungs of the smoke.

There was the sweet smell of crushed grasses and a light musky-spiciness, which she realized was Garth. She lay curled up with her back next to his back. The sky was beginning to brighten with the promise of day and there were the small rustlings of the life around them; either retreating from the coming light, or coming out to greet the new day.

Ryes tried to calm her wildly-beating heart. There were no flames, nor running people around them, only the peace of the break of a new dawn. The nightmares were becoming more intense the further they journeyed from Matlowe. She turned and inched closer to Garth's warmth, while trying not to wake him. There was a chill in her, which neither the blankets over and under them, nor Garth's warmth, could easily dispel. It caused her to shiver uncontrollably. She felt a moment of utter helplessness as she had yet to find a way of preventing the nightmares. Then she recalled who she was and that night visions were only that. Her equilibrium began to return. She exerted her will and forced her body to relax. It'd only been a bad dream, after all!

Garth began to stir; he'd felt her movements. Ryes felt a pang of guilt at having disturbed his sleep once more. She'd become hopelessly attached to this calm, confident man. She'd never been this close to anyone, even her grandfather. Living with him, even on a journey like this, was a heady experience which Ryes found she couldn't get enough of and would never willingly leave his side, ever.

"Are you all right?" Garth asked, as he turned around to face her in the early morning light. He put his arms around her and pulled her closer to him. She'd become very precious to him.

"I'm fine. It's just another one of those stupid dreams," she apologized, as she snuggled in against his chest. "I'm sorry; I didn't mean to wake you, again." The chill was finally leaving her as he held her, stroking her red-gold hair. He could feel the chill in her body and wondered if it was something more? He already talked with Sabin about it, wondering if it was related to his Visions, but he hadn't thought so. Maren was suffering them, too.

"It's time to get up, anyway," Garth assured her with a chuckle. Ryes clung a moment longer, enjoying the sensations, then pulled back a little, looking into his warm, yellow eyes. They were the color of honey in the sunlight. He leaned down to kiss her gently. Her nerves flared to life with the deep feelings he stirred within her. Her body was responding to his and she was glad the group slept apart, giving each other a little privacy! There were times, like this, when they all needed their own space.

Later, as Ryes was rebuilding the campfire from the banked coals, she thought back to the morning they left the Village. Rowan had looked so sad, but smiled as he handed her a small pouch. She missed him and worried about him, but there was nothing here she could do about it. She recalled his last words to her.

"Be careful. There're all kinds of dangers loose in the world. Stick to the Caravaner's routes as much as possible," he warned her, then as he gave her a farewell kiss and embrace, he whispered, "And bring home lots of fine, healthy cubs."

"I will, I promise," Ryes whispered back, chuckling softly. She had no idea what he told the others as he said good-bye to them, but everyone was all smiles then. She prayed he was still safe, at least. He HAD to be!

The small party set a simple goal of seeing the ruins, then finding a place to live through the winter; far away from the Village and the problems there. If they found their own, proper home, then so much the better. Everything was fine for the first several days, but now these dreams came to haunt Ryes and Maren every night. And in their exhaustion, they were leaving more of the burden of setting up camp to the rest. Ryes felt guilty, but she was so tired, so totally drained of energy. She couldn't understand it. She'd never been this way before! What could be behind these nightmares? She smiled ruefully to herself, wondering how to overcome this strange affliction, while watching the tiny bits of kindling catch flame. Garth, sitting nearby, gestured her to stillness as he quietly picked up his spear. Careful of any sudden moves, Ryes turned to see a bounder doe and two small fawns grazing nearby.

"Garth, not the mother," Ryes breathed out in warning, barely moving her lips.

"Why?" he whispered in question, a frown upon his handsome face, as the warmth of true dawn was touching them.

"Then you might as well kill all three. Without the mother to protect them, both the fawns will surely die," she insisted. His arm was taunt, ready to hurl the spear. He nodded his head once in answer, then cast. She watched Garth throw the spear, admiring the rippling play of the muscles in his chest and arm. Suddenly, she felt an intense stab of pain in her ribs. It was as if her body was engulfed in a fiery pain! Garth, intent upon his prey, didn't see her grasp her side and crumple into a ball next to the small, crackling fire.

"Got him!" he cried as he bounded up to claim his kill; his eyes never leaving the fawn. Ryes gasped out as tears sprang to her eyes. She was shaking all over and barely able to breathe. She killed many times on the hunt, but usually managed to block the pain of death from her acute, inner senses. Now something was awakening within her. She felt that spear too fully and realized she hadn't even been concentrating upon the prey! She had to regain her equilibrium before Garth returned!

"Ryes?" Shadd's voice quested, her voice filled with concern, coming from behind her. "What's the matter?" She saw her sudden collapse and knew Garth missed it as he rushed to claim his kill. She was quickly at her side, reaching out a comforting hand. The paleness of her face surprised her, as the trembling of her body deeply upset her. She realized she wasn't playing a game, as she saw the intense pain in Ryes' eyes.

"I felt that, as if it'd been me," she whispered, her face ashen. Shaken, she added more sticks to the fire. "Well, at least it'd been a clean kill, or I might now be feeling the knife, too."

"How?" Torr demanded, as he came and sat next to their small, breakfast fire.

"I've always been able to feel it to some extent, but when you need the meat to feed your family... So, I learned to block most of it out before. But with these night visions, it seems I can't block it now." Ryes sighed, trying to force her body to relax again. The coldness had returned and she was shivering as she wiped the tears away from her face, with the side of one hand.

"Good morning, Maren," Ardis said over her shoulder, as she and Sabin came to sit near the fire. Shadd put one of their larger pots over it to heat, so they'd have some fresh, hot tea. Maren appeared, sitting down next to Ryes, still shivering from the cold he was feeling.

"You again, too?" Ryes asked. He nodded his head. She saw his eyes were shadowed. "What is this? Some kind of family curse?"

"Powerful Healers run in your family, maybe it's something from that which plagues you both now? Didn't Rowan say Jana would run off for days, as if searching for something? Maybe she had the same nightmares and was looking for her own answers?" Ardis suggested.

"I only want those women to leave me alone!" Maren declared, wishing he knew how to drive spirits away. He was sure that's what they were.

"Women?" Ryes sharply questioned, frowning. "Is one haloed in a greenish light?" she demanded.

"Yes," he affirmed, seeing her quick interest. "She's the scariest one. It's like she's reaching out to catch and eat me. And I can't move to get away from her! She really gives me the chills! You've seen her, too?" he demanded. She huffed out a laugh and nodded her head.

"She also wants me, but keeps telling me I'll be safe with her. There's something about her which makes me want to be as far away as possible! Then there's another one who's more like a ghost and calls me by name. She needs my help for some reason, but I don't know why. And tonight, at the last, there was my mother."

"Was she wearing a white, flowing dress and has bluish-white light around her? She looks just like you! She's the one who blocked off old green-creeps and saved me from her," Maren told her, finally sharing what was keeping him from sleeping, lately. "Did you see a woman with golden hair and bright, blue eyes? She's been calling out to me, to save her from the cold. I don't know who she is, but if I find her, I'll surely help."

"I didn't see her," Ryes answered, smiling. "Maybe only you can reach her in time?" She sighed as her own shivering seemed to be fading, once more. They'd both been having nightmares, but never knew there was so much similarity in what they were seeing.

"She sounds strange with blue eyes and golden hair. I wonder why she needs saving from the cold? Could she be living up north?" Ardis asked, teasing him. Sabin appeared thoughtful.

"There're supposed to be people in the south, who're said to have golden hair. And if I have green eyes, I don't see why blue ones would be so outlandish," Ryes told them, diverting them from Maren, seeing a look in his eyes which she thought meant he wasn't happy with the teasing about his blue-eyed lady. "I also saw Hailys destroyed. It was horrible! All fire and thunder, with people running in absolute terror and nowhere to be truly safe," she added, feeling a chill up her back again.

"What's Hailys?" Torr asked, curious.

"The ruins which Tyra used to call the destroyed city. It was a huge city and when it was attacked, it was without warning and was utterly destroyed. The terror was unbelievable..." Her voice trailed off as she saw it, as if she had actually stood there when it happened. She truly lacked the words to express it all. And she'd been born there? Could her mother's family be living somewhere near it? The others sat and looked to each other, wanting to understand. At least they now had the proper name for the place they sought.

Garth returned with the dressed carcass of one of the fawns. He noted Ryes had the fire rebuilt and the rest were sitting around it, waiting for the water to heat for their morning tea. He smiled as he saw Ryes pull out the last of the nut biscuits to warm on a clean, flat rock next to the fire. She made them the day before, making sure there were plenty for this morning. But she looked pale and shaky as she greeted his return. Maren didn't look much better either, and the rest of the group appeared worried.

Garth was concerned. First the odd nightmares, almost every night. And what could be happening now? If it continued much longer, he'd insist the two of them and Maren return to Matlowe. Even if her season came upon her, he knew he could outmatch the other men - even Korman. He felt he'd have to. There was a closeness he shared with Ryes, which he savored and would never give up. She had somehow become a part of him. He crouched down and got to work with his knife, trying to think of a way to breach the subject with her. Everyone appeared lost in his, or her, own thoughts.

"They're seeing almost the same people in their nightmares," Sabin finally informed him. "This feels like it's more of a Talent awakening in them both. None of us has any training, nor truly knows the dangers. Ryes doesn't even know what kind of Talents Tyra had to pass onto her. Why don't we take them back to the Village?" he suggested, then shut up as Ardis glared at him, daring him to finish saying what was on his mind.

"We go forward, not back," she stated, in a no-nonsense tone of voice. "I don't want to see Metta declaring your life forfeit because of a few nightmares!"

"For heading toward the ruins, we're going in a roundabout way," Garth commented, ignoring Ardis' outburst as he cut the meat into strips to cook over the fire, glancing up to see Ryes' face. In his heart he agreed with his blood brother, but he knew that Ardis had a point, too. He'd never endanger Sabin, either!

"I didn't know the lay of the land from just the maps. Now I understand why Darman keeps such detailed logs of his journeys. It's because the maps aren't as detailed as they should be for such venturing," Ryes replied, looking up to him. He noted the quiet pain in the depths of her emerald eyes.

"What's wrong?" he asked, needing to get this out in the open. She sighed, sat back and wrapped her arms around her legs, blushing as everyone's eyes were now upon her, wanting to see if she would tell him the whole thing, or not.

"Rowan used to always tell me Tyra could do things no one else could," she began slowly, looking from Garth's eyes, back into the dancing flames, avoiding the eyes of the rest, too. "He always told me I have the old gifts of the ancients, but no real power. Now I think Sabin's right, something's awakening in me... the power. But since Maren's suffering this too, I agree it may be coming from a Talent we've inherited from our grandmother, Jana." She sighed again, acutely embarrassed. She had no way to control it! Awakening Riss' Talent hadn't been ANYTHING like this! Maren looked thoughtful at hearing her, frowning as he nodded his head in agreement. Garth looked back to his own work, threading some meat strips onto a stick.

"That's the why for the nightmares you're both having?" he asked. Ryes nodded, again meeting his eyes. "But what's gotten you so shaken now? You were already over this morning's shivers." He looked at her with a heartfelt concern in his golden eyes. She'd gotten through it as they free-mated this morning. It was as if they were back, and far more intense.

"The bounder fawn... I felt its death," Ryes admitted in a low voice, blushing. She was trembling again. She looked back to the fire, turning the nut biscuits over, as she was trying to avoid them all, but she continued, speaking to the fire. "I've never felt a death so strongly before." She shrugged a shoulder. "I'm only glad I wasn't the one to cast the spear." She wondered how she was going to be able to help provide for their future family, if she was unable to hunt. She taught Garth and the others quite a few things about hunting as they travelled, even if they'd only been out a few days. But most men only stayed with their mates to help with the hunting and cubs until the cubs were about to enter their second year. From that point on, Ryes would have to provide for herself, Rowan and her cubs, since she had no siblings to help. She had to find a way to overcome this problem!

Garth was troubled as he met Sabin's eyes, in question. He saw his shock, too. He knew she was a fine huntress, but never knew she felt the prey's death personally. Then he thought back...

He recalled the first time she made an impression on him as the Huntress. He was part of a hunting party from the Village, which had fanned-out to flush any game they could find. But she appeared out of nowhere, standing beside him. She usually avoided him whenever he tried to follow her, so was shocked speechless.

There'd been blood on her hands and it was spattered all over her tunic. Fresh blood. She signaled him to follow, a gleam of mischief in her green eyes. Not knowing why, he did. She led him to a small copse of evergreen trees. There, on a bed of old needles lay the carcass of an old, bull moss-eater. His great, scoop-shaped horns spanning more than the width of Garth's arms, fully extended. He was shocked. He'd been cleanly killed and was already bled.

"Rowan and I can only use so much. I thought the rest of you could use the remaining meat," she'd explained, as she knelt down by the beast to heft up a package she'd made, before she went to get him.

"You did this all by yourself?" he'd asked in astonishment. A beast this size took a half dozen hunters to bring down in a long, intense battle. Not one small female. It was an impossible feat!

"He was old and ready for death. It may be why he was so far south to begin with," Ryes answered him, patting the brown, shaggy-hided neck. She rose, picking up her spear. A moment's pain had passed in her eyes as she looked to him again. He remembered that more clearly, now. "Better summon the others. It'll take time to finish dressing him down." With that she'd turned and left, leaving him with a puzzled look upon his face... and her light laughter echoing through the woods.

"Garth, I didn't mean to upset you so much with this," Ryes said, quickly taking a meat-laden stick from his hands. "If you want to go back, I'll understand, but I can't. I have to go on." That scored, but he'd been thinking of returning for her sake, not his own. He saw surprise and humor in Torr's eyes at this, too.

"No," Garth spoke firmly, in a soft voice. "We'll go back, or continue on, together." There was a twinkle in his eye and a half smile upon his lips. Ryes' aching heart bounded with joy as she threw her arms around him, burying her face in his shoulder.

"I'll learn to control this. I'm sure it only takes time and trying," she promised him. "I only wish I knew what use it all is for? If I can feel the death of another creature, how does that help me?" she asked, turning it over in her mind once more, as she pulled back to look at his face.

"You'll find a use," he assured her, holding her eyes once more. "Now, are you ready for some breakfast, Sweet One?" he asked, hoping this problem would have a solution. And soon! Maren was tied up in this, too. This HAD to be related to some shared Talent they both had awakening!

"Yes," Ryes answered him, his smile easing her distress.

"Let me help there," Shadd volunteered, seeing he was about to drop the meat in his other hand. He handed it to her, letting her and Ardis take over.

"I hope it's simple," Maren commented. "I'll go check on Honey," he volunteered, as he stood up. He had some thinking to do; his mind again returning to the blue-eyed lady, who needed him so much. She was strange to look upon, but not unpleasant somehow. He couldn't believe the love and lust he felt when he thought of her. He wondered how he could save her, when he'd be too embarrassed to go near her! There was no way any of the others would understand his yearning for a practically hairless woman! Which was why he left out that one detail. But, those blue eyes seeking his, held his heart and what he hoped was her love for him, in return.

"Are you sure we should try this, Sabin?" Ryes questioned, worried. They hadn't made any progress on the trail today, establishing their camp early. Ryes was now teaching Torr and Ardis how to read the maps and use the compass. With her lack of sleep, she couldn't focus enough to keep them to their chosen route and wanted someone with some wits to have control over their destiny. Sabin had approached her, interrupting their class with his idea.

"What've you got to lose?" he demanded. "After all, it'll be tapping your other, working Talent and might actually free both you and Maren from the nightmares. I don't know if a Catalyst can use such Talent upon his, or herself, but working on Maren's might help yours to awaken, too. You were saying that it wasn't anything like Riss'. I'll monitor you both and help, if you run into trouble," he assured her. She was almost two years younger than him and totally inexperienced when it came to her Talents. The fact that she had more than one had him charged. She looked to have no idea how rare such a thing like that actually was in truth! At least he had years of grappling with his own Talent, so knew more of what they were facing in this matter. She sighed, still uncertain, but gave him a nod of her head in agreement.

"I'm willing to try it, at least," she replied, wishing she were still better rested for a task like this one.

"Maren!" Sabin called out, waving him over. He was learning how to ride Honey and looked to be having fun. And it gave Honey the exercise she needed, too. He turned the windracer mare toward them putting her into a slow canter, questions in his eyes.

"What's the matter?" he asked, as he brought her to a halt before the others.

"I asked Ryes if she could use her Catalyst Talent to try to find out if you really have a Talent, or are just having nightmares, which happen to be almost exactly like hers. She's willing, if you are. If nothing else, it might free you from all those bad dreams." Maren's eyes were suddenly shadowed in doubt. Did he truly want to lose his blue-eyed, hairless lady? Then he recalled the other, haunting terror and slid off the mare's back, walking closer as he led her by her halter.

"Shouldn't we tell Garth what we're up to, first?" he questioned in return, as he approached.

"I told him I'd ask the two of you about it, earlier. He said for us to be careful, but I think he hopes this will free you both. It's all we can do right now, anyway," he pressed.

"All right, I'll let her try. But, I've never heard of a person's Talent awakening this late. Isn't it usually as you first enter your teener years?"

"It can be later. I recall my grandmother saying the Visions didn't start for her until she was in her mid-twenties," he assured him, smiling. Glad he was willing to give it a try, at least.

"Before we do anything, you're going to walk Honey until she's cooled off, and then water and brush her down," Ryes ordered with a smile. She wanted Maren to know Honey needed some care and wasn't only around for his pleasure. She got up and walked over to inspect her water bucket. It was getting low. "I'd better get her some fresh water." She realized she was neglecting her, too.

"I'll take her down to the creek," Maren volunteered. He took the bucket from Ryes, then the mare's halter again, turning her for the small creek which ran near their camp. Cool, fresh water would be far better for her, anyway.

"Good, then I'll go with you and refill our waterskins and cooking pots," Sabin told him, smiling. Maren paused and gave him a nod and smile, waiting for him to gather up the equipment.

"Do you think it'll help?" Ardis asked Ryes in a low voice after they left, as she returned to them, sitting down again.

"I don't know," she admitted with a shrug of her shoulders. "But, I don't think it'll hurt. We'll see."

"Just be very careful," Torr advised with a smile.

"I have to. I wouldn't want to upset Garth any more than I already have," she agreed, chuckling. "Right now, I'm ready for a nap, but what do you think? Should we veer more to the southwest now?" she asked, pointing to the large map unrolled upon the grass before them.

"Definitely, it looks like we've come too far north," Ardis said, looking closely at the map.

"Southwest looks good. After all, we wouldn't want to miss Hailys by going the wrong direction. How come we can see some of the taller buildings from Matlowe and not from here?" he asked. Ryes smiled at this.

"You can only see them from the mound outside the Village, and both Matlowe and Hailys are situated atop high plateaus. We're in the lowlands between, remember?" she teased, impishly. "You keep the maps with you, Ardis," she said, rolling them back up, except for the smaller one, which was still folded. She felt better now that they had their directions set within their minds. She then handed the compass to Torr. "And you hold onto this and tell us when we're straying. I don't trust myself, anymore," she admitted.

"What do you mean?" Ardis pressed, worried. She was far too tired, for just a little lost sleep. It was as if she went out on a battle every night!

"Something's pulling me north and I don't want to go that direction. That's why I need the two of you to make sure we don't end up where we have no business being. Hailys will be bad enough with that poisoned dust!"

"We'll make it," Torr promised her, clasping her shoulder in comfort as he smiled assurance.

"Thanks, I believe you," she agreed, stifling a yawn. "I'm going to lie down for a few minutes." She got up and headed to a nearby tree. "Tell Maren and Sabin to wake me, when they get back."

"Will do," Ardis assured her, giving her a nod. She was worried as Ryes was starting to lose weight now. She wondered if Garth noticed it?

"Believe in Sabin's vision," Torr breathed in warning to her, seeing the expression upon her face. "He's never been wrong yet. There's a much better home out here, and we only have to find it."

"I do believe. And he's never been wrong. I only hope we find it soon! So, going in the right direction will help out greatly," she replied with a heavy sigh.

"So, you think she can use her Talent to awaken my Talent?" Maren questioned Sabin, as he paced the bank with Honey, seeing the mare was finally calming from their wild ride. He found he rather enjoyed riding the windracer and hoped that Ryes would breed her when she was old enough, so he could have one of his own.

"Can you imagine it? She's got to have more than one Talent. I wish I could ask Rowan more questions, now! I wonder if he truly had any idea how many Talents Tyra had? Can you imagine what it would be like if Ryes' littermates had survived too?" Sabin returned, his eyes bright with his voiced musings. Maren laughed at this, as he finally let the mare have a good, long drink from the cold, rushing stream.

"There was Tian, who was named after Rowan's mother, as my sister named her own little daughter," he began, recalling Rowan telling him about them, long ago. "And Tair, who was named for Tyra's father; Rayan, who was named for our great uncle. And Ryes was named for one of Tyra's great aunts. If all four had lived, then I'm sure Korman would've never dared to make Ryes' life a living hell, and Garth would've had a hard time ever getting close to her, in the first place. Two brothers with a spirit like hers..." he teased, grinning, as he wondered what they would've turned out like, then. Sabin laughed out merrily as he nodded his head in agreement. "I don't recall Rowan saying how many Talents Tyra had, but I'm sure it was more than two. After seeing the way she was after that fawn the other morning, I'd say it sounds like the way Empath was supposed to be like."

"Empath!" he returned, realizing Maren had to be right. "Rowan did say Tyra taught them all quite a bit about hunting. If she had Empath, it'd be easy for her to learn the ways of the animals. So, it's Catalyst and Empath, but you don't have either on your side of the family. What if you're both Healers, too?" he suggested. Maren had begun to wash down the mare, using the watering bucket and twists of grass as a crude brush, but he paused as he suddenly looked to meet his friend's eyes.

"Like our grandmother?" he questioned, barely breathing. "But I thought men never inherited strong Talents? Aren't men's Talents usually weak?" he asked. Honey nudged him, enjoying his applying the wet brush to her hide. He mechanically started brushing her again, as Sabin came out into the water to join him. There was a seriousness in his eyes which surprised Maren.

"Don't let this out, as only Garth knows about it, but my own Talent is stronger than any woman in my family line. My grandmother was utterly shocked at the strength of my Talent and told me to never utter it, unless it was to someone I trusted implicitly. So, there's no reason for you to think that you can't inherit a strong Talent. In fact, I'm sure that's partly why the two of you are having such a problem with your awakening Talents. They HAVE to be strong ones," he assured him, meeting his eyes. Maren saw he meant it! "I know my own was a long, dangerous struggle, as no one else could truly help, even if my grandmother tried."

"Then what makes you think you can help us?" he returned, doubts and questions flowing through his mind. Could he truly have a strong Talent? Could he truly be a Healer as his grandmother once was? Was he ready for it, he wondered?

"I've been there," he assured him, laughing as he thumped his shoulder. "I'm heading back up. You finish with your golden-haired lady here, and join us when you're ready," he told him with a laugh. Maren looked surprised, and then started laughing merrily with him. Honey was honey-colored after all.

"Her eyes are still the wrong color and I'm very sure she only had two legs, not four," he quipped back, as he gave him a nod. "I'll be there, shortly." Sabin nodded, then turned and gathered the pots and waterskins, heading up the hill toward their camp. Maren stood for a moment, sighing to himself.

"Ah Honey, you're a very sweet lady, whom I am quite fond of, but you'll never be HER," he told the mare, as he finished her brushing. "Let's get you cleaned up properly for Ryes. Your real brushes are up in the camp." He then rinsed out the bucket and filled it with fresh water. Next he took her halter and led her uphill, too. He wished he could give a name to his blue-eyed princess. Was it worth the risk of losing her company at night, to awaken a Talent he was sure he was too old to possess? He still had his mind a whir as he returned to the camp. Seeing Ryes napping, he went to Honey's gear and got out a good brush and stated in on her coat, making this golden lady very happy.

Flood Waters

"All right, we're as ready as we'll ever be," Sabin stated, smiling encouragement to his two younger counterparts as they sat upon some rocks at the edge of their camp. Neither of them truly appeared eager, nor ready for this venture. Shadd and Ardis were plucking the feathers from the four large birds she and Garth snared, today. Garth and Torr sat near the trio, both wishing they could help more with this operation. There was a distinct lack of confidence in Maren's eyes, while Ryes just appeared exhausted, but willing.

"I wish I could help," Garth finally said, feeling exasperated. Somehow this didn't feel like the right time for the attempt to him, but Sabin was looking at this as a way to end their nightmares. With that he could well agree that it was worth the try, at least.

"Some of us are just born with Talent," Sabin teased, smiling. "At least you and Ryes should have cubs with Talent, since she has it." He smiled and gave him a nod, while Ryes just blushed, looking to Garth. Their eyes met for a moment speaking volumes between them, and then she turned and gave Sabin a nod of her head.

"I'm as ready as I'll be," she told him, extending her hands to them both.

"I'm merely tired of running from ol' green creeps, each and every night," Maren ceded, giving Sabin a nod, too. He reached over and offered his hands to them both.

"All right. Close your eyes and relax. Ryes open up your Talent and we'll see if we can link up in a commune within," he instructed, glad they were finally making the attempt. Sabin grasped both their offered hands, quickly closed his eyes and relaxed, easily calling up his Talent and opening himself up to Ryes. Only it was Maren he felt a connection with first, then Ryes joined them. This took him momentarily aback.

"What's wrong?" Ryes questioned, sensing Sabin's surprise. She realized she could feel Maren's flow of emotions and thought, as if he were as active in this commune, as Sabin. She wondered if he should be; if his Talent was still sleeping?

"No. His Talent must already be awake for Maren to be this clear. And one of you HAS to be a Booster, as this is the strongest

and most clear joining I've ever experience in my entire life," Sabin
asserted. He felt embarrassment from both the cousins, as if it were
a bad thing, while he celebrated it in his heart.

"Isn't Booster supposed to be rare?" Ryes pressed, speaking
up first. She could feel Maren's undercurrent of reluctance, clearly.

"Very, very rare. Has Darman ever mentioned anything about
Talents from elsewhere to you, before?" he asked. She felt his elation
at the thought of a Booster Talent being among them. This surprised
Ryes, but she returned with humor, as her heart lightened.

"Yes, he has, but not very often. He's always been very
careful about mentioning Talent around me. I just never figured out
why. There're a handful of the Caravaner Talents I grew up with
during the winters at least, who have Mind Voice, Dreamer and one
Healer among them. Mind Voice seems most common. I never heard
of any Boosters being among them," she answered. Maren was now
showing some real interest in their exchange.

"In Matlowe Village, it's been Visionary and Healer, with Mind
Voice being the occasional surprise. I wonder why Talents run that
way?" Maren questioned. Sabin's humor came through clearly.

"It's in what was passed down to us from our family lines," he
replied. "The caravaners, who have always been a part of Matlowe,
still have divergent family lines."

"Yes. Rowan and Darman are more worried about the
inbreeding which is happening in Matlowe, as the Village has
practically cut itself off from the rest of the world," Ryes interjected,
glad they were talking about this before beginning the deeper probing
within. It gave them all time to relax more.

"Inbreeding?" both men returned, surprised.

"Haven't you seen it? There's a basic `look' to those living in
Matlowe. That's why I stand out so much, as well as the caravaners,"
she pointed out, amused by their disbelief. "Everyone's related to
everyone else, to some degree. If we don't interject fresh bloodlines,
there won't be anyone left to inherit Matlowe Village. Why do you
think the population's declined so much through the years?
Inbreeding doesn't produce healthy children." This caught at them
both, as they'd never truly noted it before.

"It explains why a lot of infants have been lost," Maren
agreed, flashing onto some of the monstrosities he'd witnessed being
born through the years, as he helped his mother. It was a good thing
they were rarely born alive, or only lived no more than a few hours.

"Kittis clubfoot," Sabin added, having never seen this much grief before in his own life. He wondered how Maren survived it? The horrors he had tried to help nurture, even for just a short life gave great testimony to his loving heart. "She just died this last winter. How old was she?" he somehow managed to continue.

"Seven miserable years old," Maren answered. He cared for her many times himself, and missed the child. Of all the mis-born ones, she had lived the longest and was the one he hoped would've grown to adulthood. "I wished I could've saved her. She was a sweet little thing." Ryes recalled the child and how she usually hid from everyone, too. She hadn't known she died and it saddened her. It was strange being able to see all this from Maren, and share their sorrow over the loss of this one, short life.

"Ryes, let's see if you can find out anything about Maren with your Talent. If his Talent has already been active, you should be able to get some sense of what it is and help him focus it and open it up fully," Sabin suggested, wanting to turn them away from such helpless sorrow. It did them all no good, as Kittis was well past their help, now. "Maren, I want you to relax and let Kittis go. If you have Healer, you could have helped Kittis if she were still alive. Think on that," he urged, still feeling his reluctance.

While Sabin was distracting Maren, Ryes gently delved deeper within his being, as she had with Riss. Only Maren wasn't a young teen, easily distracted. He felt her intrusion and it panicked him. He blocked her, hoping to keep her from his dream princess. But as he did so, Ryes was swept up in an image of his blue-eyed woman, fully seeing her and feeling the tumult of his emotions involving her. It stopped her cold, not wanting to intrude any deeper, now. He had the right to keep her to himself, after all. She realized he needed to WANT her to delve further, since his Talent was already budding. That was about all she could get out of it. That it wasn't fully opened, but it wouldn't be much longer.

"Ryes, you have to do this to help Maren! What is the problem?" Sabin demanded, feeling they had come to a mutual halt.

"I can't, it's personal," she replied. She felt Sabin probing, trying to seek the heart of the matter himself, but she suddenly moved to block him out, as did Maren. There were a few moments of silent contesting among them, when suddenly Sabin dropped out. Ryes gave Maren a moment's touch of understanding, heart-to-heart, and then she too let go. Maren was relieved as he opened his eyes to see Sabin lying on the ground next to him, groaning as he had a hand to his head.

"Sabin, are you all right?" he questioned, as Garth and Torr were kneeling beside him, appearing distressed.

"You two!" he declared, and then moaned out in pain, again.

"A cool cloth," Ryes suggested to Torr. "We didn't mean to hurt you," she told Sabin, noting a small amused smile upon Garth's lips.

"What did you do to him?" Garth questioned, needing to understand.

"Nothing, truly," she replied, suddenly nervous and blushing.

"Nothing? You call this nothing?" Sabin quipped back. "My head feels like it's splitting open at the seams!" Ardis had a cool, damp cloth in hand as she joined them, scowling down at her mate.

"I'm not ready," Maren added, feeling a twinge of regret for their doing this to their friend. Sabin was only trying to help them, but he couldn't let him know any more about his dream lady. Somehow, he knew Ryes would keep it to herself!

"Serves you right. Maren's stubborn and Ryes is too tired for this," Ardis scolded as she took over his care. "Why don't you rest for a while and we'll see how you're feeling, later." Garth and Torr helped Sabin up and over to his sleeping area, with Ardis trailing with both anger and anxiety in her eyes.

"Ardis, gently rub his temples, and then massage his scalp," Ryes suggested, getting an idea from one of the caravaner couples. He was prone to headaches and claimed his wife's gentle hands were the only cure. She appeared interested and let Ryes demonstrate, once Sabin was settled in place. After a few moments, she took over, giving Sabin some gentle, loving care. He relaxed a bit after a while, finally dropping off to a light sleep.

"No more experiments with Talent for now," Garth ordered, glad to see his blood-brother resting. "We have no idea what we're truly doing, so we'll just take things easy and slow. We might as well see how Sabin's feeling in the morning, before we try to break camp."

"How are you and Maren feeling?" Shadd questioned Ryes.

"I'm fine," she quickly replied, smiling.

"So am I," Maren agreed, chuckling. "Guess together we're more than Sabin can handle."

"Great. Then you two can finish plucking the birds. My hands are tired, as I'm sure are Ardis'," Shadd prompted, grinning mischief.

"I think we can handle that one," Ryes agreed, glad it was over, as she turned for their cook fire. Maren gave her a nod and joined Ryes, leaving Garth and the rest near Sabin, discussing things in lowered voices, as if wrestling with the problem still.

"Thanks, cousin," Maren breathed, somewhat relieved it was over. Ryes smiled as she met his eyes as they settled down next to the bird carcasses.

"Hairless? No wonder the cold's too much for her! But I guess you can't help your dreams," she teased in return, keeping it low, too. It didn't bother her that the rest of their group might be discussing them, as she knew there was no way she'd cross Maren's will in this matter. It was his own self, after all.

"If she feels for me, as I do for her, I don't think it'll matter," he answered with a heavy sigh. "I only hope that she's real and not a spirit."

"I'll send a prayer to the Goddess Korenda on both your behalves," she offered, smiling. "Just in case it's not just a dream, after all."

"Thank you, I appreciate that," he replied, touched by her offer. The goddess usually only listened to women, since she governed hearths and fertility. He grinned, a mischievous glint in his eyes. "Let's see who gets their birds finished first," he challenged. She laughed as she realized his was further along than hers. But she nodded her willingness; glad he was here with them.

Garth glanced over, hearing her laugh, but saw they looked to be plucking their birds as fast as possible, as if racing each other! He sighed. They could make anything a game! At least they kept each other amused, most times. It was keeping them both out of trouble which still worried him.

The next morning, Sabin was feeling much better. The rest and hearty stew they made from the birds seemed to help him get over his headache. Ryes thought Ardis' attention helped, too. A thunderstorm began early in the morning, and even as the rain was furiously pouring out of the sky, they knew they couldn't stay where they were camped. The hill was too exposed and the open land around them offered no immediate shelter from the storm. They were in an area with rolling, exposed hills, but the lowlands between still held a very few trees. Since they decided to head in a southwest direction to get back on course, they had to cross the creek. And it looked as if there were more trees on the other side, and more of a chance to find some kind of shelter.

Maren led them, carefully guiding Honey across the stony, creek bed. The now swift flow of the water had him feeling nervous. But Honey remained calm in his hands and responded to his guidance, as Shadd gave her the occasional slap on her rump, to get her moving again when she did balk. Torr was staying beside Shadd, carrying both his and her backpacks. He didn't want her unnecessarily burdened in such swift-moving water. He recalled the stream had been slow and lazy ONLY yesterday afternoon!

"We're almost halfway across," Sabin told Ardis in reassurance, as she kept an eye upstream. She stubbornly refused to let him carry her pack. She wanted his strength available, in case of need! She could always ditch her pack, if needed.

"I'd feel better about this, if I could swim," she returned, trying to smile for him, afraid it was coming out more as a grimace. She was wet and cold and her face muscles didn't feel right.

"You're doing fine," he answered her, as he wrapped an arm around her shoulders, giving her a quick hug. This seemed to make her feel better, as her smile relaxed into something more genuine.

"Keep moving," Garth ordered. He and Ryes were bringing up the rear. She had stopped a moment to pull up some water plants to put into her gather bag.

"These are excellent in soups and stews," she informed him, as he rolled his eyes skyward and shook his head.

"You could wait until either the rain has stopped, or the stream's waters have subsided," he scolded, feeling uncomfortable with the rushing water around them. She stood back up and returned to his side.

"Opportunity," she told him. "We're heading away from this stream and who knows if the next one we come upon will have them, or not?" He agreed as they resumed their journey across. Maren, Honey and Shadd had finally reached the far bank and were helping Torr to scramble up. They looked relieved to have made it across. Ardis and Sabin were almost there, too. Suddenly, a loud rumble sounded and as Ryes froze trying to identify it; Garth quickly grabbed her hand, rushing her back the way they just came, since it was the closer bank.

"We're going the wrong..." she started as a wall of water came down the course from upstream and they were immediately awash in the wild torrent. Garth desperately hung onto her, as they were thrown downstream with the rush of water. Ryes was dashed into a low-lying tree limb, but managed to grab hold of it and hung on for dear life, digging her claws deep through the bark and into the wood, itself. Garth wrapped his arms around her, helping to anchor them with his claws too, as the water rushed over the both of them, threatening to drown them. He kept his head down, trying to shelter them both with his arms and shoulders. They were battered by the larger stones and debris carried by the wild water for what seemed an eternity. The both of them gasped as the wave finally broke, allowing them to breath, again.

They used the tree limb to regain the bank, once more, dragging themselves out of the water inch by slow and painful inch; thankful it was supple and strong enough to support them both. Ryes found it almost impossible to let go with her claws, even if it was to find a new purchase further up the limb, as her adrenalin was running high. It was a long struggle for them both – to let go and find a new place to grab onto while fighting the current which still threatened to sweep them downstream with its unrelenting hammering. At last they lay upon the ground, clear of the water, helplessly coughing and gasping for air. After a few minutes, Ryes sat up, looking to see if the others had survived.

"Where are they?" she asked, her voice rough from the deluge and coughing up the water, not recognizing their vicinity.

"We have to be much further downstream," Garth told her. His voice was barely a raspy whisper. In those few moments, he was sure they were carried quite a long distance. He visually checked them both for any broken limbs, then stood and offered her a hand up. She smiled as she took it, looking upstream on the opposite bank, seeing if she could spot them.

"Let me guess, no more water plants?" she teased, as she met his eyes. Garth smiled at this and gave her a nod of his head.

"Not again. Let's walk back up the creek. I'm sure they're all right," he comforted her. Ryes then took a quick inventory of herself to make sure she had everything with her. Her belt pouch was missing, but the necklace was still upon her neck and her beltknife was still secured to her belt. Her gather pouch was fine, but open and most of the water plants were now gone.

"Awww.... the plants are gone. Is my backpack all right?" she asked, as she started checking on Garth's. His was still closed and appeared fine, but she realized a large lump was a rock, jammed just under the flap. She pulled it out and hoped the rest remained intact inside. He stopped and gave himself a quick inventory, too. His pouches were still secured, as was his beltknife, but his spear was gone. He got her to turn around and checked her backpack and saw it was still tightly secured shut, but he pulled off some plants that were jammed up under the flap, as well as a small branch that was tangled in her braids.

"Yes. Is mine?" he requested, knowing it was very important, right now. They might be fully dependent upon what they carried upon their backs.

"Yes, it looks fine. We'll have to find a good spot to dry out and make sure," she suggested, "Once we can get out of this rain."

"Let's start walking. I want to see if everyone on the other side made it out all right, first," he replied. She nodded her head and fell into step beside him. Her body was battered and bruised and she knew he was probably worse. Still, as she pulled sticks and things out of her hair, she was very grateful they were both alive, breathing a prayer of thanks, once again.

"Ryes! Garth!" They heard a shout from the other side of the creek. It was Maren, and he was waving at them as he ran downstream. "Are you two all right?" he called over the rush of the water between them.

"We're fine. Did Sabin and Ardis make it to shore?" Garth called back, pulling sticks out of his pockets, as Ryes tugged more out of his braids for him.

"Yeah, they look like they're as soaked through as you two, but they're fine. How're you going to get across now?" he asked, waving his hands helplessly at the torrent.

"We'll have to find a higher, safer place to cross," Garth yelled back. "You go on and make camp on drier ground. We'll join you, as soon as we can," he suggested. "Right now we've got to make a campfire and see what's still with us, and what got washed away." He realized he'd have to make a new spear. He hoped his spare heads were still in his pack, but none of the trees around them were the right size or type.

"Let's go upstream and find some shelter against this rain. It looks like its picking up," Ryes suggested, knowing she was too cold and exhausted to attempt another crossing right now, even if they could hope to make it across.

"That's the idea. Let's get warm and dry first, and give the creek time to drop a little, so we can cross," Garth agreed. "But I think as long it the rain's coming down hard, it's not going to subside very quickly." He noticed the bodies of two large dead bounders in the flood waters, sweeping by them. He waved to Maren and pointed upstream as Torr appeared from around the upward bend. He looked relieved to see them and stopped to talk with Maren for a few minutes. Garth took Ryes' hand and the two of them walked upstream, looking for some shelter from the driving rains. The creek was now a deep, swift-moving brown cascade of debris, rocks and trees. Occasionally, they saw more bounders had been swept up in the waters and knew they'd been lucky.

"Thank Ricmon we're all safe! When the rain stops, I'll tell the others to go on to Hollys without us," Garth decided.

"Hailys," Ryes corrected him, smiling impishly, knowing he did it on purpose now to tease her. He grinned at this, seeing her smile again.

"Then we'll scout upstream, until we find a place to cross, or we can dig in and get comfortable, until the water level drops. What do you think?" he asked, as he pulled a piece of weed out of her hair. She bobbed her head in agreement, playfully swatting at his hand. He caught hers up in his, grinning. "We were extremely lucky to escape with only a few scratches and bruises."

"That's true," Ryes agreed with a sigh. "We were favored by Aletagga. So, that'll leave just the two of us, for a while," she teased. He gave her hand a gentle squeeze and a knowing wink.

"That doesn't sound too bad to me," he returned.

"Me neither," she agreed, smiling. "Yes, a little quiet time together sounds very nice, after all." She'd never envisioned her journey to the ruins to end up with problems and opportunities like this, when she was young! "We were going to break off from the others soon, anyway," she stated. He laughed as they turned once again, looking for a path they could use to get through the rough terrain and brush.

After over three hours of picking their way along the rocky edge of the creek, they turned inward a bit and found a small copse of trees which afforded them some shelter from the driving rain. Garth helped Ryes put up an overhead tarp and then left her to finish setting up as he went back to the creek to see if Maren was still there. He was waiting for him. He had a half dozen bounders he had pulled from the floor waters sitting on the rock while he was skinning them. Garth smiled, liking that idea. Why let the meat go to waste?

"Did you find a good place to camp?" he shouted across the still raging torrent.

"Yes, we did! Did all of you find a good place to camp over there?" He stooped down and grasped the back of the neck of a bounder floating past. This one still had some kick left, so Garth tossed it up on the bank. If it lived, it would be fine. If not, it would become part of his dinner.

"Yeah, I've let quite a few go, myself," Maren shouted. "We found a great spot but are glad we had filled up our waterskins earlier as this does not look like drinkable water. We're filling the pots with some fresh rainwater right now. We're just getting dried off now."

"I'm going to need to make a new spear," Garth admitted. He snagged another pair of bounders. One dead, one scrambled up and ran off after a few minutes. He pulled out his beltknife and started in on the dead one. "We were going to split off soon, anyway, so go ahead and head to Hailys. We'll catch up soon enough," he ordered. Maren nodded, then scooped up his bounder carcasses, wrapping them in cloth he had with him.

"Then you two take good care of each other. We'll see you both soon!" he replied, grinning. "Get busy on those cubs!" Garth outright laughed and nodded.

"We will," he promised. Maren disappeared off through the trees, headed towards their camp. Garth started looking for more bounders as he began skinning the one he had already. They'd make a great dinner tonight.

"Come on, Maren, get up. You look like you're too comfortable for sleeping on a bed of leaves," Ardis protested, sounding disgusted, as she gave him a nudge to get him going. It was getting harder and harder to get him awake in the mornings. He finally stirred and opened his eyes.

"Good morning," he said sleepily, as he began to lazily stretch.

"Are you sure those nightmares are gone?" she questioned, scratching her head as she looked down at him.

"Oh yeah, they're gone," he assured her. "I don't know what Ryes did, other than give Sabin a nasty headache, but it sure helped me," he bragged, as he sat up.

"Yeah, you're sleeping out here in the wilderness, as if you're home in your own bed," she agreed. "Come on, breakfast is almost ready." She then turned and walked off. He smiled as she left. Yes the nightmares had stopped, but his beautiful, blue-eyed lady remained with him every night now. He sighed as he wished she were real and with him on this venture. He bet she'd love to see Hailys, too! The one new thing he gained from Ryes in their brief attempt to find his Talent was a look of the city before it was destroyed and its fiercely, fiery destruction. The attack had come from above and caught everyone by surprise, just as the legends said... It's a wonder ANYONE managed to escape it! And he was fairly sure she had no idea he'd seen it.

"No sign of them," Sabin stated, as he returned to camp. "And the creek's still way too swift and deep."

"You went all the way back to the creek?" Torr demanded, astonished. "What time did you get up this morning?"

"It was still dark when I left. I don't know. I haven't had any Visions, but still have a feeling that they're in danger. You don't think Old Korman's tracking them, do you? They're not camped at the creek bank."

"With that rain which fell for days? I'm sure they're fine. After all, didn't you see us all together in our new home?" Ardis pressed, meeting his eyes. Now he was going without sleep on this watch for Garth and Ryes! This truly got her irritated! "So, are you always right, or not?"

"So far, I've been right, and the waters are flooding the banks, so I'd move my camp inward away from that, too," he replied with a heavy sigh. "Garth wanted us to keep going and set up a campsite near the ruins, so we'd better go do that," he finally surrendered.

"That's the spirit," Torr told him, lightly cuffing his shoulder. "They'll be along, as soon as the waters settle down. They're both too good at woodcraft to be caught unawares and from what Ardis and I can discern from the map, there's no dangerous animals, or peoples in that area. They'll join us in a few days' time. I guarantee it." His confidence was strong and Sabin finally smiled as he realized he was right. They were both too good in the woods, to truly come to grief. And he was sure his own Talent would warn him, otherwise. They must be out hunting to replenish any food they lost from their packs.

"All right. As soon as we get packed up after breakfast, we'll head for the destroyed city and see what it's really like!"

"About time," Maren agreed, as he joined them. "Honey's getting restless, here. Even she thinks we ought to be going." The day was young and there was a lot they could be doing, he thought.

Shadd chuckled at this as she handed out the mugs of hot tea. Their fish looked like they would soon be ready.

"For all the work of keeping you men fed, I still will never regret leaving Matlowe," she voiced aloud. "I'm truly looking forward to a new place to settle into and get comfortable, soon. Do you think it could it be near Hailys," she wondered?

"Maybe?" Sabin answered with a shrug. "I'll know it when I see it."

"It won't be too much longer before our own first seasons come and we both want a home, before we give birth to our children," Ardis stated. Sabin set aside his metal mug of tea and stood up.

"I promise that we will all be there and very happy in our new home. All of us were in that Vision and laughing and very happy. And this one came with a very strong feeling that just said, HOME. I've never had that before. It was very crystal clear and strong. This one I believe in more than any other I've had in my whole life," he assured the others. "I don't know where it is, but we will get there."

"I believe you," Maren stated with a nod.

"So do I," Ardis agreed, smiling. She jumped up and gave him a hug.

"Me, too," Torr and Shadd echoed, happy grins on their faces as hope warmed their hearts.

"Something's pulling at me and I can't fight it anymore," Ryes complained, clinging to Garth's arm for support. "Sorry, I'm so tired. I can't seem to get any sleep at night." She wiped the back of her hand across her eyes, straining to see what lay about them. Her exhaustion was plain in her voice and evident in the way she kept losing track of where they were and where she was putting her feet. Her mind wandered, as if she were walking and dreaming, both at once. In all the years he'd tried to follow her through the woods, he'd never seen her behave this way. And she was losing weight. It was like she was thinning out, becoming a ghost of her true self. It panicked him deeply, but he refused to surrender himself, or her, to any fears.

Garth looked for a place to shelter them for the coming night. The terrain had changed from the familiar forested hills to rolling plains and now those plains opened up to deep gullies and small valleys, which appeared suddenly. They'd been traveling northward for the last three days, as the rain continued and the creek level was still too high to cross safely. With her acting this way, he didn't want to risk a crossing, unless it was an absolute necessity. And with the stream overflowing its banks, it was safer for them to move inland. At least the rains stopped late this afternoon, so they could see the lands about them. Ryes was struggling against whatever was haunting her. Garth wrapped an arm around her, pulling her close to his side, as he led her down a nearby gully, hoping to find some clean water at least. The stream had been nothing more than a brown flow, but they had gotten some fresh water from the rainfall. Still it didn't hurt to have a nearby source of good, clear water.

As they descended, her eyes again took on a dreamy faraway look. She was talking, as if trying to get someone's attention. Garth frowned, but kept his arm about her, leading her deeper into the barren gully. They turned a bend and he found it opened up into a deep, wide valley. The valley was lush green with a small, clear stream flowing back through it. He stood in wonder of the beauty before him, when Ryes suddenly twisted away from his support, utterly shocking him with her strength and energy of movement.

"Not here, Garth! We're in HER valley!" She'd suddenly come back to the present. She stood trembling with a chill, as a look of panic shadowed her darkened eyes.

"There's nothing here to hurt us," he assured her, taking her into his arms to comfort and calm her. He realized she was cold and shivering again! "We'll head back to Matlowe in the morning," he told her, feeling they should return home. Ryes nodded her head resignedly, allowing herself to be led under a flowering tree. She didn't have the strength to fight anyone, anymore. "Rest here while I build a fire." Garth helped her off with her pack and dropped his own beside hers, at the base of a sheltering tree.

She nodded once more, sat down and wrapped her arms about her legs, trying to tell herself that this was only a dream she was having... that they weren't truly in this nightmare place. They had to be camped beside the creek and she'd merely dropped off again. Would this nightmare never end?

Garth gathered all the kindling he could carry, hurrying back to Ryes, his mind deeply troubled over her behavior. She still sat exactly where he left her. He knelt and started the campfire. But as the tiny flames took, Ryes reached out to grasp his wrist. Startled, Garth looked at her puzzled by her action, but she wasn't looking at him. Her gaze was locked onto something she saw over his shoulder. He turned and saw a ghostly image, dressed in a flowing gown, heading toward them out of the gully they recently quit.

"Do you see her?" Ryes asked doubtfully, as she shifted over suddenly and hugged her body against his. Garth nodded his head in wonder, not believing his eyes. "It's the spirit of my mother, I think. I hope she can help free us from this trap."

The ghostly figure stepped up to them and Garth felt an intense chill travel up his spine. The hair on his neck stood on end. How could the ghost of Tyra be here? She appeared as if she must have looked in life, except for being dressed in a beautiful, flowing gown, which he had only heard of being for the rich families in the largest towns upon Tayna. Her features were distinct and Ryes clearly showed her relation in the echo of her own face.

"Ryes, you have come at `Her' summons, against all the warnings I gave you. The danger is neigh upon you." She addressed Ryes directly. Her voice was soft but steady and seemed a projection of her being, rather than just speaking words aloud, even if her lips moved as if she still had a voice.

"A clue. Could you give us a clue, so we can escape?" Ryes requested, in an unsteady voice in response.

"Two clues I will give you. The first one you bring with you, yourself." She indicated Garth. "The second one is a name. Doran of House Forental, of Kahmarr. She begins to stir; your presence is awakening her. Remember this; I escaped her once, myself. It is not beyond you, my daughter, especially since you have the power I have always lacked." The image faded into a blue mist, leaving Garth and Ryes clinging to each other, both feeling very young in this moment.

Finally, Ryes took a deep breath and let it go slowly. She tried to smile up at Garth, but her inner quaking kept her from feeling at ease.

"It's about lunch now. I think we'd better get something to eat," she suggested in a quivering, low voice, not wanting to let go of him just yet.

"Right," Garth agreed, a forced smile upon his face. He let go of her reluctantly and reached for their packs. The chill was slowly leaving his limbs. "I truly saw her?" he questioned, looking back to Ryes, feeling the world was less a known and comfortable place, as it'd been a short while earlier. Was this what she'd been wrestling with the last couple of weeks of their journey? No wonder she hardly knew where she was, much less what was happening! He wondered how Maren now fared? Was he free of his torture, or still having those night visions, too?

"Yes, you did," Ryes agreed, then hastily added, "but don't name her here. I think it'd only bring trouble down on us faster, since she escaped from here before," she warned, wondering where that notion came from, but still feeling its truth. Garth nodded as he looked about the lush, green valley. He didn't see or feel any threat around them. But if Ryes thought there was one, he wouldn't doubt her. The sun was still high in the sky, but the shadows around them were deepening. Coldness still chilled his heart and he shuddered as he handed Ryes a food packet.

"Let's eat, and then see if we can't just walk back out?" he suggested. She appeared surprised, then smiled as she nodded her head in agreement, liking the idea.

"Sounds far better than trying to stay the night here. Maybe it's not the trap my night visions have made of this place?" she ventured.

"Maybe," he agreed. "We'll soon see for ourselves."

Trap

"It's no use, I can't push through it," Garth told Ryes panting as he finally quit and turned to look at her. There was a determination in her eyes as she stood still panting, as she thought about their problem. They were in the gully, just a turn away from the lush valley, yet they were unable to go another step further due to an invisible barrier which blocked them in fully. They had both tried pushing it, throwing rocks at it and even digging under it - all to no avail. And it refused to show any signs that their efforts had damaged it, or had any effect upon it at all!

"Give me a boost," she requested, stepping over to one of the gully walls next to it. Maybe they could merely climb out here, instead? Garth smiled, hope in his eyes as he readily complied. He meshed his fingers together and held his arms stiffly out before him as he stepped up before her. She smiled and gave him a quick kiss, then put her foot into his hands and felt herself quickly lifted upwards. She dug her fingers into the dry, hardened soil and determinedly pulled herself upwards. She gained the top of the bank, only to feel the invisible wall standing there, too. She snarled out her helpless anger at this unseen menace as she struck it uselessly with her fist.

"It's there, too," Garth commented, having never seen her anger before. "Might as well come back down," he suggested, feeling fully helpless in this situation.

"My mother said she escaped! How did she get past this thing?" she demanded, pounding a fist against it again, furious at this forced captivity. She pulled herself sideways until she found the original wall, hoping she was above it here, at least. Alas, it still blocked her at this point, too.

"This is impossible! She had to have used Talent to escape," he told her. Ryes finally sighed, letting her shoulders drop. She climbed back down, tears upon her face as she reached the ground again.

"How can we get out of here? My Talents are only awakening! I don't even know what I have, or how to use them," she complained, feeling despair and exhaustion blanketing her mind and heart. Garth wrapped his arms about her, holding her close as he comforted her. He understood how she felt, feeling so helpless himself. How could this be? What was this wall they could only feel?

"We'll find a way. Your mother gave us two clues, but I've no idea how I can be a part of the answer, if I can't get us past this wall, either," he replied, as he leaned back against the unseen wall. It supported them well, at least, even if it looked odd to lean on empty air.

"Maybe you're supposed to be my inspiration?" she finally returned, smiling a little. "I'm sorry. I would've warned you not to come this way if I could've remained focused enough, earlier."

"I know. I should've stopped and just let you sleep where we were. I have no idea why I thought this gully looked more sheltering than any of the others I passed up. This is my fault, far more than yours," he assured her. She looked up to meet his eyes, shaking her head no.

"I think we both were merely snared into this trap. Ol' green creeps, as Maren calls her, took full advantage of us both. It wasn't your fault. Now I only hope we'll find a way out of this soon. How about if we scout out near where we camp, to make sure it's as safe as can be? Tomorrow morning may bring us some new ideas," she urged, hoping she was right.

"Maybe we should camp right here, in case this wall disappears with the sunrise?" he countered, but then saw a chill go up Ryes' back.

"No, it would only leave us no options to run. Who knows what she has here with her? I'd rather some room to fight," she countered. He laughed at this, nodding his head in agreement, liking her logic, as he smiled.

"Ever so wise, my lady," he replied, then bent and kissed her. "Yes, let's get a look at this valley before the sun sets," he added, after several long moments of kissing. She sighed and nodded her head.

"And we might still have a little time for some fun, after all," she replied, grinning. He let her go as he gave her a wink.

"Whatever you think best, my Sweet One," he answered. He hoped they'd find the key, because something about the valley gave him a deep, inner chill now. So different from the welcoming warmth he felt earlier when he turned the corner and saw the lush valley before him, then. Setting up a camp might be enough of a distraction to keep it from his mind for a few moments, at least.

"I just verified it. No one's seen him in DAYS!" Kovin told the small gathering of hunters, as he approached the group. He wasn't exactly their leader, but since Garth was gone, the remaining group looked to both him and Gann for direction. And Gann appeared grim as he considered the implication of this news.

"We've GOT to warn them!" Mitt declared, jumping to her feet.

"Sit down," Gann ordered her, slapping the space on the felled log beside him, the one she just quit. "Maybe, if we got one of Maren's siblings to tell us how long? Just so we can know it for sure," he suggested, as Mitt reluctantly returned to her seat.

"That's a good idea," Leand agreed, "and since they're my half-siblings, I should go talk with one of them." Teris grinned at this, nodding his head in agreement.

"I can go speak with Tars, she doesn't mind me," Mellas volunteered. "And she knows I'm her half-brother, too."

"I was going to ask Tennan," Leand countered, "at least she's old enough to understand the implications of what lies behind what I'm asking."

"As if SHE'D CARE," Mitt scoffed, scowling. "The only thing important to Tennan is that little cub of hers! I would hope Korman's not the father, but who knows with THAT family! Tars sounds like the better option. At least she's young enough to tell us the truth, outright."

"Mitt!" Gann scolded, disgusted with her attitude this morning. "We're soon to be related to that family," he reminded her. She sighed and blushed as she recalled Ryes was a cousin to Maren's siblings and any of her and Garth's children would be so, too. "Go ahead Mellas, go ask Tars if she can come out here and speak with all of us?"

Mellas gave him a nod of his head, then gave Mitt a quick wink, stood and trotted off toward the Village proper. He had to admit to himself that he was very impressed with the new home Kovin and Teris moved into. It actually belonged to Ardis and Shadd, but they were doing some minor repairs and keeping it up, until the ladies' return. Out by the Yuri was so different. He wondered if he could talk his mother into taking one of the houses here, too? They were much larger and far better equipped homes.

"I'm sure Korman's not the father of Tennan's cubs," Leand said, speaking into the peaceful silence which followed Mellas' leaving. Each of the hunters were delving into their own thoughts. "I recall hearing Tanns assuring my mother of that a few months back, before

Tian was born. And I'm sure she wouldn't lie about something as important as that."

"That's true," Teris quickly interjected. "I'm sure he has that much sense, at least."

"His daughters trust him," Sana added. She'd come out to hear the news, since her littermate was out with Garth's group. Kaytas blushed as she met Sana's eyes.

"It's true, he's never treated us the way he treats the other women in Matlowe," she admitted with a sigh. "I only wish he would stop. I can't believe that he challenged Garth!"

"No, he didn't. Garth challenged him over Ryes," Mitt corrected her, surprising many in the group around them. "I was there to see it all."

"They're not running from Korman, only seeking a place to stay until Sabin can safely return," Gann added, meeting doubtful and surprised eyes around the morning fire.

"Where did they go, then?" Leand asked, wondering.

"Why so many?" Kaytas added, needing to understand.

"Garth HAD to go with Sabin," Gann started, still recalling what his brother told him the night before they left. "Ryes went because she could read the maps and knew how to use a compass, and I suspect needed to stay close to Garth since she should come into her first later this spring."

"Then the others?" Teris questioned, knowing Kovin truly wanted to understand.

"Torr went to watch Garth's back. Maren went to help watch out for Ryes, since he's decided they're cousins after all," he explained. This was met by merry laughter all around the fire. His stubborn refusal to have any associations with Ryes through the years was well known to them all. It was amusing to see such an abrupt about face from him like this. Gann smiled to himself as he gave them a nod of his head. "Guess he won't call her a farga's daughter, anymore." This got nods and more laughs.

"And since Torr went, so did Shadd, and Ardis went to spend some time with Sabin and to keep Shadd company," Mitt finished up for them, having heard everything Garth related to Gann that night, too.

"I'm still not happy with her taking an interest in Sabin," Sana commented, biting her lower lip. "She's chased after Garth for years and has suddenly decided Sabin's all right? I think she's just playing a game to see if Garth will turn away from Ryes and accept her for mating!"

"I don't think so," Mitt interjected. "I saw the way they were acting together, before they left. She wasn't even glancing at Garth. It was as if she'd forgotten he existed!"

"How long are they going to be gone? How long is that banishment supposed to be in effect?" Kovin questioned, still wanting a try at Ardis. Gann and Mitt quietly exchanged glances, both appearing uncomfortable.

"You know something! Come on, tell us," Sana demanded, unhappy with the way Garth's siblings kept too many things to themselves. "I deserve to know! Sabin's my brother!"

"Sabin had a Vision the night before they left," Gann sighed out, still hoping this one would be wrong. He saw the eager expressions upon the faces gathered around him and knew he HAD to tell them now. "He saw them finding a new home and that they wouldn't be coming back to Matlowe. He and Ryes both saw it."

"Ryes saw one of Sabin's Visions?" Mason questioned, shocked. "The farga's daughter has TALENT?"

"Yes, she does. Remember at the Village meeting? She used her Catalyst Talent to activate MY TALENT!" Riss declared, still very pleased with himself. "I'm going to do my best to help people with my Visions, since Sabin had to go away."

"Sabin had to help, since she had no idea what she was doing," Sana threw in, disgusted with her younger cousin. He was such a pain, at times!

"I forgot about that. Then she has more than one Talent?" Kaytas asked.

"It seems so," Mitt replied, seeing Gann refused to say anything more on the matter. "So that would mean if Garth and she do mate, they'll have cubs with Talent, too." This small statement got the other men stirring. She forgot the status men seemed to take on with fathering Talented cubs. Now she was glad Garth was far away, as she was sure the whole lot would try to wear him down with challenge after challenge for the chance to mate Ryes. Now she knew why Gann had remained silent!

"I'm glad Garth's finally getting a chance to be alone with Ryes. He's been after her - just to become friends - for too many years. I think he's been in love with her, since they were just cubs. He used to help Maren take care of her, when she was very sick and she didn't know he'd even been there," Gann spoke out into the silence, reminding them that this was a deeper matter, not just one of opportunity. "And Garth's been here to help all of us for years. So, our main concern is Korman and where he is right now." He met everyone's eyes and got nods of agreement out of them - especially the men. As he finished this, Mellas appeared with all three of Maren's younger siblings.

"I ended up volunteering as protector, today," he announced to the gathering. This was met with merry laughter all around. He took his seat, putting little Rowis up on his lap. She snuggled in against his chest, smiling at the others. Karis sat down next to him, while Tars picked up his spear, pretending she was a real huntress, too.

"Are you going out hunting with us tomorrow morning, Tars?" Sana teased, grinning as she could well imagine her little daughter doing the same when she hit this age, too. She recalled always holding her older cousins' spears, when she was little.

"Can I go?" she returned breathlessly, her eyes alight. "Maren never let me go!"

"We'd have to ask your mother," Leand replied, chuckling at her youthful eagerness. "But I have to warn you little sister, it's a LOT of work to be the one to provide food for your family."

"I know, but I can do it!" she declared. This was followed by more laughter. She carefully put down Mellas' spear and threw herself into Leand's arms. "Can I go, please big brother?" She knew they were two of her older half-brothers. Her father had told her so. He laughed as he shook his head.

"It will depend upon what Tanns says about it. Maybe Maren never took you because she wouldn't let him?" he replied, making sure she knew it wasn't their decision alone.

"If she's going, you're keeping an eye upon her," Kovin told him, grinning in reminder. Cubs out on the hunt could be a handful, but since they had to train their younger siblings and cousins, they tolerated their presence from time-to-time. "And what about you, Karis? Are you going to be a hunter like your older brothers?" The child appeared surprised to be asked this, but shook his head no.

"I want to be a Healer when I grow up, like my grandmother Jana was," he replied.

"You have to have the Talent for it, first," Tavis replied, as she smiled at his solemn attitude. He already had everything planned out! "But, truth be told, your mother does very well for not having the Talent."

"Tars, we need to ask you something," Gann butted in, not wanting to get the children too stirred up over Talent, right now. She turned, meeting his eyes as she nodded her head in answer.

"Mellas said you had some questions," she stated, as she still clung to Leand.

"Yes, a good huntress would always be truthful to her team," he told her, smiling now. "I need to know where your father went?"

"He was going to the ruins. He and mother were fighting about it before he left. Will Maren be all right? He was going to help protect Ryes, but father was so very angry with him," she told him.

"When did he leave?" Gann pressed, not sure how to answer her questions.

"Nine days ago. I saw him leave late into the night. I'm so afraid for Maren," she replied, her eyes fearful. He sighed, unwilling to leave her with such fear.

"Garth and the others love Maren and would never let your father hurt him, no matter what," Mitt assured the child, smiling.

"Your father doesn't want to hurt Maren as much as challenge Garth," Gann added, "I'm sure Maren will be just fine and will come home to you, as soon as he can."

"Father wants to kill Ryes `cause she laughed at him. He doesn't let anyone laugh at him! Ev'n me," Rowis told them, in all seriousness. Tars and Karis both nodded their heads in agreement.

"Do you think Maren laughed at him, too?" Tars asked with fear behind her eyes.

"He's never laughed at your father, that I've ever seen," Sana assured her, smiling as she wondered at the trepidation she saw in the children. What kind of nightmare home did they live in?

Rowan stepped out of his house, having been listening in on the hunters from one of his open, side windows. Tennan was washing her clothes in the kitchen, so had no idea her siblings were out here being questioned. He saw he had their attention as he stepped over to join the group.

"Grandfather!" Rowis shouted out as she jumped off of Mellas' lap to run up to Rowan with her arms open. He chuckled as he picked her up and kissed her.

"You think there may be trouble? If he's gone to the ruins, there will be. Garth and the others were heading that way, I think in hopes of finding out how the ancients ran their machines. But, Sabin did have a Vision about it, too," he told them. Gann stood up, giving him a small bow in respect.

"Garth told me that Sabin saw him winning a challenge with Korman," he replied. "It's supposed to be in a forest clearing. We only thought it would be here, near Matlowe."

"Father's going to lose?" Tars demanded, not believing it. She stood up, too.

"I'm afraid so cubling," Rowan answered her. "It has to happen sometime. He's getting old, but refuses to acknowledge it."

"Sabin had a Vision about it, too? That makes two for that one day!" Sana declared, amazed. "He's never had them happen like that, before."

"And he's never been wrong, yet," Teris added, smiling to realize that Korman would finally be defeated. It was very welcome news, at that! "Can I go to warn them, he's after them?" he turned to ask Gann, as he jumped to his feet.

"Me, too! I don't want you going out alone," Kovin added, as he stood up. Suddenly, Gann had everyone around him wanting to be included in the party - even young Tars. He laughed as he shook his head, wanting to venture out too, but knowing Garth had made him promise to stay and take care of their family in his stead. That meant managing the remaining hunters, too.

"Let me think on this. A party of two should be enough to get a warning through, but I would wonder if you'd get there in time?" he told everyone, as he gestured for them all to sit again. He turned to face Kovin. "If you leave, then who'll take care of Ardis and Shadd's home?" he questioned. He appeared surprised by this question, as he realized Gann did have a point.

"I will," Minn supplied, giving him and Teris a nod of his head. "It's kind of nice out here," he added.

"This has always been the best part of Matlowe," Rowan assured him, as he sat down with the hunters, feeling their welcome. "And one of the reasons I've never felt compelled to move back in to the Village, proper."

"Isn't this where the caravaners stay?" Tavis questioned, frowning as she looked to the many, well kept-up homes about them.

"There, you can see their marks above most the doors," Kaytas pointed out for her friend. Tavis nodded her head as she saw them now.

"Yes, but they don't use all of them. Anyone's welcome to come out and live here. Most the houses only need a few repairs to be livable, once more," Rowan assured her, smiling. "What was this second Vision of Sabin's?" he suddenly pressed, as he better situated Rowis upon his lap.

"That they would find a new home and would never want to return to Matlowe Village," Gann replied, seeing he'd been left out of it. Apparently, Ryes hadn't wanted to worry her grandfather. "Except to fetch back their families, who'd want to live with them in their new place." Rowan nodded his head at this, understanding it all now.

"And he's never been wrong," he sighed out in answer.

"Not yet," Sana assured him, smiling.

"I'll let everyone know my final decision after dinner, tonight," Gann informed them. "Two can travel far more swiftly than seven, so they might have a chance of catching up to them and letting them know that Korman's after them."

"That sounds like a good plan," Rowan agreed, smiling.

"I want to go," Mitt urged, knowing she couldn't live with her sister any longer. The idea of a new home sounded like heaven to her.

"Not you. You're enough of a handful, as is. This is too important for all of us," her brother told her, knowing she'd prove to be another headache over the next several days, until she let loose of the notion.

"So, what are we hunting tomorrow?" Tars pressed, hoping that her mother would allow her to go. She knew her father could be very mean, when he wanted to be, so knew it was best they warn their friends and her brother. She only worried about Maren, wanting him to be safe. The hunters laughed at her determination.

"We're going out to snare some fat, tasty birds," Gann replied with a chuckle. "We're leaving early in the morning, so you have to get permission and get up before the dawn."

"I will!" she assured him. "Can I go hunting birds, Grandfather?" she asked, realizing he could grant her his permission, too. He laughed at this, shaking his head.

"You'd better ask your mother, first," he urged, not wanting to get into the middle of that situation.

"I'll go ask now," she suddenly decided, then jumped to her feet and ran off. Merry laughter followed her light steps, up the path.

"I'll look after her, Rowan," Leand assured him, "if she can come out with us."

"Thank you. I don't know if I could toss a spear properly, anymore. It's been a lot of years," he replied. There was more laughter as the young hunters recalled he'd once been one, himself.

"Could you tell us again, how best to approach the birds, so we don't scare them all into flying off?" Teris quickly asked, "I'm not quite sure if I can recall everything Ryes showed us before." Rowan sagely nodded at this; while thanks and small bows were granted him in appreciation from all around the circle as they saw he was willing to teach them. He chuckled as it made him happy being drawn back into a more active role in Matlowe Village, once again.

"Now it depends upon the kinds of birds you're hunting as to how you hunt them," he started, dropping into his storytelling voice. He had their rapt attention.

Later, as Ryes slept in Garth's arms, she felt a dangerous presence creeping closer. She awoke shuddering with an icy chill running through her body and sat up - fully alert. Looking around, she could make out little in the darkness beyond their fire. Garth hadn't stirred, so she shook him, trying to wake him. He didn't budge, nor groan, nor make any voiced protests. He was very deeply asleep and his body was fully limp and unresponsive.

Asleep? Ryes questioned herself. Or under a spell of some kind? She never believed the traveling wizards, who came through the Village from time-to-time, following the caravaners. Most of their so called "spells" were fake and easily seen through. She saw truth where most others saw illusion. Darman used to try out his newest tricks out on her, to see if she could unravel his riddles. She never failed and sometimes told him how to make his tricks better. But this valley was a place of power; it shimmered in the air about them. And

Garth was in a sleep, deeper than sleep. How would she unravel this riddle? It wasn't a game as she feared for his very life!

As Ryes sat thinking, a presence approached. She finally made it out, across the light of their dying fire. A viper rose up, as if poised to strike. It was huge. Its head and body were as big around as one of Garth's forearms; it's length un-guessable in the flickering firelight. She froze in panic. Garth's spear lay on the other side of his still body, beyond her easy reach. And her beltknife was no weapon to use against a serpent of such size. Then almost instinctively, she reached out to it from within. If she could feel a fawn's death, then maybe this was the way? To be able to stretch out and touch the mind of another creature... as if she were reaching out to Sabin or Maren.

In the shock of first contact she saw HE had a cold, narrow mind, but there were vast depths to his limited thinking. He was old. Perhaps centuries old. But, he was a prisoner of this valley, too. He'd been sent here tonight to take Garth's warmth and life with his fangs. He bobbed and swayed, eager to dispatch his duty; one he was well accustomed to performing.

"He's my mate and you can't have him," Ryes sent firmly, as her fingers closed around the hilt of her beltknife in reaction. She forced herself to relax her hand, knowing that using her Talent might be the only way to deter this creature.

"Mate?" Was the hazy reply, "Mate?" He seemed disturbed by the word. He looked from her to Garth and back. "You and that... mate?" he asked, full of doubt.

"Yes. We are male and female of our people," she responded. The serpent lowered himself to the ground and slid with surprising speed around the fire, coming next to Ryes. She shivered in reaction, but kept a tight rein upon her fear. To lose whatever slender control she had now, could spell the end for both of them! Thinking of Garth gave her the courage to face off this viper.

"Once I had mate," he thought to her, as he flicked his tongue against her leg, tasting her warmth and life. How very tempting it was to take her warmth for himself. "Now I do Other's wish." Ryes, feeling sympathy in spite of her known danger, slowly reached out her hand and gently stroked his head. She felt the tension leave him, but suddenly knew of his deeper yearning for a mate of his own. It was an instinct the one who controlled him was unaware of, she was sure.

"Can't you leave and find a new mate?" she curiously questioned, wondering if he could get through that invisible barrier, which held them prisoners?

"No way out. All trails go to cold stone place," he replied, distress in his mental tones. Shaysa's light had begun to fill the valley and Ryes looked behind her to the gully, which let them into the valley. Maybe it was only one way?

"There's a way out," she said, indicating the gully. "Can't you see it?"

"No." There was firmness in his reply. He doubted her, now, as all he determined was another part of the wall which enclosed this place.

"Then let me take you there and you'll see," she pressed, seeing that he couldn't even SEE the opening! The tongue flickered again as he considered her offer.

"Yes, I want see out way." Ryes shifted to her knees and lifted the heavy serpent carefully, draping him across her shoulders, barely keeping from staggering under his weight. She kept his head well away from Garth's still form - just in case. Then she cautiously rose and walked toward the gully. As she went up it, stepping around the bend, the serpent shifted his weight in apparent excitement. She suddenly realized she couldn't take another step further, as the invisible wall still kept her from passing through! She hoped he could pass through it!

"Yes! Yes! Free... find mate!" Ryes knelt and the excited viper slipped off her and down to the ground. Swiftly, he slid up the gully to his freedom. Faintly, she could feel the singing in his heart. She let go of the contact, tired, but glad she'd been of some service. At least Garth was a little safer with the snake gone. She tried to push forward again, but the wall was still solid! Frustrated, she turned for the camp, glad she'd been able to use her newly awakened Talent, after all. As she was returning, Ryes saw a flickering blue light over Garth. She ran the rest of the way, beltknife in hand, knowing it was useless. The viper had been some kind of decoy, after all?

"It is all right. I am only watching over him, for you," Tyra spoke calmly as Ryes ran up to her. "It was a good thing to do for that old serpent, but you left your husband unprotected. There are other things lurking about near here," she scolded.

"Is there a way I can free him?" she asked, looking at Garth. It broke her heart to see him so unresponsive. "Because of me, he's ended up this way. How can I save him?"

"You must go to the Temple and wrest his soul from Doran. I will stay here to guard his body for you, but I will ask a favor in return someday, my little Ryes," Tyra warned, smiling impishly.

"Anything," she vowed. "Where's this temple?" She slipped her useless beltknife back into its sheath. She loved Garth too much, to leave him to die like this!

"There are many traps set to keep the unwanted away," Tyra replied approvingly. "Simply follow the calling you've been hearing. It's your invitation and will lead you in safely. Try to keep a memory of that path for you'll need it to get back out. There are more than just physical traps here. There are other creatures who have been her guardians for uncounted years. But, you're my daughter after all, and you'll always be sensitive to Her call because of your Talents."

"You came from here?" Ryes asked, utterly shocked.

"Yes, after a fashion. Long ago, I came to this place to escape an arranged match on Kahmarr. He was a very old man and in fact I rather liked him, but never as a mate; much less my first mate. He was as old as my great-grandmother and he and his family and their plans for me were a nightmare! I was a very Talented heiress with no place to hide. But my father found the Temple of Doran, where no man could go. He brought me to Tayna and I submitted myself as one of her handmaidens; gaining asylum. That was a mistake! She and her followers have very twisted ideas on obtaining dominance over all men. I was quite young but knew that the only true way for men and women to honestly live together was to do so as equals. It was hard to live among them, but it was only supposed to be for a very few months. Father was going to rally his family to break the engagement and let me choose my own first husband."

"In the meantime, Doran found out who I was, so she had me put into a cryogenic suspension. It's an endless, cold sleep, all because I was from an important house. So I slept the years away with her and her other captive followers. I kept myself as shielded as possible, but it was hard and I lost track of time." She paused, her outline becoming indistinct for a moment. She looked up at Ryes again, becoming firmer, clearer.

"There is a great stone of power here. Through time I managed to absorb enough of its energies to escape. Doran was absolutely furious, but there was nothing she could do about it. Her own Talents and power are fading. I traveled south and east, away from the valley, when I came upon Jana. She had come under Doran's lure and was heading for the valley to be enslaved. I freed her and as she awoke, I told her I was lost and very far from my own home. So, she brought me home with her. I found much happiness in her and Rowan's family. I found the life I had been searching for all my years."

"Were you and Ronn true-mates?" Ryes questioned in a low voice, feeling the ache of the thousands of others she wanted to ask her. "Rowan thinks so."

"Yes. We were and are." Tyra looked down at Garth. "You have a sturdy man of your own. If you can win through to the stone, you can win freedom for both of you with its great power. Now go, while Shaysa's light can help you." She saw the questions building in Ryes' eyes, but had to get her started upon her quest, while there was still time. "Doran will be slowly consuming his very soul!" Ryes stepped forward, wanting to touch her, but Tyra stepped aside, shaking her head. She indicated Garth. Ryes went to him, knelt down and threw her arms about him.

"I'll get you free of this, I promise," she whispered, tears trailing down her cheeks as she kissed him. She then took in a deep breath and stood. There was a fire in her eyes as she set her determination upon saving Garth. She tuned in the lure, which she had finally managed to block out of her mind. Without a word she left quietly, as a huntress on a hunt.

Tyra watched her go; her only surviving child. She had courage, a good heart and quick mind. She wished she could've been the one to have raised her. Yet, she was proud of the job Rowan accomplished in her stead. She longed for freedom from this quasi existence and to be with Ronn's spirit, as they should be together. She felt him waiting for her - so far away from this unhealthy place. Soon, she hoped... Ryes would be fighting for freedom for all four of them.

Battle of Wills

The silvery light of Shaysa was waxing to fullness, casting eerie patterns of light and shadow upon the lake's water, as Ardis sat upon the rocks, enjoying the sounds of the night and the gentle slap of the water on the bank. They were finally camped in the outskirts of Hailys' itself! She saw orange Menna was low to the horizon with his light adding little. Small, blue Porr was trailing below Shaysa, his light washed out by the greater moon's brilliance. She loved the sky at night. The dancing moons and bright stars were her longtime friends. But tonight she wasn't looking up at them. Tonight she was watching for Sabin's return. He'd gone out again and it was well past dinner time, with no sign of him. She knew he and Garth had taken a blood-brother oath when they were cubs, but this was starting to annoy her. Sure she'd been pursuing Garth since they were early teeners, but finally realized there was some true promise in Sabin, after all. She closed her eyes for a few moments, striving to relax, but her mind and spirit were too restless. A huff of breath sounded near her, startling her. Ardis' eyes were instantly open and her beltknife in hand as she stood, ready at the guard.

"It's only me," Sabin assured her, sitting down and she settled down next to him. "I caught a strange scent a little earlier and wanted to make very sure the area was clear, before I relaxed." She smiled ruefully as she sheathed the knife and leaned against his shoulder. His solidness comforted her.

"I worry about you, even so," she told him. He chuckled, as he put an arm around her, pulling her in close.

"I want to do everything I can to make sure you're safe. I want to see our cubs someday playing in a field of flowers, safe from harm, and you smiling at them in happiness," he told her, sharing his heart's desire. He had the Vision on their journey out here, but was afraid to jinx it. It looked too perfect a scene to him. She laughed at the picture he painted for her.

"Cubs? Are you thinking I'll put up with you THAT long?" she teased, laughing lightly as she looked into his eyes.

"You must, because I've seen us with four cubs to look after," he said, practically holding his breath.

"You're kidding?" she questioned, her mouth open as she wondered about his Talent? Four at once? It seemed impossible!

"It's the one Vision I've been most afraid of not coming true," he painfully admitted, as he met her eyes in the bright moonlight. "It seemed there were two little ones and two older ones." She stretched up to him and closed her eyes, kissing him passionately.

"Well, we wouldn't ever want you to be wrong," she told him breathlessly, as she leaned her body against his. "We'll just have to see where this does take us. My season should only be about a month or two away, I think." She started undoing the lacing on his tunic, teasing him as she did. He wanted to yell out his happiness, as he started pulling her tunic lacing free, too.

An old carrion eater turned up next, snarling and snapping, not daring to come any closer, as it slinked in a circling path around his prey. He was another slave to the will of the "goddess" of the valley but recognized power when he saw it. Tyra looked at him and waved her hand. He left immediately, as if he'd been dismissed. She looked to the moons above, knowing she held power here even in her spirit form, because she'd been a long time resident and could still draw it from this place without tapping the stone directly. Still, it wasn't a comfortable place for her to be... She wanted to rest with Ronn. She felt his calling, but knew he understood their duty to their lone surviving daughter. He'd be here in her place, if he held enough power to handle the demands needed. His power lay elsewhere and she was never so happy as when they discovered his Healing Talent and awakened it, just a few months before the birth of their cubs. Because of him, their birth had been a joy, instead of a pain-filled uncertainty. She missed his warm gentle touch more than anything else!

She felt something about Garth, so gently probed him, not wanting to alert Doran to her presence, but she was curious. And she discovered he had Talent, too. She wasn't sure, but thought he might have more than one. But his Empath Talent was ready for waking. So, she nudged it, hoping she could use it to help free him a little from that evil woman's grasp. It wasn't enough to awaken his Talent fully, but it gave him an awareness of himself. As she backed out, he stirred just a little, so knew it was working and might help anchor him more to his own body again. At least he'd know the path back, now.

Garth stirred, moaning a little, giving her a small feeling of reward. She knew Doran was "teaching him a lesson" for trespassing

in her valley. It was forbidden for any man to tread here, much less
camp out as if he were in his own land! She felt sorry for him and
Ryes, both. If she could win their freedom from this place, they still
had so much to accomplish, ahead of them. She knew Ryes' first
season would soon be upon her, which would make their cubs due at
the end of the winter. They needed a safe, secure place to call home,
since it didn't look as if they intended to go back to Matlowe. There
was little else she could do for them, except what she was doing now
- keeping the valley denizens at bay - and giving Ryes her chance to
save her own love.

Ryes traveled quietly through the garden of a thousand
deaths, sensing the many traps and misshapen denizens only
peripherally, through the deep shadows the arching, overhead
branches created. Her mind was focused upon one thing - to free
Garth. He was her anchor as her Talents had awakened, nearly
driving her mad. She had to save him! He was a part of her and his
absence would cause a painful ache within, far more than losing Tara!
She loved him so very much! So she held onto Doran's call, trotting
through the weaving way it indicated, trying to hasten her footsteps
while noting the pathway for later. She turned often to look behind
her to landmark the path back in her mind.

The animals here amazed her. They were, for the most part,
deadly-looking but there were others which hadn't appeared to be so
fierce. Still, she didn't doubt their danger as she knew of quite a few
animals in the wilds near Matlowe which didn't appear to be overly
deadly, but were still so in truth. She kept her distance while they
sometimes inspected her scent, but never once tried to harm her.
They were under some type of direct control and might prove a
hazard, she was sure, on her departure. She noted them clearly, as
well as her path back.

There was a wide open, stone-paved walkway at the end of
the outer gardens and she paused at it, wondering. The inner drive
had her turning off it to a much smaller pathway which ran parallel to
it. On an impulse, she grabbed a nearby loosened stone, which
seemed hefty enough, and threw it hard at the middle of the wide
path. Immediately the stones in the middle swung down and a huge
opening gaped almost at her toes. The moonlight revealed heavy
spines sticking straight up, far down below. After several long,
panicked heartbeats, the pathway panels rose back up into place;
ready for the next victim. She nimbly stepped over to the smaller
path and started down it cautiously. So far she'd seen numerous
dangerous animals and a wall that shot out darts, when she

deliberately tripped that trap. She had no idea how many other dangers lurked in this place, but she was making sure she followed the indicated pathways closely.

After an eternity she finally emerged from the outer gardens into a large clearing with a neatly-kept verge of grass. There were flowering bushes all along the entire edge of the square-shaped grassy area. Strangely-shaped stone statues with stone seating near them were in small arranged gardens in the corners of the clearing nearest the building. And above it all arose a great, white-marbled temple before her. It was centered on the far side of the massive clearing. The building was the largest she had ever seen in her entire life and was a bit intimidating as she stood back and away before it. The stone of the building was pristine. There was one huge double doorway at the top of the wide, long flight of stairs. And she noted there were several other smaller doors spaced around it – both at the ground level and above on the same level as the main doorway. The building rose up for many levels above. There were many tall, wide windows to indicate each of the levels within the structure. Ryes had studied the books with all the drawings and paintings of the great cities upon Tayna and this appeared to dwarf all the ones she'd seen in the books Darman had given her. There was a broad, wide porch which looked to encircle the building up above. She thought it would be a perfect place for people to stand upon and throw spears down at anyone here below. An icy chill travelled up her back.

The building itself had massively tall figures carved into the marble. She was still far enough back that the details were not quite clear by moonlight, but from the little she could make out that they appeared to be women torturing men. She felt oddly insulted with such depictions. She felt men and women should be partners in life, not enemies.

She strolled carefully across the open expanse, approaching the building slowly and carefully. Even if the calling was clearly indicating this was the way to go, she was not going to fully trust it. She saw there were tall columns about the lower porch, each of which were carved with images of plants and animals. She truly appreciated the detail of the work involved in their making. It was a deadly, yet amazing place.

There was a pause in the luring song in her mind as an old, bent, richly-dressed crone emerged from the building, slowly shuffling toward her. She was shorter than Ryes and her back was half twisted with a strange, lumpish deformity. Her hair was a slate-gray color and tied back, revealing a very-wrinkled withered face. She wondered how old this woman was? Surely far older than the oldest elder in Matlowe Village!

"A gift to you from Our Great Sleeping Goddess," she cackled out in a strangely accented voice, as she held up a garment made of a thin, filmy, white material. It looked far too fragile to even be worn! It looked as light as if one could make a garment from web spinner silks!

"She'll have to accept me as I am," Ryes declared firmly, looking closely at the crone's face. At least she wasn't the second image from her reoccurring dreams, she noted in relief! Her eyes appeared a little unfocused, which was a bit unsettling. Was she using some kind of medicine, or was her mind under full control of someone else? It gave her a shiver. She wondered how many years she'd been enslaved in this nightmarish place? And where upon Tayna had she come from? Her accent was not one she knew. The old woman's own dress was a simple design, but made of a rich material with a few colorful scarves tied about her middle as a belt.

"Oh, but it is so pretty and you will look so nice in it," she fussed, thrusting the garment toward Ryes. "All first comers must adorn themselves before presenting themselves to the Goddess for their initiation. And it would be so much better than those stained rags you are wearing!"

"My clothing shouldn't matter. I'm not going to a party," she retorted. Ryes resisted looking down at her own clothes. They'd been on the trail for quite a while, so knew she didn't look her best. But she wanted nothing from this "sleeping goddess," except freedom for Garth and herself.

"Come with me," she protested. "We will bathe and dress you and prepare you for your glorious meeting with our lady!" She was indicating a nearby doorway on the ground level.

"No!" she replied firmly. She turned and rushed up the stairs and into the huge open doors of the temple, ignoring the prattling old woman, who hurried to follow.

She stopped as she found herself in a long corridor of white marble. The floor and ceiling were of dark alabaster tile, rich with riotous colors in small streaks throughout. It was well lit with strange torches which didn't flicker, nor give off smoke. She passed a hand close to one, noting very little heat came from it. They looked as if carved from crystal and in their cold, bright light Ryes clearly saw what adorned the walls. Weapons! Weapons of every make and design. Half of them she couldn't even guess their use, they looked so outlandish. The luring voice, which had fallen silent when the old woman had confronted her, now laughed gleefully at her surprise. The old woman had trailed her and stopped a few paces behind her, suddenly quiet, the filmy gown still in her claw-like hands; as if a puppet which had been discarded.

"Why would a `sleeping goddess' of such great power need such things?" Ryes questioned aloud, her arm's sweeping gesture indicating the walls about her.

"You like my toys?" The voice reverberated within her mind, uninvited. "They are the trophies my followers have gathered after putting them to use to put disgusting men into their places." There was again the gleeful, hysterical laughter. Ryes continued down the corridor, feeling unsettled. She HAD to find Garth and get them BOTH out of here! The maniacal laughter was bad enough, but the ideas behind the founding of the armory sent icy shivers up her back. She went around a couple of sharp bends and stopped face-to-face with the haunting figure from her dreams.

The hall she stepped into was wide and deep, with numerous columns and alcoves lining its length. A great dome of crystal formed most of the ceiling. It let in the bright light of Shaysa and the fainter, bluish light of Porr. There was a large empty space between the alcoves and the center of the hall. In the middle of the hall was a great, stone monolith, lavishly decorated with gold and glittering gemstones. Upon a pedestal before the monolith was a very, large lifelike carving of the cold enchantress she'd been trying to run away from in her dreams. It seemed to be made from a green-frosted glass. It might have been why she'd seen her wrapped in greenish light in her nightmares, before.

"I happen to like most men," Ryes declared to the statue, as if she were talking to her face-to-face, feeling a direct confrontation was best. And if she thought men were disgusting…

"How could you? You have not known your first season yet, child!" The voice was shocked, yet condescendingly mocking. Ryes smiled mischievously, knowing she'd been right.

"There's still free-mating. That can be enjoyed ANY TIME! And I'm plenty old enough to do it and have enjoyed it immensely," she taunted, mocking the voice in her turn. She felt a wave of horror wash over her, almost drowning her senses. She stood and managed to block it out somehow, remembering the way she had helped Maren block out Sabin. "You have something of mine and I've come to claim him, Doran of House Forental!" Ryes shouted out, her anger roused. There was an outraged shriek from the voice that returned to her mind, at the mention of her name. Ryes felt her anger, too.

"How do you KNOW ME? You have never been off Tayna! All the starships were destroyed in the great battle! Daughter, I claim you. And you shall NEVER leave my abode; dead or alive," the voice answered Ryes' challenge.

The old woman had stepped into the chamber behind her. She no longer carried the filmy garment. Now she held a weapon. It was like a short walking staff with two, flat, fan-shaped blades, one on each end. She meant business; those blades looked razor sharp. Ryes silently cursed herself for not bringing along a weapon of her own. Garth's spear would've been her best choice, now! She drew her beltknife to help deflect the blade and defend herself. The old follower deftly swung at Ryes, but she jumped back - just out of reach. She surely didn't move as if old and crippled anymore. Where did this energy and grace she suddenly displayed come from?

"I am the vessel for my lady's power. Let her light fill me and guide me," the old crone intoned, chanting over and over, as she advanced upon her. Ryes danced out of the way of that deadly arc of metal, backing toward the monolith and down the stairs to the bottom of the center of the chamber, skirting the cold statue. She gave it no more than the barest glance, having had her fill of this twisted woman already. Her mother had mentioned a stone of power. Where was it hidden? Did she need to touch it, or just get it into view to find a way to tap it? This place was too large!

"Two fair cubs were a dancing, a prancing `round the Winterfest tree," she sang out loudly in counterpoint to the crone's chant, hoping to distract her. She slowly retreated further from her as she sang. Her heart was pounding as she was trying to find something around her she could use in defense. The old woman paused in her advance for a moment, looking puzzled, as if trying to recall which voice she was supposed to be listening to.

"Here is my Winterfest gift for thee,

Please dance with me about the tree.

She laughed and gave him her gift,

Smiling as he gave her a kiss.

He gave her his gift with glee.

Take my hand said she,

Take my hand said he,

And together they twirled `round the Winterfest tree."

There was a sudden rush of anger, which Ryes was hard pressed to block out. It came directly from Doran. Then the crone's confusion cleared as she gripped the weapon's shaft more surely, advancing once more. Apparently dancing with a man, even if he were a cub, around a tree at Winterfest was something Doran didn't like and she was responding to it with anger and action.

Lacking any weapon with reach, Ryes finally reached out with her mind, as she had with the serpent earlier. She was blocked, but not very well. Doran was using her puppet only and was not protecting the woman from any attacks. Or maybe she couldn't see someone attacking in this manner? As Ryes tried to redouble her efforts, she stumbled as she dodged a swing of the weapon and her forearm was gashed open. The pain gave her the added strength she needed, as she struck at the follower with her mind, with all of her inner might. There was a horrible shriek of pain. Then she watched in pain-filled horror, as the crone stumbled back and crumpled limply to the floor. The weapon clattered loudly as it tumbled from her hand and away from the body. Ryes sheathed her knife then rushed to her side so see if she still breathed. She was twitching in her death throes with her eyes wide in terror, as she passed. Ryes was not going to reach out to her with her mind in such a moment, partly out of fear and partly to allow her some personal room in her passing. Then the old woman was no longer breathing and the muscle spasms mostly stopped; just the few twitches that followed after death.

Mad laughter filled her head as tears filled her eyes. She truly hadn't meant to hurt the old woman. She only wanted to keep her back and away! The pain partly blocked the maniacal mirth from her mind, as she cradled the bleeding arm against her chest. She fumbled to find the strength within to block out Doran again, but the focus eluded her. She finally stood up and for several long moments, leaning against the side of the monolith, struggling to recall what she was doing... What she'd been searching for... For a space of time, nothing but pain and cold laughter filled her reeling world.

Then his face flashed in her mind. His warm smile and bright golden eyes. That special look he had for just her. The warmth of his strong arms about her. Garth! She let memories of his presence flood her mind, heart and soul. Every minute they had spent together since that hunt on that fate-filled day flowed through her being. It was almost as if she could feel him nearby. She fought to regain control of herself as she clung to the thought of Garth and a stone of power, which could free him from Doran's greedy grasp. She didn't think she had the power to do it by herself, alone. It had to be what was giving Doran her strength!

"Come daughter and sleep away time with me. I have many ladies here in my keeping. We truly are a delightful group and I'm sure you'll find a few kindred souls among us," she crooned using a luring voice again, having no idea Ryes thoughts were fully centered around a man.

"Never," she breathed out, barely above a whisper. Ryes shook her head and blocked out its alluring quality. She was learning things she could do with her Talents as she strove to keep Doran at a distance and away from probing her thoughts, or taking control of her will. With her puppet dead, she didn't think Doran had any direct way to affect her now.

"If not, then you can DIE!" Suddenly what surely seemed like all the weapons from the hallway were flying through the air - aimed at her. Ryes ducked down into a ball and covered her face and head with her arms. She concentrated and willed the blades away from her with all her being. Her stomach was clenching as she ground her teeth and praying to her favorite deities in the back of her mind. Then the first one to reach her clattered to the floor nearby. Sweat ran into her eyes as she held her will and kept up her inner force to keep the rest of the weapons away from her. Some got through and she felt deep cuts but she was very sure they were far less than what it would have been without her efforts. Finally, the loud clanging and clattering noises stopped and silence reined in the hall again.

She sighed relief as she then turned her will to her own body, thinking if she truly had Healer Talent, she should be able to mend her body, too. Then the laughter started up again. She stood back up and saw the pile of debris only a few feet away from her. She was amazed to see only three of the weapons had actually reached her. She took in a deep breath and let it out slowly, calming herself once again. She had to get out of this place!

Ryes closed her eyes to concentrate, seeking something of power. There had to be a way to find it without having to touch it. What would it be like? What would it feel like? She strove to extend her inner senses and found Doran tried to block her, as if she stood in her path. Still, she was not very effective. She was not a physical presence and she could not truly block her Talents. Ryes wondered at that as she continued to search. There was something ahead... beyond this gaudy monolith. It was a brilliant white light... as bright as Shaysa at full moon. And she could actually see the light it cast through her closed eyelids. That small promise excited her and drew her onward.

Ryes stumbled toward it, her shoulder sliding along the cold, lifeless stone of the monolith with a hand outstretched before her, almost stumbling as she reached its end. She continued onward toward the brightness and finally opened her eyes as she banged her shin against something hard and cold. It was a low stone wall, built into a ring. In the center of the ring lay a stone which was raised up upon a tall, white marble base. It was shaped like a huge globe. Shaysa's light made it bright and sparkling - like a star -so much so that it was hard to look upon. The light hurt her eyes!

"After my great treasure, daughter?" Doran demanded in a wicked tone. "It is the most well-guarded object in my chamber. You shall never reach it!" She sounded so sure. Ryes was determined to not respond to her taunts. She didn't want to be drawn out and off her guard. She had to remain focused, so kept quiet.

Ryes shifted her eyes from the stone to study the ring around it. There were circular-shaped indents along the inside, about the size of her hand, at regular intervals. The outside was richly carved, as the monolith, except it lacked the gold and gemstones. The scenes depicted women free mating with other women. It made her wonder as that was something she had only heard about in the largest cities, but it was better than the ones of women torturing men in viciously cruel ways, which adorned the monolith itself. How can this be so well guarded? It didn't appear to be anything other than simple stone. Still, there were many wondrous machines the ancients had, which were legend only now. And this place looked at least that old, especially with crystal, fireless torches! She stumbled back along the monolith, stooping down to pick up the old crone's weapon, which was easier to find than sorting through the pile of weapons thrown at her. She didn't look upon her face, not wanting to see if death had freed, or cursed the woman. She ripped a length of the filmy cloth she wore and wrapped it around her arm as a bandage. It made a poor one, but was better than nothing. It didn't seem to be bleeding now, nor did the others on her arms or shoulders, but still it gave her a better feeling to wrap them up as she could.

Ryes returned with the weapon and thrust it over the edge of the stone ring. Blades sprang up from the top of the ring, piercing the shaft, while bright beams of light punched myriad holes in the blade. Well-guarded, indeed! Ryes pondered this problem for several long moments, trying to think of how to bypass the defenses, as she peered at the light through the new holes in the blade. She'd never seen anything like this before! Light which could puncture metal? And cleanly. The holes were perfectly round! Warily, she walked about the perimeter of the ring, looking for a break, or way to disable it. The crystal dome above and the stone walls of the building protected it from the weather, but didn't anyone ever dust it?

"I'll have you yet, daughter," Doran vowed. Ryes held her chin up defiantly, tired of this ancient nag and her incessant taunts. She truly had had enough.

"You couldn't hold my mother; you won't be able to keep me. You're weak, old ghost!" she challenged her. Then there was dead silence. It rang in her mind, more loudly than the laughter! Ryes noted the many alcoves lining two of the walls inside the room. She wondered what they held? Could they hold something useful in defeating this thing's defenses? As she stepped away from the ring, crossing the floor, a ghostly figure, haloed in a greenish light, blocked her path. It was Doran and the absolute fury painting her face caused Ryes to step back in startlement.

"So, you are actually Tyra's daughter? Have you come here merely to taunt me? And you think I am powerless? CHILD! What do you know of true POWER?" She shrieked in outrage. Ryes suddenly found herself flying through the air, light as a wind-tossed leaf, thrown painfully upon the stone steps before an altar, which was on the opposite end of the room from Doran's statue. The pole weapon clattered down the steps to the main floor. She picked herself up and faced the ghostly visage. Doran again voiced her mad laughter.

"I never wanted to come here!" Ryes yelled back, finding her own anger rising in response. "And all I want now is my husband free!" But the laughter continued, as if she never heard her. Tyra freed herself without touching the stone. She said she was encased. How did she do it? What is the stone's secret? She wished they had more time to discuss things, but she now understood her urgency to free Garth, as quickly as possible, from this shadow of a mad woman! How was she holding him captive? Doran noted the anger upon her face and drifted closer. With a wicked laugh, she made a pushing motion with her hand. Suddenly the weapons were flying through the air again, aimed straight at her. Ryes ducked under the alter stone, itself and pulled up her will again to hold them off. She was toying with her! The weapons clattered loudly against the stone, scaring her but it fired up her determination all the more. At least she hadn't aimed the weapons very well! Still, she poked her head out only after the clatter settled.

Her arm was throbbing painfully and she was badly cut and bruised all over, but she crawled out, to face the ghost once more. She wouldn't quit. There was nothing to go back for, if she didn't win. She had to free the both of them. As she pulled herself out, there was a distinct "schnict" sound and a small piece of the decorative carving gave way, receding inward and a stone bench sank below the flooring with another piece of the floor rising to hide where it had been. Doran, mad with her own amusements, failed to hear, or see. Could this be a key to disabling the ring's defenses? Ryes quietly hoped. Otherwise, there was little other hope to hold onto. For all her practicing to control her newly, awakened abilities, they were feeble against Doran. She couldn't throw objects the way this mad woman could. She was a Manipulator! No wonder she had ruled these other women so easily! She briefly wondered what she'd been like in her prime, if her mother considered her weak now? What had Tyra been like?

As she thought she could move about freely again, the weapons lifted from the floor as well as several stone benches from around the altar. She threw herself down next to one of the massive supports for the altar as they were all thrown her way, again. The stone shattered upon the stone and the weapons tore at her. She rolled herself into a ball and willed everything away from her. When it all settled again, she found herself in a hollow formed of the broken stone with some of the weapons thrown into the mix. And she was more bruised, but still whole. It might have been the mad one's poor aim, or perhaps it was her own Talents protecting her. She wasn't sure. She found a way through and carefully crept out into the open again. Doran was not looking her way. She seemed to be talking to the alcoves across the side of the great hall.

Ryes slowly crept down the steps, still crouched, letting Doran continue chatting and laughing to herself in her insanity. Hoping not to attract attention, she reached the old woman's weapon, grabbed it, and sprinted for the stone circle. She used it to vault over it, using that part of her to push everything away from her, which she used during the attacks, and landing within safely. She had soared over the sharp blades and the cutting lights had not touched her. She was breathing hard as she looked back. Doran had turned and was pointing at her, laughing even harder. As if she were the fool acting out a play for tonight's entertainment for her court. Ryes frowned. Was this the stone of power her mother mentioned, or not? Doran didn't look upset that she had managed to cross to the inside of the stone ring.

"You only fool yourself," Doran gasped out. Her eyes were full of hate and looked cruel. "It still lies beyond your reach, Child!" Ryes turned to look at the stone, puzzled. She turned her back upon the ghost and stepped closer, only to find an unseen wall keeping her away from what she sought. She sank down to the floor. Tired, in pain, and feeling despair. What was this barrier? She was sure it was the same which kept them prisoners in this valley!

"I warned you!" Doran maliciously declared.

"Shut up," Ryes muttered, trying to think it through. She'd come so far and was still shut out. There weren't any secret stone switches here that she could find.

"Do you give up? Do you not know? Did not your mother tell you of such things? Then I shall tell you what it is. It is called a shield barrier! Long ago, when there were starships visiting every world, shield barriers were used to protect the ships, the passengers and crews from the dangerous forces of the starship engines. The projector for the barrier lies within it, beneath the stone, and safely out of YOUR REACH." Doran grinned wickedly, triumph and madness in her cruel eyes.

"Curse you, you witch," Ryes voiced the pain she felt from within. "We want nothing to do with you, nor your valley. Let us go!" she ground out, demanding. She looked at the ghostly image. Her icy, glittering eyes were appraising Ryes; the cold evil in them giving her a sudden chill.

"We have not had a proper sacrifice in such a very long time," she said. "Did your mother tell you of those? You will offer up that... MAN... you brought with you upon the alter for our appeasement and delight," she ordered. "After you clean up the temple and repair all the damage."

Ryes closed her eyes upon the horror before her. That was what the altar was used for? Those torture scenes were real and had been visited upon their captives? What kind of women did such things? And her mother had been captive for a while, too?

"Never," she vowed in a low voice. She reached down, deep within herself, seeking her own, small Talents. Slowly, she let go of her pain, her exhaustion, and even the hopelessness of her situation. There had to be some way to free them from this mad place! Her own Talents were her last and only hope left. She'd take her own life, before sacrificing Garth to anyone! His face burned like a warm flame within her mind and heart.

Then she realized there was a bright fountain of intense energy flowing ceiling-ward, beside her. She reached out to it from within, strangely drawn and instantly found herself almost drowning in its wild energies. At first she struggled against it, trying to pull free so she could understand it better, first. And now that she had touched it from within, she was unable to back out, or let it go. She was awash in severe pain from the intensity and purity of the energy. Unable to stop it, she let it flow through her being, its purity burning within, as a hot iron would against her skin. The pain was excruciating, but far better than trying to block it out! So, she let it flow unhindered. The pain lessened quite a bit. Now to see if she could use this energy as the tool she needed. There was only one way she knew how to use it. Her Talents burned with power, ready for her to use them, as she never had before in her whole life. This was Doran's true secret! She opened her eyes and stood to face Doran again.

Doran shrieked, suspecting what gave Ryes her courage. She caused a discarded weapon to hurtle through the air, straight at her. Ryes stopped it easily; consciously with her will. It clattered to the stone floor inside the ring. There was no triumph, only acceptance. She did possess the tool she needed. She had figured out how her mother freed herself. It was her Talents and this flowing energy. She didn't need to touch the stone, as she thought before.

"Doran of House Forental," she called to the frosty-eyed image before her. "Release my mate, now!"

"I do not give up my playthings," she snapped back. "I need the soul you want to help replenish my own," Doran added with a pitiful whine. Ryes recoiled in horror, shuddering from a deep cold born of the depths of hell. To use the souls of others to feed upon, while their bodies wasted away? It was the worse evil she could ever imagine! Her killing the old follower might have been a blessing for the woman, after all. She might have been the next one she planned to use to support her unnatural life!

"Not while I live and breathe!" she swore, "He's MINE!" She bent the flow of energies, aiming them at the visage, as a wave to overcome her and wash her evil from this place. Doran laughed loudly as she absorbed the power, her ghostly image growing brighter, more distinct. Ryes mentally cursed herself. She was feeding her more power, not attacking her by doing this! She stopped instantly and instead reached within and felt for the other streams of force from the stone, looking for those which fed Doran. She found there were several. She tried to cut them off, but they wouldn't obey her. In desperation, she called the energy streams to herself, wondering if she wouldn't go mad herself with so much power channeling through her being. They came reluctantly, one-by-one, blending their flows with the torrent already rushing through Ryes. Then they were all under her command and bent to her will only.

"NO!" Doran screeched with agony in her voice. She finally drifted closer, and then broke a "charm" off a bracelet she wore and handed it across to Ryes. Her outline was very faded and her face was losing its clarity. "Here, he is yours again. Stop, please stop," she pleaded in a low whisper.

Ryes took the "charm" and held it close to her heart. It seemed to pulse in rhythm to her own heartbeat. She knew him as well as she knew herself! She let it go. It fluttered for an instant, like a flutter-wing playing with a capricious breeze, then vanished. Free! Slowly Ryes released one the flows which originally fed her. Giving it back to her, now that she had part of what she needed. Doran's outline grew clear again, but was still a little faded, as if the drain was not something she could recover from now.

"He will only use you," she warned, a deep hatred in her
eyes for her. Ryes laughed as she shook her head no.

"No. He's a part of me and I'm a part of him," she assured
her. "Why all of this?" she asked, gesturing to the cold room about
her. For the first time she noted there were glittering eyes watching
them from most of the alcoves about the room. One spot was most
obviously empty. Tyra's place, she wondered? Only through the
stone's power, which flowed through her, could she see Doran's
followers. Didn't any of them crave their freedom, as her mother
had? What were those women like, who had spent countless years in
cold storage here with this mad woman leading them?

"If you must know the reasons, you must go into rapport
with me. It's a joining of two minds. All memories shared, all
experiences felt together," Doran replied. Ryes was loathe to share
any of her life with such a mad creature, but she craved the answers
to a thousand questions, and she needed to be sure they could safely
escape the valley without her interference. Garth was free and she'd
soon be with him. They could quit this place for all time. She could
manage it, she thought and now she had the stone's energies to draw
upon. Her own Talents were the key. Suddenly, she got another idea
and reached out to the watchers. Maybe they wanted to escape too?

"Look, you don't HAVE to stay here in this darkness," she
told the followers around them. "My mother escaped, found her true-
mate, and gave birth to me and my siblings. She and my father were
very happy together."

"Men always use women to their own ends," one finally
spoke back, after several moments of silence. Was it that they forgot
how to speak, or weren't they used to being directly addressed by a
stranger? Doran looked angry, but was still too weak and indistinct.
Ryes hadn't returned all her original energy, yet... just in case.

"And you think women don't do the same at times, too?" she
demanded. "Not all men are as you say. I'm sure you've all known
men in your lives, which you do still love and miss!" With this, Ryes
opened herself up to only them, feeling their strong resentment and
doubt. She projected the memories of her grandfather and his loving
care and discipline. She showed them Darman, as he taught her how
to read and write, of the sciences, and of the world around them. She
showed them the love and strength she found in Garth and his
willingness to lay down his own life to win her freedom from Korman.
And finally, her cousin Maren and his warmth and playfulness and the
different kind of love she felt for him. There was a stirring as they
responded to what she shared. "Not all men use others, as not all
women use others," she stressed, picturing Doran and her need to
consume other souls and to call women into her service. This simple

projection caused an intense feeling of outrage, which she expected from these women of hers.

"The goddess does NOT use us!" she finally got in response from one of women. The tone was firm but there was a small note of doubt echoing behind it.

"Then why doesn't she let you go, if you will it? She wants you here to prove to her she's right, and so she won't be alone in her isolation. I don't know if her imprisonment was just, but why has she chosen to hold all of you captive here with her? Does she consume your souls, too?" she demanded in question, in return.

The anger was now visible in the air and Ryes was glad she still controlled the energy streams! They fell into shouting at her and at each other, as if she had just started some kind of revolt. Through all this, Doran had taken up her mad laughter again. Maybe it was hopeless to try to free these women, who chose to go on with this endless, pointless existence after all? This must be where they felt they belonged. Maybe the world had changed too much for them and this was their one safe hiding spot? It just didn't feel right to Ryes. She had hoped she could get the information she needed from one of them, instead of having to go through their mad leader.

"Alright," Ryes voiced her agreement to Doran. "I'll enter rapport with you. I need answers to understand things and it looks as if you're my only hope, now."

Doran smiled her icy, wicked smile. The child was so naive and trusting. She might win this contest, yet. She drifted closer to the ragged waif to begin.

A New Dawn

"Ryes, watch out!" Garth shouted as he awoke with a start.
He opened his eyes and sat up, seeing the campfire still burning bright
against the terrors he now knew this valley held. Had it all been a
terrible nightmare? But if so, then where was Ryes?

"I think she will be fine," Tyra assured him, looking toward
Doran's temple. "Ryes now controls the flow of the Stone of Power's
energies and is not as naive as that witch believes. She only lacks
proper training." He looked up at her ghostly form hovering next to
him, near the firelight.

"Then, it wasn't just a nightmare?" he questioned, feeling
lost without his mate. He felt so weak, as if that witch had been
feeding upon his flesh! "She's facing off that monster, alone?"

"She has already triumphed once and won your freedom,"
Tyra smiled as she looked back to him. His need for her daughter was
as plain to her eyes, as hers for him earlier. They may not have
spoken a true-mate vow, but it was there between them already.
"Now she is making sure you both have your freedom from this place.
She is trying to discover a way to seal the power away from Doran's
reach for all time, and keep the valley open, so anyone can come, or
go, without her interference. She does not want anyone falling into
her snares, again," she informed him. Garth felt strange talking with
the ghost of his wife's mother as if she were alive, but she was all he
had in this moment.

"Maybe I should go help her?" he questioned, tightening his
belt and reaching for his boots.

"No! She is far safer if you stay right here. But, you might
want to have some hot tea ready for her when she returns and have
your things ready to go. Do not spend the rest of the night here,
even though Ryes has succeeded. There are still things about, which
mean to take your life, no matter what has transpired in the last hour
up in the temple. They will not easily find their way out of the valley,
and will now die of natural aging, since Ryes has removed the
unnatural power, which kept them alive so long, from them."

"Then, her nightmares will now be over?" Garth asked,
hoping, but not fully understanding all she was telling him.

"Yes," Tyra smiled, her eyes shining in the moonlight. "She will only have more `normal' concerns, from now on."

"That'll be a relief," he sighed, smiling at last. Yes, Ryes did look like her mother, very much so, he thought. Garth then reached for his pack and dug into it, looking for his pouch of tea leaves. Their supply of honey was getting low, but he wasn't going to deny it to her. With this battle she'd been through, she deserved it!

Tyra chuckled to herself at seeing this man of her daughter's so worked up over pleasing her. Yes, they were well matched.

"Garth! Ryes!" Maren awoke suddenly in the middle of the night, sitting up before he even opened his eyes. He was breathing hard and his heart was pounding, as he tried to clear the formless nightmares from his mind. He realized he's been ready to jump up and run to help them. What had THAT been all about, he wondered?

"What's the matter?" Sabin asked in a low voice, coming over to kneel next to his young friend. They decided to set a night watch, since they had no idea what lay in this new land about them and wanted as much warning in case of problems, as possible.

"Some kind of a nightmare. I thought I was done with those," Maren told him, realizing it might almost be his turn at watch, anyway. He rubbed the sleep from his eyes as he stretched and yawned. Feeling he was starting to feel more normal, once more. It was only a dream, after all. "What time is it?" he questioned, seeing Shaysa almost to the horizon. Sabin chuckled as he placed a hand atop his shoulder. Suddenly, he saw a scene where Ryes was facing off an evil ghost of a woman in a chamber of bright light and stone. She seemed to be holding her at bay, while she was urging the other ghosts to rebel with her. Then it shifted to one of Garth sitting and making tea, while another ghostly figure was keeping him company. There was something about that place which gave him the chills! Sabin shuddered as he released his shoulder, sitting down on the ground - hard. Just becoming aware of the world around him, again.

"What was that?" Maren demanded, having seen it all, too. Now he understood Ryes' attitude about sharing Sabin's visions. They were strong! "Are they all right?"

"Garth seems to be, but I'm not sure about Ryes. She might still be in danger," he replied, feeling suddenly drained. Maren didn't give him the added power Ryes had, but the Vision had intensified again. He had to have a Talent, he was sure of it.

187

"We've got to go help them!" Maren declared, reaching for his boots. Sabin put out a hand to stop him.

"They're beyond us, wherever they're at. This is something they had to face and settle without us. We'll wait. They should be with us soon," he advised. "Anyway, it's your turn for the watch and I truly need the sleep, now!" Maren chuckled, seeing his friend's exhaustion. It was more than just the time spent on watch, he was sure!

"You go on to bed. I'll take it from here," he promised.

"Were those the women from your nightmares?" he suddenly asked, needing to know. Maren's eyes looked shadowed.

"Yes. The first one was old green creeps and the one with Garth was Tyra. I got the impression she's protecting him while Ryes is fighting green creeps. The others I have no idea who they are, but I'm sure she'll tell us everything, when they do get here."

"That's what I felt, too. No wonder the two of you were having nightmares with something that evil after you! I hope Ryes will win. I don't think Garth will be the same without her." Maren met Sabin's eyes, levelly.

"She will. You saw us all together in our new home, after all. She wasn't a ghost like Tyra was she?" he demanded, worried.

"No. Ryes was very real, and was kissing Garth as we returned from a hunt. I think she was pregnant, too. We were all there, as well as a few others standing back in the doorway, who I didn't quite see. It was hard to tell from that small flash of a Vision I had that night," he admitted.

"See? Then they'll be back. You go to Ardis. I'm sure she needs someone to cuddle up to," Maren teased, grinning. Sabin chuckled.

"She has trouble settling down to sleep without me, now," he admitted. "How quickly we've become attached to each other." There was contentment in his voice which Maren found wonderful, and that he envied, too. He clasped his shoulder in understanding.

"Then don't keep her waiting," he scolded. Sabin nodded his head, stood up and dusted his breeches off. "Goodnight," Maren wished him as he reached for his boots, again.

"Goodnight," Sabin replied, then turned and hurried back to Ardis' side. It was where he belonged now, too.

"Someday, my blue-eyed princess, either I'll be able to put you aside for the real thing, or I'll find you. I hope you're all you seem to be, and that you find in me what fulfills your needs," Maren whispered to the stars above him. "This is so strange. I love you and don't even know your name!" He chuckled to himself as he went over to the banked coals, to see if the pot of tea was still warm and drinkable.

"You're not supposed to be here!" Kovin scolded, seeing Mitt had snuck into their camp and was cozied down between him and Teris. She stretched and yawned, then looked him in the eye.

"I would've died crossing that stream last night, if it weren't for you two and that rope," she answered him. "Where am I supposed to go? I can't go back to Matlowe with that stream so swift, and I can't just stay out here alone. What if Korman's lost and finds me out here?"

"She does have a point," Teris agreed, unwilling to abandon her out in the middle of nowhere. Who knew what kind of monsters roamed these grasslands? This close he realized Mitt's hips had developed and she was probably old enough for free-mating! It would be very bad to leave her alone with someone like Korman on the prowl!

"Garth and Gann are going to be livid," Kovin answered, then sighed in surrender. "I guess it's safer for her with us, than alone out here. We'll let your brother decide what to do with you, when we find him."

"Yes!" she declared, and then sat up. "I won't slow you two down, you'll see! I may not be quite as good at woodcraft as Ryes, but I'm not totally helpless, either," she assured them. "Be right back," she added, as she jumped to her feet and realized she needed a few moments of privacy.

"Don't go far," Teris urged, then sighed as she disappeared into a small copse of nearby trees. "How old is Mitt? Did you see her hips?"

"Don't get any ideas," his friend warned him. "Just treat her like a little sister. Gann told me she'll be ready for mating next year and that he's pretty worried about it, already."

"Don't worry. I like my women to act like women, not like overactive boys," Teris chuckled out, as he sat up and stretched.

"She'll have a heck of a time getting anyone to believe she's ready to mate, when the time does come." They both laughed at this, knowing it was the truth of the matter. Ever since Mitt was barely old enough to drag along a spear, she spent every moment of the day with her two older brothers. She usually slept over at their place, too. She didn't like staying with their parents, nor liked living with their older sister. She loved her brothers and did her best to act just like them, and it was strange to see her out here, so far from both of them.

"It's almost full dawn. It's best we get up and get ready," Kovin prompted. Teris nodded as he got up and went to see if their banked coals were still hot.

"So, we'll just head straight for the ruins and find them there?" Teris questioned, wanting to be sure of their course.

"Yeah. We'll pick up their trail enroute. I still don't know how we lost it, yesterday. With that windracer and the whole crowd to follow, we shouldn't have been able to lose it if we tried."

"You're the tracker," Teris reminded him with a laugh. "We'll find them and hope we don't find Korman, first."

"Don't worry, we won't," Kovin replied, sure on that score. "But if we do, he's never getting his hands upon Mitt!" Teris glanced back to his friend, hearing a note in his voice which promised a real fight, if Korman tried anything with her. He did regard her more as a little sister, after all.

"We'll both make sure of that," he replied, willing to back him, if ever needed. "Fine pair we make. A tracker who can't track and a gardener who's left the gardens behind." They were both laughing at that, by the time Mitt returned.

Expecting the assault as soon as they started the meld, Ryes found she was not disappointed. She then called the last power stream away from Doran, but held their contact open so she could clearly see who now held all the power in truth. She strove to overcome her mind, but Ryes found she could now rebuff her attempt easily. Finally, calling up her own mind meld, she reached down into Doran and read her memories and knowledge in her mind, seeing how black her heart truly was now.

Doran hadn't started out as an evil woman. She was exceptional and esteemed by her family when they discovered she held more than one Talent, when she was very young. But as she grew older, she became aware of her family's plans to breed her to one of the lesser royal houses; to help her family have better lives and richer coffers. She had been intimidated by the elders and their plans. She was a young teenager and was being trained to use her three Talents more effectively, so she started to use her training as a lifeline to offer a path for escape, before they could bring their own plans to fruition. They praised her for her diligence in her lessons, never knowing her heart in truth.

In her eighteenth year she was wed in a simple, civil ceremony to a man four times as old as she. He abused her horribly both physically and using his Talent. Finally, she found her chance while out on a holiday and trapped him and tortured him for days until his life was finally exhausted. She tried to hide his body, but it was discovered and she was caught and tried for his murder. And then her family intervened, as well as his own family. She was pregnant and they wanted her child, so got a small stay of execution. Upon his birth, she cursed him and tried to kill the infant, too. Hoping for a healing of her mind and heart, they put her into a cryogenic suspension. Then to put her away from being able to influence any other young women, her encased body was put out on a faraway colony world. Still, other women took up her cause against the cruelty of men and she was protected and venerated and gained a cult following of women, who built this huge temple for her and thought it was an honor to be entombed in suspension chambers like hers; communicating with each other only with their Talents. The discovery and theft of the Stone of Power and bringing it here only gave Doran the ability to extend her evil more effectively.

Ryes back off, seeing how black and evil she had become through the years and how sick it was that these women thought she was a symbol to be worshiped. They were sadly mistaken and she saw through Doran's memories how she abused them, too. Just pulling away her power did nothing to stop her abusing the others, nor did it stop her from really calling anyone nearby to her aid and bidding. Glimpsing Doran's training, she got an idea. She called up her Catalyst Talent fully, but instead of trying to delve into Doran's being to help call up any new Talents she might have, she twisted it and used it to fully burn out all her Talent, leaving her perfectly normal. For the first time in her life, Doran was just herself and nothing more. She screamed out in her own mind, but only Ryes, still connected with her heard it clearly. She backed out to leave her to her own peace.

"Please," she pleaded, turning to her handmaidens nearby, "please give it a thought to seek out a new future for yourselves. Don't spend what vitality you still have in such dark isolation."

"What have you done with the goddess?" one of them questioned, finally, after several long heartbeats. "I don't hear her voice anymore." There were suddenly a flood of panicked questions. Ryes held them off, using the power of the Stone to help her sort it out.

"I've only done what should have been done long ago. She's all right, but is now Talentless. She will need time to readjust to her new reality, but she will," she assured them, "Her heart was black. She needs time to heal it once again."

"You can take Talent away?" one questioned out of the silence that had reined for several long moments. There was fear there now in many of them.

"I just figured it out," she admitted, smiling ruefully. "I couldn't see letting her continue to hurt and kill others so horribly. It had to stop and it's the only way I could see to do that."

"So, are you to free us this very minute from our suspension chambers, or will we be given time to decide things for ourselves?" another woman clearly voiced after a long, stony silence.

"I have other things to take care of first and a new home of my own to establish with my husband and our friends and family. I promise that I'll return to set free those who wish to so be freed. Those who wish to stay, we'll have to find a way to make sure you're safe from any harm and can continue to live out your lives as you wish," she finally offered.

"Your man and your cousin?" another one asked her, sounding like she was trying to twist it into an insult. Ryes laughed in return.

"For all the time you have been alive, you have a lot to learn about others and how to live peacefully. I will return when I can, but it won't be too long." She then broke off, having had enough of them, too. She was tempted to let them stew in their cold prison, too, but realized that would make her less than what she truly expected of herself. She'd abide by her promise to them, as soon as she was able. There had to be some good hearts in there, somewhere. Her mother had come from here too, she reminded herself.

With a smile, she turned to the Stone. She needed this one thing to be safe and away from others who would abuse such power, too. She found the deactivation sequence for the defenses and stepped out of the ring safely. She then extended the force shield until it stretched out further to encompass the whole circle. The power systems for this place were far below ground and very dangerous. Still they were self-sufficient and would keep the temple running for hundreds more years to come. Now that she understood them, even if only rudimentary, and she felt she had stepped beyond being a simple villager. How would she be able to hold a spear and go on a simple hunt again? Still a part of her knew that all this was not her true life and being able to set her own course was far more important than all these machines.

She pulled the Stone's power away from the denizens of this valley so that they would again go back to nature and live out their lives as should have been long ago. Their lives were no longer extended and they would now age and die, too. She toned down the Stone's power that fed the Sleepers. She did not want any of them being able to call other women to serve them in this nightmare place, either. They were safe and maintained; they did not need to Stone's power, either. Finally, she figured out how to release the energy streams herself. She found she was fully exhausted now, but still had much work to do.

She had to make sure to get the old woman's body out and buried in some fashion, so to at least accord her some dignity now. She pulled her away from the pile of weapons, towards a chamber, which she now knew had a ground level doorway nearby. She got her over to one of the corner gardens and then shifted some of the decorative stones to build a simple cairn. That done, she sat down for a few minutes to catch her breath and get a few sips out of her water skin. She finally got back up and deactivated all the traps in the whole valley, closed and locked the doors around the temple using switches she now knew where to find.

Ryes finally stood in the hall of weapons, trying to make up her mind. There were a few weapons still up on the walls. She pulled down a crossbow and quarrel of darts and then on an impulse, she took down a fine rapier. She was going to be crossing the garden of death in Shaysa's fading light and needed to go armed. She was too tired to call up her Talent to keep the animals at bay. She knew Doran kept a charm of warding, but she refused using it as it hadn't felt "right." It gave off a sickly, green glow, which appeared unclean to Ryes', now-sensitive, eyes. She reached out to Doran one last time, to see if she had calmed down a little. She was met with cold hatred.

"You must hurry; there's little moonlight left!" Doran's admonishment would sound as if she cared, but Ryes knew better. She only wanted her gone from her temple and valley. She now wanted this powerful, willful young woman and her man gone as quickly as possible. She hated her, to her very core, but other than urging her upon her way, she could do nothing! She felt like crying, but was more furious than anything else. Ryes broke off and turned to leave.

Doran's handmaidens were restless, debating the confrontation from what Ryes had opened up to them. It seemed they remembered things they thought were banished from their memories, long ago. Ryes was glad to be departing this mad place. The things she saw through Doran's mind would never be forgotten. She was glad she'd fixed it so they couldn't lure any more women to their service. Her handmaidens were stirring and maybe some would find the courage and strength to escape, as her own mother had long ago.

By the time Ryes neared the huge, flowering tree, all the darts in the quarrel were expended and a green ichor dripped from the blade of the sword. She could see the fire was built back up and the ghostly image of her mother's spirit still hovered near. The coming dawn was beginning to lighten the sky above and a weariness was settling upon Ryes like a mantle. It'd been no easy trek and she was now stumbling, not feeling her own legs and feet, anymore. Suddenly she was enfolded by strong arms and she smelled the light musky-spiciness that she knew was Garth. She relaxed her hold upon the weapons, letting them drop to the ground. All the nightmares she'd lived through the last several hours dissolved, as Garth scooped her up and carried her over to the fire. He forced a mug of hot tea into her chilled hands.

"You're all right!" she cried out, as tears filled her eyes.

"Because of you, Sweet One." There was a moment's pain in his eyes, an echo of the tortures Doran must've put him through while she had him at her nonexistent mercies. But a smile broke out upon his face as he pulled her toward him. "I'll never doubt your senses, again," he assured her with intensity.

"You were correct Mother, I could do it," Ryes said sleepily, relaxing into his arms. "Now what kind of favor do I owe you for your help?"

"Yes, you did, Ryes," Tyra agreed, as she picked up the ichor-stained rapier. Sadness painted her face as she looked at it. "As for the favor, I shall save it for later." She and the sword faded into a blue mist, which dissipated with the first rays of the rising sun. The dawn of a new day.

"Drink your tea," Garth reminded her. "We're ready to leave, as soon as you finish it."

"I'm too tired to walk any further," she started to protest, and then saw the look in his eyes and understood his fear. "All right, I think I can manage just a bit more," she concurred. "We still need to get out of here, don't we?"

"We're not going to rest here," he insisted. "What was this about a snake you set free?" he questioned, as she sipped the tea. It tasted so wonderful! She smiled up to him, her eyes merry.

"I tried to put some of that ability to feel an animal's responses to use and managed to mind talk with a viper. He was enormous! First, I convinced him not to bite you, then set him outside the valley proper, so he could find his own mate. He went right through that invisible wall, as if it didn't exist, but I still couldn't pass it. I did disable it, and the others around the valley, so we can leave. But I don't think he'll be waiting around for us," she assured him. He looked doubtful, since something like that would need to hunt, too. He was only glad they were far from Matlowe!

"See, I told you you'd find a use for that Talent," he replied, standing up. He gathered their packs and doused the fire, making sure it was out. He then picked up his spear. "Come on, you can finish that as we leave this place behind us."

"Right," she agreed, feeling better. She stood and walked with an arm around his waist, her head against his shoulder. "Let's go back downstream, closer to where we originally tried to cross. I want to see if there's any more of those water plants left," she teased, grinning merrily at the thought.

"You and your water plants!" he scolded with a laugh. She laughed with him. They entered the gully and threaded its way with nothing to stop them now. As they came out the other side, it felt as if they'd been freed from a dark, depressing cage. They both stopped in surprise, looking to each other, seeing they each felt it.

"We've got to get word out about this place and make sure it's marked upon every map made with the symbol of death! I don't want anyone ensnared by that witch, nor her handmaidens, ever again," Ryes swore. The vehemence in her voice startled Garth, but he realized she was right. He stopped, dropped their packs and his spear, and then started looking for stones in the vicinity, puzzling Ryes. She held her peace, seeing he was serious about it. Once he gathered enough stones, he placed them at the entrance of the gully forming the map's symbol for death.

"That might help," she said, smiling her approval. He was having no problems with the reading lessons she was teaching him, while on their journey, but this surprised her. He was picking it up, very fast indeed!

    "Let's cross the creek, find somewhere we can feel somewhat safer, and get some real sleep," he advised, seeing her support for his project. He smiled as bent down to check everything else was still in order and well packed. Ryes stood holding his spear for him, as he passed it up to her for a moment, and she had passed him her now empty mug. She found she needed the spear to stand more steadily. Ryes smiled her agreement, overjoyed she had him back and them both free from this place at last.

The End of Book One

Winterhaven

Reunion
(Chapter 1)

Garth bent to finish repacking his pack, as Ryes stood holding onto his spear. She surveyed the lush green, peaceful grassland before her. The apparent peace was fragile with Doran's Valley of Death too close for the unwary. As she stood in thought, still exhausted after her ordeal, she felt a strange lurch and a reeling surge of power, as if something within her had been unleashed. Panic gripped her heart as the very air shimmered, blurring all before her eyes into a green and gold mist. Her insides felt as if they were twisted around! Then as suddenly as it happened, it steadied again. Was this some kind of aftereffect from holding and directing such immense energies from the Stone for so long? Her mind was reeling and her heart still beat strongly in panic as she saw what lay before her eyes, once more.

She was standing back in the valley, near the tree and the open area around it, which they'd just left behind them. But instead of it being empty, there was a cavalcade of brightly dressed and armored men in front of her. Almost akin to some of the images captured in one of Darman's old books, which she had read when she was little! There were at least a dozen soldiers. Their uniforms were red with black and white contrasts. Gold ropes and buttons completed their look, drawing her eyes in with the details they created. The windracers they rode were all white and tall at the shoulder; more than able to carry some of the heavier muscled men riding them. The trappings on the windracers were extravagant, also a red cloth with the black, red and gold accenting them. They stood in such well-mannered patience, as if long accustomed to such situations. She could feel the power in them as they stood at the ready, to do as they were bid on an instant, both the soldiers and their mounts.

Their leader dismounted and drew his sword as he approached a middle-aged woman, who stood between two willowy trees. Ryes didn't know her, and wondered where she came from? She thought she had stopped Doran's calls. Was she one of her Handmaidens, who had just awakened? She was dressed in a softly-flowing green gown, but there was a vagueness in her eyes which looked all too familiar to Ryes. A thousand questions arose in her mind as she watched. Where had these people come from? And so quickly and quietly! How was she back in the valley, when they had finally made it clear of the gully? Was this something Doran or her followers managed to do, to get back at her for her victory?

"I have come for my betrothed," the officer stated loudly, his face diffused with his smoldering anger. He was an older man, who appeared older than Rowan. He was very neat in appearance; every hair in place as if he tamed it, first. His ears had strange coloration, as if some kind of special rank. She wondered about such a neatly groomed man. The woman did not respond.

"Release Tyra of House Li to us, immediately!" he ordered, raising his sword to point it in her direction. This was her next surprise. How could he be betrothed to her mother? This didn't make any sense. Tyra was long gone from Tayna now and had been married to Ronn before she died. How could he come here to make such a claim?

"She is sheltered with the Goddess now," the woman replied in a mocking voice, a sneer upon her face. "No man may violate this valley, unpunished," she stated loudly in return, then turned away, as if dismissing his threat and walked down the path leading toward the temple; the matter dismissed to all appearances. The presence of the men were not a danger by her behavior.

"Then so be it! We'll take the head of your so-called goddess and still bring Tyra home with us!" he shouted at her retreating back. He signaled his men forward, leading with his drawn sword. A now-familiar, insane laugh filled the air, surprising them. The uncertain men paused, looking around them, trying to find the source.

"It's only someone with strong Mind Voice," he declared, barely glancing back at his troops. "We have a job to complete. Mental barriers up. Forward!" The old officer refused to pay it heed, as the others stood in doubt. He pressed onward, leaving them behind, now.

"Watch out!" Ryes shouted in warning as she saw the almost invisible hand of Doran reach out and roughly push the old leader. His face registered shock as he was grabbed and shaken by an unseen force, as if he were a rag doll. His sword was pulled from his grasp and rammed through his chest to its hilt, then run downward, until he was practically cleaved in two. His screams were horrific to hear and died as suddenly as he did. His company stood with horror reflected upon their faces, as mad laughter rang out from the air around them. Doran was daring them to continue and try to take revenge.

Ryes strode forward in anger and slapped aside Doran's grasping hand, as she reached to claim the unfortunate man's soul. There was a loud, shocked shriek at this, which slowly faded. The freed soul vanished, to wherever souls fled at life's end. Ryes looked down sadly at the body of the brave officer. Two members of the company dismounted and hesitantly stepped forward.

"Who are you and what do you want?" one of the men demanded, a strange weapon in his hand. It appeared a short barrel with a grip shaped to fit the hand comfortably.

"I'm called Ryes and am the daughter of Tyra Li and Ronn," she answered. She looked back toward the gully, but Garth wasn't standing there, so he didn't know she had been swept off, yet. "We won our freedom from this valley just a few hours ago, but I seemed to have misplaced my husband," she stated with a puzzled frown. The time of the day was even wrong. It was late afternoon, not early morning.

"How can you be the daughter of Tyra Li?" the man demanded, his eyes narrowing and looking angry. "You're lying. Tyra only arrived here three months ago."

"She has no daughters and is far too young to have one as old as you!" a second one agreed as he reached to grab her arm. Ryes felt a shock at his touch, but his hand passed through her arm, as if she were made of air. She was startled by the pain this caused and her insubstantiality. What had happened to her? Why was this happening? The men appeared as surprised as she when she looked up at their faces.

"I'm more lost than I thought!" she declared, looking to them for answers. They backed away, their fear naked on their faces. Another, older man stepped forward. He was clearly unafraid and had a determined set to his chin. He gestured for the others to secure the fallen officer's body. They reluctantly stepped forward again as a pair of others came over to help. The older officer turned to face her squarely, his face a controlled neutral.

"You are Time Walking," he explained to Ryes in an oddly accented voice. She frowned at this and he glanced back to check on the progress of his command. "No, leave that cursed blade lie," he ordered, as one of the men stooped to retrieve the fallen sword. "It has betrayed the Family and will never again cause another such death."

"What is time walking?" she asked, puzzled. The officer's gaze returned to her, looking her directly in the eye.

"Only one of royal blood could fully answer that. I am only an officer of the guard of the House of Oftirrin and have a very base knowledge of the Talents," he told her. He had noted her simple dress and braids, as if she were a puzzle he was going to have to remember later for a report. "Ah, a Forester."

"How do I get back to where I belong?" Ryes pressed, questioning as they prepared to leave, bearing their sad burden. The man's windracer was brought forward to bear his now-wrapped body.

"It is a very rare Talent and none are now living have it, that I have heard. And I have never been versed in how it operates. I am sorry," he told her. The old guardsman only shrugged his shoulders, then turned upon his heel, remounted his windracer, and left with the rest of the company. They filed up the gully, disappearing around the bend. She looked down at the bloodstained sword, a sense of helplessness claiming her. Then she raised her eyebrows in surprise. It was the same sword she used last night to fight her way free of Doran's deadly garden. She shook her head sadly, bewildered.

"At least it served its final duty for me and helped free us of this place," she said into the resulting quiet around her, then sighed.

Ryes turned and walked back toward the gully, feeling very tired and alone. When she reached the top again, she stepped over to the tree she had been standing near. Even it was younger looking! She needed to get back to Garth! She closed her eyes and imagined everything as she last saw it. She strove to listen to the sounds of Garth packing his backpack. In her mind she pictured his face as clearly as she could, putting all her will into the image. Again there was a wrenching feeling within and the air about her caused her skin to tingle. Suddenly she felt his spear was solidly in her hands once more, and Garth's strong arms about her. She let herself collapse against him, dropping the spear. She was back and safe with him, again. She began to shiver with an intense cold as tears of relief sprang to her eyes.

"Are you all right, Sweet One?" His voice was tinged with desperate concern. "What can it be? Is that witch making another try for us?"

"No, she can't. I took care of that. And I'm fine now," she breathed, trying to control her shivering, opening her eyes to look into his. A warm smile sprang to her lips. "Let's get well away from this valley. Right now!" He finally chuckled, a smile of his own lighting up his eyes.

"Whatever you wish, Sweet One," he told her. He released her to pick up the dropped spear and backpacks, then wrapped an arm around her. They cut across the grassland before them, heading away as quickly as they could manage.

"I feel a million years old," she quietly commented as they began to head south and west. Garth smiled to himself. Ryes was more herself, again. "And we're going to have to replenish our food supplies soon," she added, her practical side coming out. He laughed heartily and stopped to hug her to him, again.

"Of course, Sweet One, whatever you want." There was a lot of affection in his voice and Ryes' heart beat with joy.

"Whatever would I without you?" she asked, as she returned his hug, holding onto him tightly. She needed no answer. She knew it already.

www.ingramcontent.com/pod-product-compliance
Lightning Source LLC
Chambersburg PA
CBHW070353200726
48294CB00003B/896